A MESSAGE FROM CHICKEN HOUSE

Isn't it amazing? The more we learn about the creatures who share our world, the more we realize that animal intelligence is about feelings and emotions as well as astonishing survival skills. And when her missing mother's story starts to unravel, Vinnie has to forge an extraordinary bond with such a creature: a special eight-armed friend. Lindsay Galvin's beautiful thriller is fast, fishy and funny – but also moving and resourceful.

BARRY CUNNINGHAM
Publisher
Chicken House

My Friend the
OCTOPUS
LINDSAY GALVIN

Chicken
House

2 PALMER STREET, FROME,
SOMERSET BA11 1DS
WWW.CHICKENHOUSEBOOKS.COM

First published in Great Britain in 2022
Chicken House
2 Palmer Street
Frome, Somerset BA11 1DS
United Kingdom
www.chickenhousebooks.com

Chicken House/Scholastic Ireland, 89E Lagan Road, Dublin Industrial Estate,
Glasnevin, Dublin D11 HP5F, Republic of Ireland

Cover and interior design by Steve Wells
Typeset by Dorchester Typesetting Group Ltd
Printed and bound in Great Britain by CPI Group (UK) Ltd, Croydon CR0 4YY

For Mum and Dad,
the song and the sea.

Also by Lindsay Galvin

Darwin's Dragons
The Secret Deep

The existence of gigantic cephalopods is no longer an open question. I, now, more than ever, appreciate the value of the adage:

'TRUTH IS STRANGER THAN FICTION.'

THE END

HENRY LEE
THE OCTOPUS: OR, THE 'DEVIL-FISH' OF FICTION AND OF FACT (1875)

A note on the word 'tentacle'
In zoology (the study of animals), the octopus' eight arms are not considered tentacles, as they have suckers all along their length and technically a tentacle only has suckers at the end. However, the word 'tentacles' is the common word used for octopus arms by scientists and non-scientists, alike.

PROLOGUE

Alfonso gazed back at the shimmering island of Madeira longingly as it disappeared over the horizon. Soon the sun would join it.

'We'll start around here, my good man,' said the English gentleman, Senhor Bickerstaff. He dabbed his forehead with a purple silk handkerchief, although the evening was cooling.

Alfonso's father released the sails and the boat rocked as it dropped speed, but Bickerstaff repeated his instruction loudly.

'*Aqui, aqui. Compreendo?*'

Alfonso suppressed a smile at the man's exaggerated

Portuguese accent, and his older brother shot him a glare. This *estrangeiro* had paid very well.

His father nodded at Bickerstaff. '*Compreendo, senhor.*' He unspooled the rope, and the net hit the water and sank.

'Deeper, man, I need something that hasn't been seen before. *Profundo!*' He circled his finger, eyes wide and bulging, as if showing the fisherman how the pulley worked.

With a nod from his father, Alfonso tugged the rope so just a breath of breeze caught in the sail, edging them forward, dragging the net behind them in the deep. If the English gentleman wanted to waste his money cruising empty seas at night, it was his lookout.

The boat gave an almighty lurch to one side so the sea surface was in touching distance for a few brief moments, and they all grasped something to stop themselves toppling in. A cry of alarm from Bickerstaff. They must have hit a wayward shoal after all. Alfonso leapt to release the sails as his brother and father heaved on the winch.

This really was a haul—

But Alfonso's first glimpse was not of a mass of writhing silver fish.

The net was swollen, but what filled it was darker and denser than the ocean below it. Something huge.

Not the shape of a deep-water fish big enough to feed the whole village.

Not a shark, dolphin or young whale.

Alfonso heard his father gasp, '*O meu Deus*', his brother curse, and Bickerstaff bark a stream of orders . . . but all he could do was stare. He turned his head this way and that to try to make sense of it.

As the net met the surface, something slipped through. Something . . . long. An eel? The skin was smooth like one, but too big. Far too big.

His father called for his brother to stop and hold, and took over the winch alone, turning the handle more slowly.

His brother gasped. '*Polvo!* Turn it back, it is—'

'No!' yelled Bickerstaff, bouncing up and down. 'This is *it*! A large Octopoda will do nicely.'

Alfonso's brother shook his head, making the sign of the cross. '*Não. Polvo, senhor*, this devil-fish. Too big, too big.'

The boat rocked, sea slopping over, and Alfonso's father muttered to his brother.

It didn't make sense. Devil-fish were small, soft crawling creatures, wrapping their ribbon legs around their heads as they hid in crevices of the reef just offshore.

This creature was a thousand times bigger.

'Looks to be a giant Pacific *Enteroctopus dofleini*, but

we are thousands of miles from their usual—'

Alfonso helped Bickerstaff roll over a barrel, which when righted was taller than the boy himself.

The boat creaked and shuddered as the devil-fish shifted. More arms emerged from the bulging lattice of rope, exploring the surface of its prison, as it hung suspended above the open cask. Alfonso caught glimpses of circular suckers pale in the moonlight, silken arms in constant movement.

It was Alfonso's turn to make the sign of the cross as the animal was dropped unceremoniously into the barrel and the boat rocked with the new weight. The devil-fish retracted its arms in alarm and Bickerstaff and his father slammed the lid. His brother bashed in the nails, swinging the hammer as if he were sealing the entrance to hell.

But Bickerstaff rubbed his hands together. 'This beast will suit me very well indeed.'

THE FIRST HEART

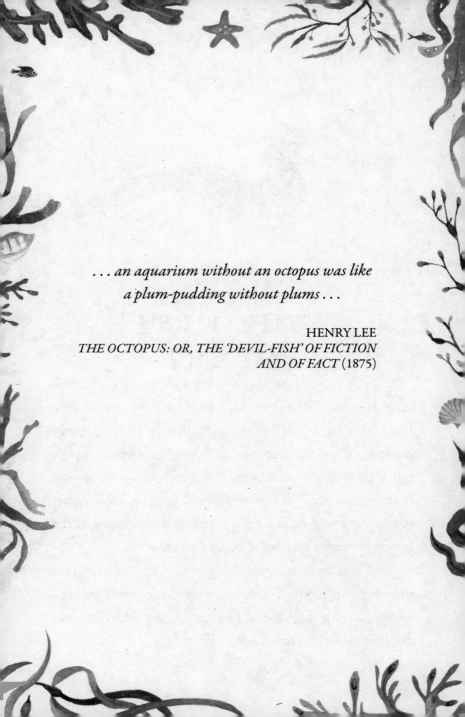

*. . . an aquarium without an octopus was like
a plum-pudding without plums . . .*

HENRY LEE
*THE OCTOPUS: OR, THE 'DEVIL-FISH' OF FICTION
AND OF FACT* (1875)

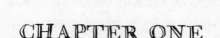

CHAPTER ONE

My pencil lines blurred, my eyes gritty with tiredness. Mother's voice could have been coming from another room, it was that muffled. We were working by candlelight, a few crumbs of ginger cake and the remains of my bedtime milk – laced with honey and brandy – on a tray. It was so cosy working together in her four-poster bed, but now I wished we'd continued at the bureau where it was easier to stay awake.

'Oh, you are fit to drop,' said Mother, 'that's enough for tonight, dear heart. We haven't even done your hair yet.'

She swung out of the blankets and padded to her dressing table to fetch the bundle of rags.

I shook my head and the drowsy fog cleared enough for me to inspect the lines of my sketch. I was pleased with this hat design. Mother had said that the loops of gauze ribbon down one side would balance the large silk peony bloom that covered the entire base. That was what I had intended, but I didn't say that. Mother had such an eye and I was happy she had taught me so well. That was why Fyfe's Milliners had become so popular with the fashionable set. I smiled up at her.

'What colour?' I said, and hunched forward as her deft fingers wound my long hair around strips of cotton.

'Tell me who you see wearing it, picture her.'

I closed my eyes. 'She's just married, taking a stroll through Hyde Park with her husband—'

'Oh no. I'm afraid this creation is going to be very . . . expensive. Too much for most young wives.'

She waited for me to go on. I tried not to sigh. Truth was, I saw colours and lines, not the people who might buy the finished headwear. My head felt filled with cotton wool. But I'd heard enough society women describing the occasions where they would build their look around one of Fyfe's designs to be able to cobble together an answer.

'Madam is attending her first grandchild's christening,' I said, 'but thinks of herself as young.'

Mother laughed. 'Yes, yes, they all like to think of

themselves as young, clever heart,' she said, and her cool fingertips wound the last curls at the top of my scalp. 'Too tight?'

I shook my head, and my thick snakes of hair bobbed as she kissed my forehead. I stifled a yawn.

'Colour?' said Mother.

She had said expensive.

'Paris Green?'

'Yes. Both the base and flower in Paris Green, the ribbons in chartreuse.'

'She must be at least a countess, then?' I said.

'I should hope so,' said Mother, and we both laughed.

Mother's customers were becoming more and more elegant since we had moved to Grosvenor Square half a year before. I knew this shop and apartment were much more expensive, but Mother had ambition. She wanted to rival the famous Parisian milliner Caroline Reboux.

Suddenly I was so exhausted I could do nothing but nod as Mother led me out of her warm bed and into my own, at the front of our first-floor apartment above the shop. The sign hung directly below my window: *Mrs Rosamund Fyfe and Daughter*.

Mother tucked in my covers and checked the window was open just a crack at the top to allow some air in. Moments later I was asleep in a haze of green silk.

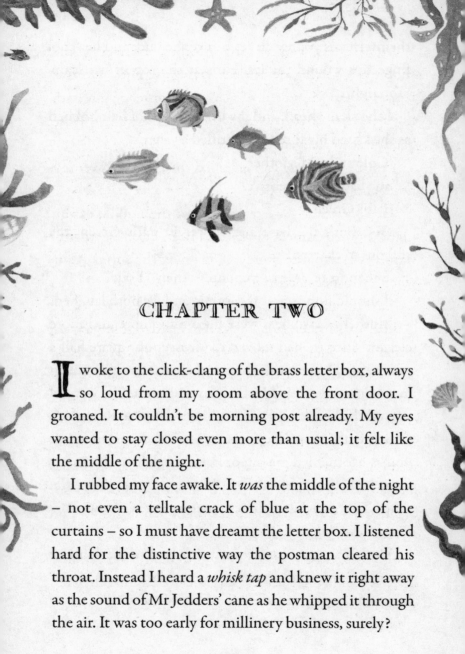

CHAPTER TWO

I woke to the click-clang of the brass letter box, always so loud from my room above the front door. I groaned. It couldn't be morning post already. My eyes wanted to stay closed even more than usual; it felt like the middle of the night.

I rubbed my face awake. It *was* the middle of the night – not even a telltale crack of blue at the top of the curtains – so I must have dreamt the letter box. I listened hard for the distinctive way the postman cleared his throat. Instead I heard a *whisk tap* and knew it right away as the sound of Mr Jedders' cane as he whipped it through the air. It was too early for millinery business, surely?

Mr Jedders worked for Mother, managing the shopfront, sorting deliveries, buying supplies. He was younger than Mother and I thought him very conceited, but he knew how to charm the customers, even if he barely acknowledged me.

I rolled on to my front, pulled the blankets over my head, and fell back to sleep.

The next time I woke it was *still* the middle of the night. But this time a candle had been lit on my night-stand. I was about to bundle back under the covers again when a whisper startled me.

'Lavinia, get dressed, we are taking a trip.'

I sat up. Mother, fully dressed in her dark-blue travelling suit, was buckling my suitcase at the end of my bed. The wardrobe at the other side of the room hung open, empty. Travelling clothes were laid out for me on the chair.

I yawned. Had I forgotten something? Was there a wedding fair we were attending? We had to get up in the middle of the night for those – but Mother was so organized, we always packed the night before.

'Where are we going?' I said.

She looked up and her eyes glittered in the candle-light. She pulled me gently from the bed and handed me a cloth to wash my face.

'A trip, dear heart.'

I frowned, still half asleep and feeling suddenly out of sorts.

'But it's night . . .'

'Perfect time for an adventure,' she said and put a finger to her lips.

I let Mother help quickly dress me even though I was far too old for that. She unwound the rags from my hair so my curls tumbled over my shoulder, and pinned them in place, then held me by the tops of the arms to inspect me, and gave a quick nod.

When Mother led me out of the apartment she didn't turn towards the front door. Instead she beckoned me to the staircase that led to the apartments above.

'Mother?' I whispered. 'What are you—'

But with a sharp 'shhhhh' she was already on the staircase. I followed her up three tall flights of stairs – corridors leading off into the other apartments – until my calves ached, the suitcase seemed double the weight and I couldn't think what on earth Mother could be up to. Finally she opened a small door on to an even smaller landing. An attic. I didn't even know this existed. Dust tickled my nose as I peered into the darkness. I held Mother's arm but before I could speak she pulled me close, whispering in my ear, 'My clever heart is wondering what sort of trip begins with spiders.'

I smiled at her despite myself. 'And bats. And mice.'

She widened her eyes and gave an exaggerated shudder. 'You know how nosy people can be, I don't want everyone knowing our business. Will you trust me and ask no questions, dear heart, so as not to spoil the surprise?'

I nodded. Of course I would. I slipped my hand into hers and she led me through the dark attic. We tiptoed across the floorboards and soon we seemed to have walked much further than the boundary of our apartment; I judged we were now in the attic of the next house. I started to wonder if Mother was quite all right – she didn't seem unwell, but I'd heard so many ladies talk of their nerves in hushed whispers.

I rushed to catch up with her just as we came to a door. She pushed it open, releasing a gust of colder air, then beckoned me down a very narrow flight of stairs that surprisingly brought us out in a yard, which belonged to the end house in our square. We trod lightly across the mossy flagstones and left through the gate, still silent.

I squeezed Mother's hand. She really did need to tell me what this was all about. Who was going to open the milliners tomorrow? We would have customers—

Once again a finger at her lips, then a repeated whisper of 'Trust me.' What could I do?

The streets were deserted, aside from one carriage, waiting for us.

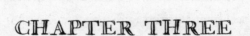

CHAPTER THREE

We were on the first train of the day, quarter to six in the morning, and weren't just the only people in the carriage, but the only people on the train entirely. Mother was attempting to close the window. I yawned and yearned to question her about exactly what sort of adventure this was, but I didn't want her to think I didn't trust her or that I wasn't grown-up enough to try new things.

'Gracious me,' she said, 'this window is completely jammed. Lavinia, please pass me the umbrella, I might be able to—'

Without warning Mother ducked so she was crouching

at my feet, then pulled me right off my seat so I fell on to the floor beside her, bumping my elbow. The two of us squatted amid our bulky travelling skirts and petticoats.

'Mama! What are you—'

'Shhhhhhh!' She pressed her fingers to my lips. Her eyes were wide, and for a moment she looked scared as she pulled my head towards her and spoke in my ear. 'Quiet, stay down,' she said. I gripped on to her arms and her dark-blue eyes sparkled again.

We waited in silence, huddled together.

Then I heard it. *Whisk tap, whisk tap*. It was the same sound I had heard outside the shop earlier. Mr Jedders. I couldn't help it, I craned up just as a man passed the window. Mother dragged me down but I had already seen him, a well-cut suit and a brown bowler hat at just the perfect angle, about to peer in at the next carriage window. A hint of blond curl over his ear and that slim ebony cane that he always whisked through the air. The cane had a carved ivory handle in the shape of a head with a horrid gargoyle sort of face on one side and a smiling face on the other.

'It's only Mr Jedders,' I whispered, now completely confused.

'Did he see you?' hissed Mother.

I shook my head and she nodded, seemingly relieved. I really needed to know what was going on here. If Mr

Jedders didn't know we were off on this trip, then who was taking care of the milliners while we were away?

We both leant against the carriage side, below the window. I listened out for the *whisk tap* of the cane and eventually it started up again and grew louder. More pauses. The only explanation was that Mr Jedders was searching for us, and Mother didn't want him to find us, and that was no explanation at all.

The sound of the cane grew more distant then disappeared, after a few minutes replaced by passengers gathering at the platform. I noticed Mother gripped one of her longest hatpins – topped with a bead of onyx – in her fist, the point facing upwards.

She caught me staring at it and quickly threaded it through her hair and hat.

Rather than sit down opposite, I perched next to her. 'Mother, what was Mr—'

'Mr Jedders is no longer in our employment, dear heart,' she said, dropping her voice as an elderly woman entered the carriage. 'He's a little . . . disgruntled about that and must have somehow tracked us to the station.'

This was news to me. Mother relied on Mr Jedders – he organized most of her deliveries and communications, and I'd seen him in the shop only the previous day. Could I have missed some sort of argument?

'What happened?' I said.

'We simply do not need him any more, dear heart. The business is named Mrs Rosamund Fyfe and Daughter for a reason,' she said, giving my hand a squeeze, 'and between you and me, Mr Jedders was becoming a little too big for his boots. I decided to let him go.'

'And he's . . . annoyed about that? So he is following us?'

I remembered the *whisk tap* of his cane outside our letter box in the middle of the night and told Mother so. She shook her head but didn't seem surprised.

'It's men's pride, that's the problem. There's really nothing for you to worry about, Lavinia, but it's as good a time as any for our little adventure,' she said. 'Remember, no one needs to know our business but us.'

I nodded. But my eyes strayed to her clasped hands, and I recalled her white-knuckled grip on that hatpin.

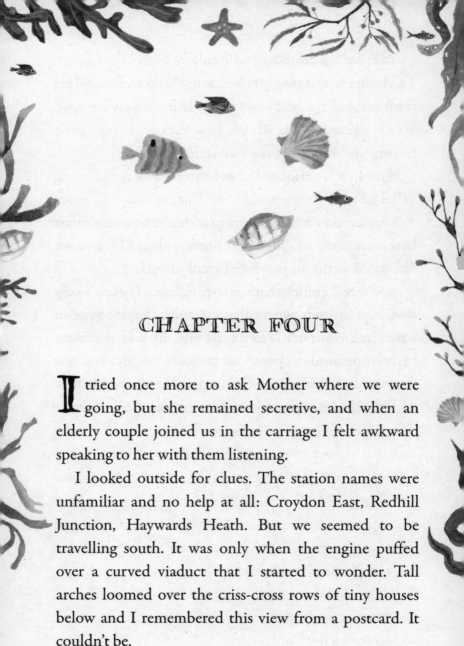

CHAPTER FOUR

I tried once more to ask Mother where we were going, but she remained secretive, and when an elderly couple joined us in the carriage I felt awkward speaking to her with them listening.

I looked outside for clues. The station names were unfamiliar and no help at all: Croydon East, Redhill Junction, Haywards Heath. But we seemed to be travelling south. It was only when the engine puffed over a curved viaduct that I started to wonder. Tall arches loomed over the criss-cross rows of tiny houses below and I remembered this view from a postcard. It couldn't be.

'Is this *Brighton*, Mama?' I said.

Mother just smiled slyly. I bit my bottom lip, stifling my joy, scanning her face for clues that it was really true. We were finally going to visit Aunt Bets.

'Really?' I said, my heart pounding.

'I told you to trust me, dear heart,' she said.

I'd almost given up asking to visit the sea – we never even made it as far as the Thames flats. I couldn't count how many times I had asked Mother to take me to see Aunt Bets, our only surviving relative.

Aunt Bets and I had been writing to each other every couple of months since I was able to hold pen to paper. I pictured the postcards I kept tied in a blue ribbon at home. Donkey rides, beach huts, swimmers, the promenade and pier. And the photo of Aunt Bets herself, standing formally outside her tea shop, Ruggles Terrace Tearoom, looking much sterner than she sounded in her letters. I wished I had that photo with me to look at her now before I finally met her in person. Why hadn't Mother told me about this? I would have savoured the anticipation. As we rattled around the curve of the track I was jolted forward and my nose pressed against the window.

'I hope those windows have been cleaned,' said Mother. I quickly wiped the fog from my breath off the window with my handkerchief.

The elderly woman sitting opposite tutted. Mother gave her one of her stern looks, one eyebrow raised, and when the lady puffed out an exaggerated sigh and turned back to her knitting, I worried I might giggle.

The train slowed and shuddered, and both Mother and I perched on the edge of our seats adjusting our hats. I hardly recognized Mother in such a simple chapeau and veil. I wore a straw bonnet lined with lace and decorated only with folds of lilac ribbon, my long ringlets released down the side.

When the train halted I went to stand and Mother directed that I must sit back down as the other passengers departed. Then she whipped the curtains across the window now facing the platform.

'Isn't this Brighton?' I said, fearful I'd misunderstood; after all it did sound too good to be true.

'Just a moment, dear heart,' she said. 'Stand by the door, and tell me if anyone is coming.'

I did as she said, but when she unbuttoned the neck of her blouse I gasped, for it was so out of character. She drew out a tiny key on a chain, unlocked her case, then reached into a side pocket to draw out a twist of silk.

'Is there anyone there, Lavinia?' she whispered as she unrolled the fabric.

I peered through the doors into the carriage corridor

and shook my head. When I looked back at Mother she was clasping a pendant around her neck and a pale glow caught the light.

When I stepped forward to look closer, her palm closed around it.

'Can I see?' I said.

She gave an impatient sigh. 'It's a simple heirloom, dear heart, but I have decided I would rather keep it about my person.'

Mother unfolded her fist to show a creamy-blue pearl, but I had never seen one even half that size; it was like the pickled quails' eggs she sometimes served during her special soirées. I reached out a finger but she closed her fist and slipped it into the neck of her dress, quickly buttoning up.

I had never seen this piece before. Mother's jewellery was always understated, tasteful. I would have remembered something like this.

'Now, I expect you are ready for Brighton?' she said.

'I am, Mother, I really am,' I said.

She laughed that tinkling laugh I loved so much, and drew the curtains back to reveal the passengers on the platform had cleared away. Mother peered up and down before leading me from the train. We hurried down the platform to the airy station atrium, where pigeons swooped and light filtered through the domed glass ceiling to bathe us.

I took a deep breath in and out. The air tasted clear and bright, and suddenly I didn't feel tired at all.

CHAPTER FIVE

Outside the station a straight downhill road stretched ahead of us. I blinked into the distance, searching for that first glimpse of the sea, but the road met the sky above, with houses and shops either side. The early morning wind whipped at us, so clean and clear compared to London, it stung my nose. Mother had already found a tram stop, bought the tickets, and was calling for me. We sat at the back of the tram, Mother's veil still pulled low as I stared ahead. I was never even awake at such an early hour. The milliners didn't open until eleven and it was still only nine o'clock.

'Is the sea going to be ahead of us?' I asked, as the tram trundled downhill.

'It is only a few minutes to the Brighton Aquarium and then you'll have your fill of the sea. It is right on the promenade,' whispered Mother close to my ear. 'Never understood the fascination with the sea, myself. It is quite unpredictable.'

'Are we going straight to the aquarium now?' I said, confused. Wouldn't Aunt Bets still be at home at this hour?

'Oh yes, Elizabeth has always kept utterly unholy hours, dear heart. The life of a baker,' she said with a shake of her head.

When the tram squeaked up a shallow slope and reached the top, I gasped.

The sea didn't look real. It was almost too like the postcards, completely flat and the deepest blue. Nothing above, no houses or trees, just all that water . . . I felt dizzy looking at it. As the tram gathered speed, I saw the flat blue was dotted with dashes of white and my fingers itched for pencil and paper. Then the tram bell rang and Mother stood. My attention was wrenched from the sea and on to the next excitement. We were finally at the aquarium I'd heard so much about, soon to meet Aunt Bets.

Mother gripped my hand, leading me out of the door.

A clock tower stood proud, surrounded by fancy balustrades, carvings and statues, and beyond it steps led down to a courtyard and a huge arched entrance with a carving above it: *The Grand Aquarium*. I had never visited an aquarium before. Would I be able to see the . . . creatures? I shivered. Any free time we had, Mother would take me to parks and stylish squares, where we'd wear our best creations like walking advertisements. She would observe the latest fashions on society ladies, and I would draw them as soon as we were home. Sometimes we would call upon customers she had befriended for afternoon tea.

I'd seen nothing like this.

A flight of stairs to the side of the clock tower led upwards to the terrace on the aquarium roof, and that was where Mother headed.

Ruggles Terrace Tearoom was at the far end of the paved area covering the entire roof of the underground aquarium. A blackboard stood by the top of the stairs.

Breakfast rolls served 6–8 a.m. weekdays.

I scanned the terrace; to my left there were four arches with alcoves, and the counter for Ruggles Terrace Tearoom occupied the final one. The others were boarded up. Tables and chairs spilt out from the counter, covering over half of the terrace.

To my right was the sea, underlined by the promenade,

stretching to white cliffs in the distance. There were two piers – one long, one short – and rows of bathing machines along the pebbled beach. Above the sea was only sky and more sky all the way along the endless horizon.

My mouth watered at the smell of fresh bread and crisp bacon, but I was suddenly fearful that I wouldn't even recognize Aunt Bets in person, let alone know what to say to her on our first meeting. I needn't have worried as I spotted her right away in the far corner, serving tables, even though she bore little resemblance to the stiff and washed-out photo. In reality Aunt Bets was as bright and clashing as the basket of offcut ribbons in the milliners. She wore a buttercup-yellow blouse and a skirt in a blue linen stripe – with only the smallest hat that could be respectable, in purple. I noticed bloomers in the same stripe beneath her skirts and blinked. My fine navy taffeta dress with the sailor collar beneath my travelling cape suddenly felt both stiff and babyish.

Mother wound through tables and chairs occupied by men and women in sturdy working clothes, her back ramrod straight. Their eyes followed my fine, dignified mother.

When my aunt caught sight of us she nearly dropped her tea tray. I frowned. Were we earlier than expected?

Mother ignored Aunt Bets' shocked expression and

pecked her cousin-in-law on the cheek. My father – John Fyfe – had been a prominent tailor on Savile Row but died in a coach accident when I was less than a year old. We had one photo of him and Mother barely spoke of him. The only one from his side of the family that Mother had kept in a little contact with was his favourite cousin and my godmother, Elizabeth Ruggles, at least until I was old enough to keep up the correspondence myself.

'Elizabeth, you do look . . . well,' said Mother, surveying Aunt Bets' lurid but rather dusty-looking hat for a beat too long.

'As do you, cousin. And this is Vinnie. Finally, Vinnie! Here, let me make sure you are real, girl,' said Aunt Bets and gave me a brief but enthusiastic hug. I grinned, glad she was real too. She smelt of cinnamon.

The photo I had of Aunt Bets made her square jaw look rather stern, but in person her large features looked just right together. I liked the way her whole face, eyes, cheeks, chin and mouth lifted when she smiled.

'Well, this is a true surprise. Now what are we about, Rosie?' said Aunt Bets.

Through my pleasure at Aunt Bets' welcome I began to feel confused. *A surprise?*

'Could we partake of some of your fine tea before we talk?' said Mother. 'Maybe somewhere a little quieter?'

Aunt Bets showed us to a table under the arches next to her counter and out of sight of the tables outside, then reappeared with a huge pot of tea and a plate of tiny biscuits.

'Are marzipan petits fours still your favourite, Rosie?'

We'd had no breakfast and the plate of biscuits was soon gone, and the sweet tea refreshing. I wondered if there would be time for even a short visit to the aquarium before we went to Aunt Bets' house.

Mother dabbed at the corners of her mouth. 'The air is so stimulating here. A tonic, really,' she said.

'I've always said so, haven't I?' said Aunt Bets, a crease forming between her narrowed eyes.

I made a pile of crumbs with my fingers, beginning to feel awkward. Aunt Bets had seemed shocked to see us. Mother couldn't have sprung this trip upon her, could she?

'Thing is, Elizabeth, and I do apologize for the lack of notice, but as you can see Vinnie is quite pallid. A girl of her age needs good clean air once in a while. I'll only be leaving her for two weeks, a month at most, just while I carry out some business in Paris. I can't very well drag her to another city when she is so ... wan.'

My head shot up. Leaving me? Did she say *leaving* me?

CHAPTER SIX

What was Mother talking about? *Wan?* I had barely had a day's illness all winter and it was now spring and . . . well, I must have heard her wrong. She couldn't intend to leave me in a place I'd never been to before, with a person I only knew through letters? I opened my mouth, but with a pointed look from Mother, I snapped it closed again.

Aunt Bets was clearly as astonished as I was, although trying not to show it. She spoke slowly.

'As I've said to you many times, cousin, I'd love to have Vinnie to stay.'

I had the impression that Aunt Bets would have had a

whole lot more to say if I hadn't been there, and I felt the same way. Aunt Bets' letters were wonderful and I had been desperate to meet her, but I'd never been apart from Mother.

Finally I found my voice and chose my words carefully, although panic rose in my chest when Mother began pulling on her gloves. She couldn't be leaving me here, right now?

'It is so kind of you, Aunt Bets, to offer to have me to stay, but I would really like to come with you to Paris, Mama. I promise you I am quite well and ready to assist you as always.'

'You haven't told the girl?' said Aunt Bets, colour rising in her cheeks. 'Really, Rosamund, that is quite—'

'Now, Elizabeth, you just said you were happy to have her. In the fashion world we move quickly to maintain our edge. I must visit Paris this season.'

I was beginning to feel desperate, head spinning with the fall from excitement to fear. 'But, Mother, who will do your sketches? Who will help you . . . ?'

I trailed off.

Mother took my hands in both of hers. 'It will not be for long, Lavinia, and you will have a wonderful time.' Her blue eyes held mine like a pin to a feather. 'Won't you, dear heart?'

Was she giving me a choice? Was now my chance to

tell her I wasn't ready for this? No. Mother expected me to accept this. So I swallowed the lump in my throat and nodded, hoping I looked braver than I felt.

'Now, Elizabeth, as you know Lavinia is a budding couture designer. It is imperative she keeps her fingers soft and sensitive, her eyes sharp and clear. She'll need to avoid too much sunlight or time outside.'

Aunt Bets rubbed her chin and nodded.

'Thank you, cousin, you are the only one I would trust with my precious girl,' said Mother and took Aunt Bets' hands.

'It will be a pleasure,' said Aunt Bets, voice tight.

What if Aunt Bets didn't even want me here?

Mother turned to me and we held each other's gaze. I loved her so much. She was beautiful and clever and admired and I wasn't used to ever being without her. Other mothers could easily have found a husband to replace my lost father, but Mother wasn't interested in men, she was only interested in Fyfe's and in . . . us. How would I do without her for a whole month? Without our work and long evenings together, designing, experimenting with combinations of ribbons, silk flowers, feathers and ruffles, reading about how our creations had been worn at all the best society occasions, the gas lamp fizzing late into the evening?

She took me by the shoulders and leant close to my

ear. 'When I have completed my research, we will be in a position to appeal to the highest society. We will rival the best in Paris. House Fyfe, set to become the most exclusive couture milliners in London, showcasing the designs of rare young talent, Lavinia Fyfe,' she said.

'But what about our salon here . . .'

'A short break in trade will pay off in the long run,' said Mother. Her tone was brusque, her mind clearly made up.

'I love you, Mama,' I said into her dark hair, my voice catching.

'As I love you, my dear heart,' she said. 'You are my Lavinia Fyfe.'

I nodded, but as Mother turned tears started in my eyes. One day I would have a straight back, the raised chin, the poise of Mother. My eyes followed her brisk step across the terrace, then one wave before she disappeared down the stairs. It took everything I had not to run after her.

Aunt Bets tapped my arm. 'This is hard on you, Vin. I'm sorry. But let our Rosie have her Paris. She'll have a grand old time this month, just you see,' she said, 'and so will you.'

CHAPTER SEVEN

I sat in the corner of the terrace attempting to sketch a whimsical headpiece with a daffodil design, but Mother's voice arrived in my head, directing me, praising me, and my eyes filled with tears. I turned my attention instead to the pier and the sea beyond. I'd longed to see it but with Mother gone so suddenly I couldn't appreciate it.

I wondered briefly if I could draw it but flipped the sketchbook closed. I wouldn't know where to start. The most infuriating thing was I had been desperate to meet Aunt Bets and to visit the seaside for many years, but now I was here, even a whole pot of sweet tea to myself hadn't washed away the lump in my throat.

Aunt Bets must have noticed that I could barely keep my tears back because she closed the tea shop as soon as there was a lull in customers, and we walked to her white-painted terraced house, which was only a few roads back from the seafront.

After we had hung our outer clothes and hats in her hall, we passed what I supposed would be used by most people as a parlour, but which was lined with deep shelves floor to ceiling, packed with sacks, brown bags and jars of dried fruit and preserves. I glanced at the small table with its one chair in dismay. Our parlour at home contained the large bureau which I used for drawing and where Mother did paperwork. The curtains were rich velvet and Mother's pianoforte sat in the corner. By the fire, Mother would sit in the brocade wing chair with my matching stool at her feet and I would sharpen my pencils and sketch dried flowers for practice, while Mother cut out designs from the magazines for her scrapbook.

Aunt Bets must have noted my expression. 'I hope you like the smell of baking,' she said, shepherding me through the hallway to a warm back room that she'd made her bakery, where a range took up the whole of one wall, every size of mixing bowls were stacked, and copper pans glinted beneath rows of hooks for utensils. A sugar cone was like a monument in the centre of a scrubbed table.

The vinegary yeast smell coated the inside of my nose and trays draped in cotton covered a huge butcher's block table. She peaked under the edge of one of the cloths and I spotted pale mounds.

'The rolls have risen perfectly. That's good luck,' she said and gave me a squeeze, 'but of course it is, because you're here.'

I forced a smile. Aunt Bets was just being nice. She hadn't exactly been given a lot of choice in me being here.

'Don't worry, Vin, I don't get much call for entertaining but I have got a room for you upstairs,' she said. 'Just give me one moment.'

Once she had shown me up, I decided I liked the small bedroom with an embroidered bedspread and views of the sea. I sat on the bed. Now I was finally alone and could let the tears come, my eyes were hot and dry. I changed out of my travelling clothes and padded downstairs again.

'Now, why don't you help me weigh out these ingredients?' my aunt said. 'If we are quick, everything will be ready before bed.'

'I've never—'

'Oh no, of course you haven't,' she said. 'Doesn't matter a jot, we just get doing.'

I looked at the tiny print in the recipe book with dismay, but when Aunt Bets called out the first letters of each ingredient, I found I was able to find them and tell her the amounts. Numbers were always easier for me than letters, and I was glad Aunt Bets didn't rush me.

Once she showed me how to measure, I was soon distracted from missing Mother by the swaying tip of the scales, the tickle of the flour up my nose, the cinnamon spice and sugar on my tongue, then the sticky sweetness of the dried fruit on my fingers. I liked the way the mixture held the shape of my stirring wooden spoon, as it spiralled around, although my arm quickly tired, and I was a little in awe when Aunt Bets rolled up her sleeves, muscles cording in her forearms as she whipped the spoon around in the stiff batter. I even managed a sense of satisfaction when the huge round fruitcake was finally lifted from the oven.

Aunt Bets made a smaller cake in a square tin with the last of the mix and now served me a slab, steaming and glistening with raisins and candied peel. She added a chunk of cheese, a heel of fresh buttered bread and an apple.

'It's tempting to just eat bread and cake but I do try,' she said with a rueful grin.

I wanted to smile back at her, but I was considering the night ahead, my first ever without Mother, and the lump was back in my throat despite the food being delicious.

'Time to turn in,' said Aunt Bets after I had helped with the plates. 'It's baker's hours here, I'm afraid.'

I checked the clock. Eight thirty. Often this was the time Mother and I had our supper. Sometimes it was the time guests would arrive.

I lay awake trying to picture where Mother was now, to feel happy for her on her way to Paris, but all I could see was her walking away from me, alone.

Swish, swish. Swish, swish.

It was so dark. And for a moment I thought I'd dreamt it all, and I was back in Grosvenor Square with Mother just in her room next to mine, and Jedders outside swinging his cane and waking me far too early in the morning. But this was no *whisk tap*, more of a low pounding, and I realized it must be the sea. Then the sound of water much closer and the scent of steamy lavender. My eyes adjusted to the dark and I made out Aunt Bets' figure pouring water into the washbowl. When Aunt Bets had said baker's hours I hadn't under-stood what she meant.

'No need to get up now, Vinnie,' she whispered, 'I've

got scones and bread to bake plus the breakfast bacon, and then I'll be off to feed the aquarium and pier workers before we open up to the public. But you can stay here, you'll be quite all right to make your own way down to the tea rooms when you're ready. Can you remember the way?'

At that I blinked properly awake. Being Mother's constant companion meant that I was never really alone, and the thought of finding my own way to the aquarium filled me with new dismay, mainly at myself. I now realized I'd got to twelve years old utterly ill-equipped to deal with this adventure. It had never really dawned on me to do anything by myself; we were a partnership. Mother had always said Fyfe and Daughter were perfectly complete – with my designs and her business sense and eye for a trend – but really I was like a ribbon to Mother's hat. The hat could do perfectly well without the ribbon, but the ribbon was just a scrap of fabric without the hat.

I sat up. 'No – I'll get dressed now and come with you, I'd like to help,' I said.

As soon as she left I washed, wrinkling my nose at the smell of the ivory soap bar. Mother always used Pears. But what about my hair? I'd tried to wind it in rags but most of them had fallen out overnight. I brought the candle close to the dressing-table mirror, feeling a lump build in my throat. I always wore my hair the same way. I didn't look like myself at all.

'Vinnie,' called Aunt Bets, 'time to go.'

Already? I took a deep breath, then plaited my hair as I always plaited Mother's before bed.

The hairstyle looked plain, and I felt undone without coils of hair in pins that pulled at my scalp, but it would have to do. I pinned on the simplest of my hats, jabbing the sharp end into my head, then wincing. What was I trying to do? Pin myself down? I then ran down the stairs. The front door was open, blue dawn light pouring in, and Aunt Bets stood just by the front step holding a bicycle with a huge basket attached to the front and a smaller one to the back, clearly labelled *Ruggles Fine Cakes*.

'Ah, there you are,' said Aunt Bets. 'We're running late and it's all downhill, so I'm going to take the bicycle.'

She shook her skirts with the strange bloomers beneath. Now I knew where I had seen Aunt Bets' outfit before – on ladies cycling in Hyde Park. Mother did not approve; I think mainly because these sporty young ladies were not her customers, tending to wear rather small and subtle hats.

'Would you prefer to walk? I'll meet you there. You know the way, can't miss it. If not, just swing on to the saddle and keep your skirts held tight. I'll pedal up front.'

I felt the horror show on my face; it probably wasn't a polite expression, but I couldn't disguise it.

'Me? To ride a . . . bicycle?' I said, staring at the contraption.

'Of course,' she said. 'Best way to travel!'

CHAPTER EIGHT

Before I knew it Aunt Bets was helping me up on to the leather bicycle saddle, directing me to hold on to the rim of the basket behind me, and most surprising of all . . . I was doing as she said. When she gripped the handlebars and rolled the bicycle out into the street, I yelped, legs swinging, trying to keep my balance. The machine hadn't looked so very tall, but now the street seemed a long and painful way down.

'All set?' said Aunt Bets.

She didn't wait for my answer, but swung her own leg over in front of me so she was hovering over the crossbar as she pressed on the pedals. With a petrifying wobble we lurched down the street, the front wheel drawing a wavy line. I stifled a scream and closed my eyes tight, braced for the impact then agony when I inevitably toppled off. But as we gathered speed, the wheels fell into line and when we hit the downhill, wind streamed through my hair. I grew brave enough to open my eyes to slits, only to see the dawn-lit world rushing by. I immediately snapped them shut, tight. By the time I'd drawn the courage to open them again, Aunt Bets was slowing, and we had arrived at the aquarium.

Aunt Bets sprang from the bicycle and helped me stumble down, my knees jellied.

'All right now,' she said, surveying my face with a concerned look. 'You really did tremendously well, Vin – I never thought you'd agree to get on the bicycle with me. Your mother never would've.'

I wanted to say I hadn't known I had a choice. Aunt Bets' teeth were large and stuck out a little, but it just made her look like she found it difficult to contain her smile. She was laughing at my expression – I must have looked as petrified as I felt – but it was a kind sort of chuckle, and I found myself grinning with her, despite my heart still hammering in my chest. She tucked some stray blonde curls back into her bun.

'Now, howsabout you go down into the aquarium and tell the keepers that breakfast has arrived? Ask for

Mr Lee, he's the aquarist, the man in charge of the animals.'

I swallowed. Another new thing. I wasn't used to being sent on errands – that was Mr Jedders' job at Fyfe's, or he'd pay an errand boy – and on my own in the aquarium? I didn't know how to tell Aunt Bets that I was worried about a task she made sound so simple, so I nodded, rehearsing in my head: *Pleased to meet you, Mr Lee. Breakfast is ready.*

Or should I say: *Good morning, Mr Lee, I am Elizabeth Ruggles' niece. She wanted to let you know that breakfast is ready.*

The dawn light grew brighter but the arched entrance to the aquarium was still shadowed. When I turned, Aunt Bets had parked the bicycle and was carrying the huge basket of baked goods up the outside stairs to the terrace where I had followed Mother the day before.

I rolled back my shoulders, smoothed my skirts and stood in front of the grand archway in the centre of the clock tower, looking upwards at the sharp spire that crowned the clock. Below it, on the corners surrounding the clock face, perched life-size sculptures of women, gleaming dark brown, like the bronze drinking fountain near our shop in London. I wondered who they were supposed to be; the two I could see both seemed to be wrapped in robes. One woman was holding a bunch of flowers, one a sheaf of wheat. I crossed through the archway and turned to see two more of these bronze statues on the other two corners above me. One held a huge bunch of grapes and the other held nothing, just an extra bundle of clothing, a veil over half of her face. This final one seemed to look down on me, expressionless. I shivered.

'They are the Four Seasons,' called a voice from above, and I stepped back startled, to see Aunt Bets peering over the side of the terrace above the aquarium entrance. She grinned, pointing at the doors below.

'The fancy Roman ladies aren't hungry, but Mr Lee will be. So get doing, our Vin,' she said, and disappeared.

CHAPTER NINE

I paused at the tall wooden doors that led into the aquarium, and stared at the inscription carved into the stone arch above. I wanted to know what it said but the letters jumped around and there were some long words. Mother had taught me to read, impatient when it didn't come easily to me, even though she tried to hide it. If she were here now, she wouldn't want to wait, she would read the words for me. Much easier.

And God said, Let the water bring forth . . .

I took a deep breath – all of those words had come quite quickly, but I felt a familiar prickle of anxiety at the next one, and sounded it out: *ab-un-dant-ly*. I knew that word's meaning – like when a hat was piled high with decoration, it would be abundant.

I felt more confident now . . . *the moving creatures that hath life.*

Surprised at myself, I breathed out, then thought on the words again. Had God meant the waters to be contained beneath the ground, or the creatures to be locked behind glass? What kind of creatures would be here? I'd dreamt of seeing the sea, of the beach, but I'd never really thought about what lived in it, *under* it. One door was ajar. I took a deep breath, feeling a thrill of anticipation as I pushed through. No tanks or creatures in here. My footsteps echoed in a cavernous entrance area, big enough to hold a tea dance. No sign of any keepers. I headed through a second door and found myself in a vast gallery.

The aquarium.

It was like stepping into a different world. The vaulted ceiling criss-crossed above and the tanks that lined the walls glowed blue-green. There was no one here.

I breathed in cool, clammy air, a world away from the breezy seafront and terrace. It was underground like a cellar, or mausoleum – I shivered at the thought – but it was the opposite really, because behind the glass it flickered with life. My ears filled with the bubbling of what must have been the pumps and the burble of the waterfall at the far end of the gallery. I didn't know where to look first; it was as if another world existed that I had known nothing about, a tranquil watery realm.

Ornate columns held the place up as if it were an ancient temple to the creatures of the sea. I smiled as I passed tiny slim fish darting in and out of the sand. I read the plaque – *Pipe Fish*. I traced my finger along the engraving letters, forming them with my mouth at the same time as my mind, glad I was alone and could take my time. *The Great Spider Crab, Hyas araneus*. I wondered if the last two words were in a different language. The creature's stalked eyes were capped red, quite a sight with its spiny back covered in a thatch of moss and weed, and long spiky legs.

I followed the colours and shapes that caught my eye, my steps zigzagging across the gallery. *Paradise Fish from China* were bright orange, striped with iridescent turquoise, with fins like ragged flags. *Spiked Anemones* looked like cushions filled with black hatpins but their vicious points faced outwards. *Pacific Sea Stars from the Americas* littered a giant rock formation, some vivid purple, others blue to pale pink. Most had five arms but some seemed older and were mottled and pale with missing arms. Even animals I already knew of were different and fascinating – *Common Shrimp* had bulging eyes and swivelling antennae, and there were glistening salmon and spotted trout. Among the animals that caught my eye were others much more plain, some even scruffy-looking. A brown shore crab with no pincers . . .

My fingers itched for pencil and paper, although I wouldn't know how to begin capturing what I saw. So much movement, but contained behind glass like photographs come to life and colour. Between the brighter animals were bigger tanks. I stared in wonder at a *Giant Turtle and Young* and the *British Sharks*, some of which were very large and swam around their tank in brisk circles with dead eyes and gash-like mouths.

At the very end of the gallery was a display that spanned the entire back wall. It was less than half full with water, and contained mainly huge boulders; it went back much further than the other tanks. As I drew closer, one of the rocks shook a fine set of whiskers and I saw four slick shapes lounging, one much bigger than the others. *North Pacific Sea Lions, Family and Infant.* I started back as one slid into the water and swam over to the glass. Up on the rocks I spotted a much smaller animal – mottled grey and with huge eyes like jet beads – and gasped at how sweet it looked.

The tanks were decorated not only with the animals they held, but with arrangements of sea plants, weeds, stones and impressive sculptures. The whole place flickered with movement against light that shone through from behind.

There was so much to see I'd almost completely forgotten Aunt Bets had given me a job to do. Trouble was, I could hardly call the keepers to their breakfast if I couldn't find them. There seemed to be no one here.

I scanned the other tanks again with a thrill of excitement. With Aunt Bets' tea shop directly overhead, surely I could come down here often. I wondered again about sketching the creatures, although I doubted I would have the skill. But I could certainly use some of the colours to inspire my designs.

The biggest tank was in the centre of the gallery. This one was strange. For a start, it had barely any water in it. It was also at least double the size of any of the others, but aside from a collection of seaweed swaying in a back corner and what looked like a sunken temple in the centre, it was empty. There was no brass plaque, just a darker patch on the wooden frame where one must have once been.

A clamour of voices at the far end of the gallery – were these the keepers to invite to breakfast? I swallowed and straightened my back.

Five men manhandled the biggest barrel I'd ever seen – big enough to fit at least two of these men inside it – through the doors and rolled it slowly across the tiled floor towards me.

CHAPTER TEN

I stepped out of the way, leaning against one of the columns, as with a huge heave the men tipped the barrel upright. Three of these keepers wore grey-blue uniforms with epaulettes on the shoulders; a fourth was a gentleman wearing a gold brocade waistcoat that set off a florid face with rather fleshy lips.

'Have a care!' said the fifth man as the cask rocked slightly before settling. He stroked the wooden lid. I pressed myself against the column, wondering what could be inside. Something alive? This man looked like he might also be a gentleman but was dressed rather shabbily, and had a mop of brown curls and long sideburns. His smile seemed younger than the wrinkles around his eyes.

'No need for kid gloves, Lee. Trust me, these beasts are *quite* robust,' said the gold waistcoat man, slotting thumbs in his waistcoat pockets and thrusting out his chest. 'We've got real monsters here.'

Lee. So the curly man was Mr Lee. He pinched his lips shut as if he wanted to reply, then he noticed me.

'Oh, I didn't see you there, miss. Can I help—'

'The aquarium is not yet open to visitors, child,' interrupted the waistcoated gentleman, looking down his nose at me as he checked his pocket watch.

All I needed to say was the message for Mr Lee about breakfast, but my words had dried up completely.

Just then the barrel juddered. By itself. None of the keepers were standing near it. A couple of them stepped back and I did the same, sliding round the side of the column, eyes fixed on to the giant cask which was still vibrating. The wood creaked ominously, and everyone seemed to hold their breath, only letting it out when the movement and sound stopped. Whatever was inside . . . was alive.

'Good morning, sirs,' I said in a half-whisper – I could almost hear Mother telling me not to mumble – then I dropped a half-curtsey, still eying the barrel warily. 'My aunt wanted me to tell you all that breakfast has arrived.'

'Your aunt? Why then, you must be young Vinnie. Honoured to make your acquaintance. I'm Mr Lee, the aquarist in charge of the animals, and this is Captain Bickerstaff, the aquarium director. Captain, Vinnie is the niece of the much-appreciated Betsy Ruggles, who runs the tea rooms on the terrace.'

I took Mr Lee's offered hand. It was cold and soft, but his smile was warm enough to make up for it. Captain Bickerstaff didn't offer his.

The barrel trembled again.

'I think we'll give our new guests a chance to calm down after a long journey,' said Mr Lee. 'They seem rather agitated.'

'Nonsense, no time for dilly-dallying. Fetch them out of there now, Lee. I've waited long enough to get a good look at these slippery beasts, and I need to be getting back to London, drum up some business. Lord knows we need it,' said Captain Bickerstaff.

Mr Lee tipped his head to one side and I thought he looked a little sly. 'You're right of course, captain. Sure we can do without Mrs Ruggles' famous fresh-baked buttered rolls and crisp bacon for one day.'

Captain Bickerstaff had a sudden change of heart.

I followed the men out of the aquarium, but found myself glancing back at the barrel until the door closed on the strange bubbling aquarium world. I'd seen more new things in the last five minutes than I'd experienced in years. But that huge trembling cask gave me the shivers – so why was I already determined to get back to it and find out what was inside?

CHAPTER ELEVEN

aptain Bickerstaff strode ahead and I walked beside Mr Lee, the other keepers following behind, muttering among themselves.

'How to safely settle our new guests is giving me quite the conundrum.'

I wasn't sure if Mr Lee was talking to me or to himself. I desperately wanted to ask what was inside the barrel, but didn't dare.

'If you promise to stay well back, you can watch us unload, Vinnie. Charlie is coming – he's my nephew.'

We climbed the stairs up to the terrace where the smell of bacon and fresh bread rolls led the keepers to form a queue at Aunt Bets' counter. Boiled eggs were piled in a tall mound, bacon was dished out by a rosy-faced Aunt Bets from a large platter, and they helped themselves to rolls. Other people were scattered around the terrace tables, eating, and I watched two girls in nurse's uniforms collect bread and bacon, wrap them in handkerchiefs, place them into their carpet bags and head back down the stairs arm in arm.

A boy with copper-red hair sat at the table closest to the counter, taking a huge bite of a bacon roll, melted butter dripping on to his plate.

'Charlie, you are here, my boy,' said Mr Lee over his shoulder, already on his way to join the queue. 'Our new guests are going to be transferred to their home as soon as breakfast is finished. You'll be joining us with your notebook?'

Charlie nodded and raised a hand to give me a sort of wave as he finished a mouthful. His face was thin and pale, making his thick dark eyebrows stand out like punctuation on a page. Bright-blue eyes gave me a direct, but not unfriendly, stare. There was a scattering of freckles across his nose and his bristly hair needed a trim.

Mother would have expected me to wait quietly as she introduced me, so I'd just stand at her side and wait, never a worry. But Aunt Bets was behind the counter,

Mr Lee was in the queue and Mother – well, she might already be in France.

I tried a smile and shook the rather inky hand that Charlie held out.

'I'm, er . . .' Mother always introduced me as Lavinia, but I much preferred Vinnie. Now I looked like I didn't even know my own name. My cheeks grew hot. 'I'm Vinnie. Vinnie Fyfe. Mrs Ruggles is my—'

'Aunt. Yes. I know,' finished Charlie, not seeming to have noticed me stumbling over my words, 'and your mother, Rosamund Fyfe, is a society milliner, who has disappeared causing a minor uproar in fashionable circles.'

I started, knocking the table so the teapot wobbled. 'But how do you—'

'Sorry,' said Charlie, swallowing another mouthful. 'Should've said. In the newspaper.'

'Mother is in a *newspaper*? She only left yesterday . . .'

'Oh, it's only a very small column in the fashion section of the *Thames Star*. Here . . .' Charlie stuffed in another huge bite of the bacon roll, then reached into a large leather satchel and drew out a bundle of newspapers. He started paging through them so quickly and with such energy, I found myself staring.

'I'm going to be a journalist,' he said. I tried not to raise my eyebrows, as he barely looked older than me.

'I'm just starting out, so writing small articles for the local papers, investigating current affairs.' He shrugged and added as an afterthought, 'Of course, I still have to have lessons with Uncle. But I get to keep up with the news. Your aunt has an edition delivered each morning, and Uncle orders the main London broadsheets for the reading room in the aquarium. I read them first, but don't tell old Bickerstaff. Ah – here.'

He pointed to a small column.

FYFE'S MILLINERS CLOSED FOR BUSINESS

Mrs Rosamund Fyfe has left her exclusive and loyal clientele quite bereft, with her shopfront closed until further notice and no forwarding address. She is reputedly in Paris working on an Autumn Collection. A loyal customer who wished to remain nameless, but who was dressed in a towering Fyfe's creation in emerald green, commented: 'There would never be a good time for us to do without Mrs Fyfe; her designs will be greatly missed for the summer season. But we eagerly anticipate her return from Paris, sure she'll add a continental twist to her already impeccable style.'

My shoulders slumped in relief, although I wasn't sure what I had been afraid of exactly. The column was just a tiny block in a sea of other stories. Mother would probably be pleased to see what had been reported. When she sent me her address in Paris I could cut this out and send it to her.

'You can keep it if you want,' said Charlie.

I mumbled my thanks, still feeling a bit shaken to have seen Mother's name in print, the newspaper already knowing something I'd only just found out myself.

CHAPTER TWELVE

Mr Lee joined us at the table with bacon and buttered rolls plus a fresh pot of tea.

'I'm glad you two have been getting acquainted. Charlie's father is a friend of mine from my time studying in Edinburgh and he's staying for a while.'

'Truth is, I'm the youngest of six sons and my father has had quite enough of us boys,' said Charlie.

'Oh, Charlie, that's not true,' said Mr Lee.

'Father works for the post office, and three of my brothers do the same, two at the main exchange in London. Another works on the railways, one left for America. We aren't exactly a family of books or writing,

Vinnie. I'm a bit of an . . . oddity. That's why Uncle Henry and I are so suited,' he said with a buttery grin.

'I shall endeavour not to be offended by that comment,' said Mr Lee, although he didn't look offended in the least.

The queue had disappeared and I looked around to see most of the tables were empty. Aunt Bets was wiping them down and placing a small bunch of flowers in a vase on each one.

'It's always amazed me how quickly Mrs Ruggles clears the breakfast shift. Watch—' Mr Lee pointed to where Aunt Bets now took the teapot from a table, one hand on hip, and gave the customers a brisk nod and waited a moment. Sure enough the two men gulped the remains of their tea, tipped their caps and left.

Mr Lee raised his eyebrows at me. I wasn't sure how to respond, as I didn't want Aunt Bets to think I was making fun of her, but I gave him an uncertain smile as Aunt Bets joined us.

'What are you two smirking about?' she said.

'I'm just hoping we don't get the same stare your last customers did. We don't want to be turned to stone.'

Aunt Bets flicked Mr Lee's arm with her cloth. 'Are you comparing me to a gorgon, Henry Lee?'

When I was smaller I had sometimes persuaded Mother to read to me from a book of illustrated Greek myths, and the thought of Aunt Bets as the fang-toothed Medusa with a head of snakes tickled me. I stifled a giggle and saw Aunt Bets notice with a wide smile.

'Of course not, Mrs Ruggles,' said Mr Lee, blustering now, turning pink right to the tips of his ears which poked through his curls.

For a few moments we tucked in. The rolls were soft and warm, the bacon salty and crisp. I could see why Aunt Bets had so many workers join her for breakfast, even with the gorgon stare. Then Aunt Bets wiped her hands on a napkin and tilted her head to one side.

'No rest for the wicked,' she whispered. 'My early ladies are here.'

I turned and saw three older ladies in colourful but rather flouncing dresses – Mother would note the fabric as only of middling quality. They were all pale in the flat way that suggested too much face powder. With them was a girl with dark skin, wearing a boater with a blue ribbon. The girl whispered something to one of the ladies, who waved a hand, still talking to her companion, and the girl chose the table next to ours although all the others were now free. The women swept over to look at the cakes on the counter.

I saw the girl's shoulders rise and fall in a sigh, and then she slipped a hand into a pocket in her skirts and drew out a small booklet covered in blue brocade and a pencil with a tassel on the end. When she caught my eye I quickly turned round.

Charlie leant forward, indicating with a flick of his eyes to the girl. 'That girl is here plenty, her guardian can talk for England and brings all her friends here. It's a good place to hear society gossip, especially on the weekends when the London crowd arrive. Then she can spend the rest of the week spreading it around. The girl is always scribbling in her diary.'

Charlie had lowered his voice but not by much. I wondered if the girl could hear us anyway.

'How do you know it's a diary?' I whispered, thinking of my sketchbook. Would strangers notice me sketching and wonder about me now I wasn't with Mother?

He shrugged. 'I heard her tell one of the other women.'

It felt wrong to be talking about the girl when she was right there, even though our voices were low. I tried to think of a way to change the subject. Mother was always so good at this, keeping up a seamless flow of conversation with the millinery customers. I was beginning to fear I had learnt nothing from her.

'So – are there plenty of articles to write, down here . . . in Brighton?'

'My brothers share an apartment near the Victoria Sorting Office in London, so I can visit whenever I like,' said Charlie, 'but Brighton suits me for now.'

'And Charlie needs to keep learning. There's no rush,' said Mr Lee.

Charlie glanced at Mr Lee out of the corner of his eye. 'Besides, Uncle Henry's house is a lot nicer, and a writer needs his comforts.'

'Well, thank you very much, I'm sure,' said Mr Lee. 'There might be a story for you today, if our new guests are as magnificent as Captain Bickerstaff claims.'

'Can't wait to see them, Uncle, whatever they are, and I'll write a story better than any advertisement.'

Mr Lee sighed. 'I fear you are working against the tide, dear boy. Aquariums have become a victim of our own success.'

I didn't know what he meant and he must have seen my expression.

'Ten years ago a well-stocked aquarium was a huge draw for tourists, but now there are just so many. You know what they've now filled the last few tanks at the Crystal Palace Aquarium with?' said Mr Lee.

He waited for us to answer.

'Mussels for eating?' said Charlie.

'No. They've drained the tanks completely.'

'Rare breeds of cat,' said Charlie.

Another shake of Mr Lee's head.

My turn. 'Erm – chickens?' I said, feeling a little silly but pleased when they laughed.

'They've made it into a monkey house,' said Mr Lee, with a sigh. 'Monkeys. I ask you? I just cannot understand it . . . not so long ago an aquarium was the most popular of diversions but now all and sundry have a tank in their front room and think that makes them an aquarist.' He took the napkin from where it was tucked into his shirt and straightened it. 'Time to greet our new guests,' he said.

The barrel. I swallowed, remembering how it had rocked and creaked. I could simply refuse Mr Lee's offer – no one would blame me, I was sure, and Mother would certainly expect it – but I found myself following.

As we crossed the terrace an arm slipped into the crook of mine. I spun around, for a moment thinking it must be Mother come back after all, for who else would be so familiar? But it was the girl who had been writing in the diary. I tensed at the unfamiliar touch and she dropped my arm.

'Sorry – I couldn't help overhearing,' said the girl, calling out loud enough that Mr Lee could hear. 'Do you have a new animal arriving, sir? I adore any and all creatures, and I would so love to see it.'

Her words rushed out so quickly I blinked, trying to keep up.

Mr Lee turned to her. 'I'm afraid the aquarium isn't yet open to the public, miss, but if you come back—'

'Please, sir, I have an uncommon interest in many subjects, the natural world being one of them . . .' She paused with a pleading sort of sigh, shoulders slumping. 'And I am so *incredibly* bored.'

Charlie frowned, but I couldn't help but smile at the girl's words and saw Mr Lee do the same.

'Very well, if your guardian agrees,' said Mr Lee.

'Mrs Heap,' called the girl, 'can I join these respectable people in the aquarium for a short while?'

The woman peered over her glasses at us. Her grey hair was in a fringe of tight ringlets. 'Yes dear, that is a fine idea,' she said.

'All right then,' said Mr Lee, 'but you are to stay with Vinnie and Charlie here. What is your name?'

'They call me Mary Randall Rose,' she said, linking her arm in mine again. This time I didn't flinch, although it felt strange. I liked this outspoken girl. She glanced behind her to where the three ladies were now sitting and lowered her voice. 'But my name is actually Temitayo.'

CHAPTER THIRTEEN

It was only after we had bounced down the stairs and through the atrium into the main gallery of the aquarium that Temitayo dropped my arm. Some of the keepers must have gone ahead of us because a cream canvas tent had been erected around the largest tank, and there was a clamour of voices inside. I guessed the barrel must be behind the canvas.

'This tank has always been one of the main attractions,' said Mr Lee. 'It once housed a manatee—'

Temitayo gasped and interrupted, 'That's a sea cow as big as an actual cow,' she said. Charlie shot her a glare.

'That's right—' said Mr Lee, but she interrupted again.

'I only know that, sir, because I've read your pamphlets,' said Temitayo. 'I ... read a lot.'

I flushed. She was the opposite to me.

Mr Lee flashed a wide smile at her. 'Well, well. You've read my pamphlets? Then you are in somewhat of a minority, dear girl. So you might know that most of our tanks are filled tidally but this is one of the few habitats heated by pipes running underneath, which means we can control the environment for more delicate creatures.'

Captain Bickerstaff thrust his head around the curtain. 'No time for a lecture now, Lee. And I'm not certain *delicate* is quite the word for them.' He glared at us as he held the canvas aside so we could enter the small space. The three other attendants gathered around the barrel. 'Is an audience really necessary?' he said.

'My nephew is going to take some notes and we thought—'

'Never mind, let's get on with this,' said the captain.

The barrel I'd seen earlier was in the middle of the enclosed area.

'Lately we've had a lot of our creatures supplied by amateur collectors,' said Mr Lee. 'They acquire bigger and more exotic animals to impress their neighbours but cannot look after them. The animals ail as their owners hadn't realized that their tanks needed to be cleaned so regularly, the water changed and ideally filtered continuously on a pump. What with the precise foods particular species need, it all becomes too much work. Fish corpses are the opposite of ornamental – not to mention smelly.'

'And yet Mr Lee continues to take in any ailing waif or stray no matter how unimpressive, as if we are a charitable home for unfortunate specimens,' said Captain Bickerstaff, 'so I've taken matters into my own hands, found shipping reports about unusual creatures, and procured some entirely myself. I might yet turn this business around.'

He raised his nose in the air and gave a self-satisfied sniff. For a man who hadn't wanted an audience, Captain Bickerstaff seemed to have a lot to say for himself in a very loud voice.

I noticed that the tank was filling, the water now rising more than halfway.

'Now stand back please. You too, Charlie and Miss Temitayo,' said Mr Lee. 'Right here.' And he directed us to the edge of the canvas tent where we had entered.

'What are they?' I said.

'They are water creatures, Miss Vinnie,' said Charlie. 'Ain't going to be much risk to anyone on land.'

I narrowed my eyes at him and he smiled, mischievous. I didn't know whether to smile back; I wasn't used to being teased.

'Well, that's not strictly true, as you might call an anaconda or a crocodile a water creature, but I definitely wouldn't want to meet one of those on land,' said Temitayo. Charlie rolled his eyes at Temitayo but if she saw it, she pretended not to. She whispered to me, 'An anaconda is a huge snake.'

At the mention of *huge snake*, I wondered if this was such a good idea. Should I go back up to Aunt Bets? Mother would most certainly think so – she wouldn't have wanted me down here in the first place – but Mr Lee wouldn't put us in danger, would he? Aunt Bets and he seemed to be friends. Ignoring my racing heart, I did as we were directed and pressed my back to the heavy canvas that divided us from the rest of the aquarium.

Mr Lee turned to the three keepers – and they gathered around him. They were all holding implements: a stiff brush for scrubbing the floor, a cloth on a pole, and a stick with a hook on the end.

This tank had a section of wooden frieze above that could be removed, resulting in a wide space. This was now open.

'My dear friends, these are rare and sensitive creatures so please remain calm, no sudden noise or movement.' Captain Bickerstaff folded his arms.

Mr Lee gripped a wrench, his shirt sleeves rolled up and eyes shining.

When the lid was prised open a fishy stench wafted past me. Mr Lee raised both his hands and one finger to his lips.

The reactions of the men peering into the barrel were intriguing enough that both Temitayo and I almost stepped forward to see, but then I pulled her back. All three keepers seemed somewhere between confusion and fear, and the oldest of the men made the sign of the cross. Whatever it was, it was frightening these men who were used to unusual creatures, and my heart now thumped in my chest.

Captain Bickerstaff remained still, as if he had seen this all before.

'Wait. Give them a chance to acclimatize to the light, the change,' said Mr Lee.

Nothing happened. Everyone seemed to be holding their breath.

Charlie broke the silence. 'Are they alive?' he whispered.

'We had a lot of movement from them not so long ago,' said one of the keepers.

'Do get on with it, Lee,' said Captain Bickerstaff.

Charlie, Temitayo and I edged forward with a nod from Mr Lee. Finally I went up on tiptoes to peer into the barrel. A pale mass filled the huge space inside, covered with only a few inches of water. I didn't know what I was looking at. I had never seen anything remotely like this.

The creatures didn't look like creatures at all.

CHAPTER FOURTEEN

The shapeless pale mass filling the barrel pulsed, like a muscle being tensed. I stepped back, wanting to pull Temitayo with me.

Then something unfurled into a long shape and quicker than seemed possible became a gigantic grey – what would you call it? Arm? There was just time to glimpse a flash of grey flesh studded with a pattern of circular rings within more circular rings, then the arm – or was it a leg? – flipped over the side and clung to the outside of the barrel nearest me, sliding across the wood like a monstrous slug. I yelped and clapped my hands over my mouth. One of the keepers poked the creature's arm with the blunt end of a broom handle and it made a dent in the jellylike flesh before it sprang back to shape.

'Enough of that,' said Mr Lee, grasping the stick, 'let them settle.'

'What are they?' said Charlie.

'Giant octopods. Some similarities to the giant Pacific *Enteroctopus dofleini*, but a bigger specimen and well outside of its usual habitat off Madeira,' said Captain Bickerstaff.

'Octopuses have always been a popular attraction, but you can see common British specimens in every aquarium. The captain suspects this is a new species,' said Mr Lee.

'I am quite certain, Lee. I've already contacted the Royal Society.' Captain Bickerstaff twitched his moustache. 'There's a pair of them, possibly one male and one female, I caught them together.'

I couldn't take my eyes off the creature's arm as my mind raced to what I knew of octopuses, but all I'd really heard was the word. The tentacle was pale grey and then – it wasn't. Deep red spread across the flesh – a wash of colour. I gasped. It wasn't only a colour change. The flesh of the creature's arm was no longer smooth and slug-like, but textured, raised in small lumps and bumps, like a toad I'd once seen hopping across a damp path at Hyde Park. It looked like something totally different to the creature I'd first seen. Like a trick that couldn't be real.

'It can change colour?' I said.

The thick arm that clung to the outside of the barrel transformed again – this time to dark brown, banded with grey. Exactly the same colour as the barrel, and again, the same texture. I could even make out the shape of a rivet on its skin. Impossible! How did it see, how could it possibly know the colour of the barrel? Did it even have a head? Eyes?

For a second, the tentacle was completely disguised against the wood. I wanted to get away from it as much as I wanted to get closer.

It was almost invisible now. Imagine that, to just be able to disappear, take a rest from the world, unseen.

'It's a blooming . . . kraken,' said one of the men.

'Ungodly thing,' muttered another.

'Nonsense,' said Mr Lee. 'I've had a devil-fish before, although I admit, nowhere near this size. They are intelligent and engaging. This is good for us – no other aquarium will have anything remotely like them.'

'That's the most sensible comment I've heard from you today, Lee,' said Captain Bickerstaff.

'Uncle Henry wrote a pamphlet called *Sea Monsters Unmasked*,' Charlie said to me.

'Yes – explaining that the monsters that sailors write myths about are simply animals like any other,' finished Temitayo.

One of the keepers jabbed at the octopus' arm with a metal hook, despite Mr Lee's earlier instruction. The end flicked up, displaying its array of circles underneath. Mr Lee snapped at the man and at the same time the octopus reacted. I would say it shot out, because it was that quick, but the movement somehow didn't feel hurried. The arm tilted upwards, swaying, like an eyeless snake. The men all staggered back. The thing seemed to suck back into the barrel and Mr Lee directed the men to quickly heave the lid back into place.

The men looked at each other. One ventured, 'We can't lift the barrel.'

Mr Lee shook his head. 'Not full of water. I admit that I hadn't calculated for the sheer size of them.'

I suddenly felt cold. The octopuses were trapped back in the dark. They wouldn't leave them there, would they? If they couldn't get them into the tank?

'The winch won't take the weight?' said Captain Bickerstaff.

'It won't, I'm afraid,' replied Mr Lee, 'and if it were to fall—'

'Why is this place such an utter shambles?' interrupted Captain Bickerstaff. 'Not at all prepared for the type of attraction that could really turn the tide.'

Silence again. I looked around. There was a drainage grating in the floor just in front of the tank. An idea arrived but I waited for someone else to think of it and say it before I did. No one said a thing. Mr Lee stroked his whiskers.

I gave a little cough to get their attention, like I sometimes did when I could tell the colour a customer was leaning towards would not suit her at all and she might need a little pointer in the right direction. 'Would it work to make a small hole in one corner of the barrel and tilt it – let the water out first?'

'. . . then put the barrel with no water, and the animals still inside, in the tank together?' Charlie grinned at me, then at Mr Lee.

Captain Bickerstaff looked at the floor and pointed. 'That grating must lead to the main storm drain connecting to the beach, so just drain some of the water, making a small aperture . . .' He continued to repeat what I had just said. I felt suddenly doubtful of my idea, but they were already prising open a hole in one of the seams of the huge cask, tipping it and allowing the water to drain.

I tried to picture the octopuses inside, in the dark, water being sucked out from around them, because the water was like air to these animals. I almost felt the dank walls of the barrel around me.

'Sir! Something – the water is . . . wrong,' said one of the attendants.

'What do you mean, wrong?' snapped Bickerstaff.

'It's . . . black.'

He was right. The water pouring from the crack was now black as tar. Black as Indian ink.

'I can feel the beasts moving,' said one of the attendants.

'This is causing these creatures great stress. Despite their size they are delicate and the release of ink is a defence mechanism,' said Mr Lee, a note of panic in his voice.

'Don't dawdle, men, make the hole larger, time is of the essence!' bellowed Bickerstaff.

One of the attendants burrowed the claw end of a large hammer into the existing gap, and levered it open so the wood splintered to make a hole bigger than my fist.

Mr Lee pulled the man's arm back. 'Not that much! Have a care, man, that's too—'

Water gushed out. The smell of the sea, that high stench of the fish market. An ocean animal shut up somewhere it didn't belong. All at once something astonishing happened.

A pale bulge at the gap in the barrel and then . . . the animal inside *poured* out of the hole.

CHAPTER FIFTEEN

It was as if the octopus had somehow turned itself into a paste, the way oil paint squeezed out of a tube. One tentacle, then two, both through a hole no bigger than my fist.

The creature really was enormous. It was impossible that it could fit through a hole that small, yet it was happening, and so quickly, in a mass of suckers and flesh and weird sliding movement, more water than an animal.

'Tip the barrel back up—!' shouted one of the attendants.

'Get the winch tied, we'll have to hope it holds,' said Mr Lee.

None of the attendants shifted; all were pointing their broom handles at the octopus. I felt Temitayo's shoulder against mine but didn't move, horrified but mesmerized. Could this really have been my idea? Two gigantic tentacles were out of the barrel now, which meant six more were still in the barrel, and then there was the other creature as well.

'Is it poisonous?' said one of the keepers.

'No, I shouldn't think so. It's not likely,' said Mr Lee, 'but the suction is surprisingly strong even in smaller specimens, so we need to act quickly so we don't allow it—'

An escaped tentacle curled tight around one of the keeper's ankles and before he could scream, it spiralled up to his knee then his thigh.

The octopus yanked the man clean off his feet.

The keeper grasped the pole he'd been wielding and stabbed the tentacle now winding around his leg like a snake. Mr Lee crouched by the man, and Captain Bickerstaff's yells merged with the man's frantic curses. I watched in horror, my hand searching behind me for the flap in the heavy canvas tent, but unable to take my eyes off the battle taking place. The keeper slipped and slid on his back in the inky water on the floor, battering at the tentacle, mangling the flesh, until with a gush of the animal's dark blood, he was free.

The octopus' arm was sliced almost through, an ugly wound. Temitayo released a whimper and covered her mouth. I felt frozen to the spot. It took a few breathless moments before the undamaged tentacle crept across to the mangled arm and somehow sucked it back through the hole with it, leaving a trail of blue down the outside of the barrel.

The creature had blue blood.

Mr Lee threw off his jacket and the other keepers bundled it into the hole and were directed to hold it there.

'This is a very valuable specimen,' roared Mr Bicker-staff. 'How dare you damage it!'

'Damage it? What are you doing bringing us that cursed thing? Look what the unholy beast done to *me*!' screeched the attendant as he scrambled to get to his feet. His britches were torn and I gawped the marks on the man's leg. No blood, but red circular suction marks in tracks of neat lines.

My idea.

'Looks like the octopus came off worse to me,' said Charlie, pointing at the pooling blue blood around the grating.

'He's right, Gerald,' said Mr Lee, helping the man to his feet. 'The suction hasn't broken the skin, the bruises will heal in a few days—'

'But your employment will be terminated as of now,' said Captain Bickerstaff, his face scarlet, eyes bulging.

The keeper pushed through the canvas curtain and staggered off. The other attendants were already attaching a winch hook to the ropes around the barrel.

Mr Lee mopped his brow. 'That seems a little harsh, Captain, as none of us expected—'

'Are you questioning my actions, Lee? This is an absolute shambles, man. You do realize that aquarists are ten a penny—'

'Now hang on a minute,' interrupted Charlie, 'it's not Uncle's fault—'

Now Captain Bickerstaff's face had turned white and his voice was a menacing rumble. 'You had best silence your collection of impudent children immediately. If it hadn't been for this one's suggestion' – he turned to point at me – 'my prize specimen would not have been damaged.'

Mr Lee hung his head. I felt sick.

My fault.

'Your employment here is hanging by a thread, Lee. I will be back in two weeks and if that creature isn't pulling in crowds . . .'

The captain didn't finish. He checked his pocket watch and cufflinks, then raised his nose to give a gutsy sniff. He flounced out of the tent and was gone.

'Charlie, please escort Vinnie and Temitayo back up to Mrs Ruggles,' said Mr Lee. 'Some sweet tea for the shock.'

He didn't seem angry, but surely this was my fault. It was my idea to make the hole. Temitayo and Charlie turned to go, but I had to say something.

'I'm sorry,' I whispered, but Mr Lee had now turned to help the attendants guide the barrel to the aperture at the top of the tank.

Despite my guilty feelings, I was still fascinated and now desperate to see the animals in full. Were they both the same size? How could they each have eight of those huge arms?

I'd done enough damage.

It was very difficult to imagine how a creature like the octopus was going to *settle* anywhere, let alone in that tank.

CHAPTER SIXTEEN

Temitayo's guardian Mrs Heap met us halfway down the stairs, flushed and blinking. She clutched at her heart.

'Mary! You must not wander off like that, dear, I was quite frantic.'

'Sorry, Mrs H,' said Temitayo sweetly, 'but I did tell you.'

Mrs Heap's round glasses were steamed up. 'Did you? I must have been quite distracted. Mrs Drayton's daughter has just had twins and her sister is . . .'

The lady trailed off, removing her glasses. Temitayo took them from her, swiftly polished them and gave them back.

'This is Vinnie, she's Mrs Ruggles' niece, and Charlie – who is Mr Lee the aquarist's ward. They kindly offered to show me the aquarium.'

'Well, I don't suppose there is any harm,' she said.

I guessed she had missed the injured keeper limping his way out, and then the furious Captain Bickerstaff, or she might have had a quite different impression.

Charlie caught my eye, his lips pressed together, suppressing a smile. I wasn't ready to laugh about any of this. That keeper had been injured and then made un-employed, the octopus was hurt and Mr Lee's job was under threat, all because of me and my idea. There was a good reason why Mother always did the talking.

Mrs Heap took Temitayo's arm and hurried her up the stairs. The girl glanced behind her and gave me a despairing look. At the top of the stairs Temitayo was ushered to the table where the other two older women were sitting, but she didn't sit.

'I wondered, ma'am, if I could spend some more time with Vinnie and Charlie. They are quite suitable companions . . .'

Mrs Heap looked me up and down with what I thought was approval, but her eyes lingered on Charlie's inky fingers. 'I've always thought it right you spend time with those your own age,' she mused, 'but remember, Sir Edgar is sending a coach for you next week, and he had asked that you practise both that French song on the pianoforte and the poem in ...'

Temitayo frowned. 'Greek? Latin?'

'I don't know as I can remember, just practise both?' said Mrs Heap.

My voice seemed to come from nowhere. 'I could help with the French, *certainement*.'

What was I saying? Mother had taught me a few words. I certainly couldn't help Temitayo, and it wasn't at all like me to lie. I felt like covering my mouth to stop anything else coming out and causing trouble, but the delighted look on Temitayo's face made me feel better.

'We could take a walk on the promenade?' said Temitayo.

Mrs Heap's companions had already started their conversation again and she quickly agreed. Aunt Bets brought over a handkerchief containing some broken biscuits, which Charlie pocketed.

'*Merci*, Vinnie,' said Temitayo as the three of us headed across the terrace to the steps leading down.

'It's low tide, we could walk on the sand?' said Charlie.

I had brought two pairs of boots and one pair of dress slippers in my case. I was wearing the sturdiest of my boots but the soft tan suede would be ruined by sand. But this was real sand on a real beach, and I'd dreamt so long of being here that I found I didn't care one jot about my boots as we stumbled down the pebbles.

'I don't actually speak French,' I said to Temitayo.

'I could tell,' said Temitayo. We smiled at each other.

'So you are going to perform a song in French and a poem in Greek? Which ones? I studied both at school,' said Charlie, plopping himself on the stones and untying his bootlaces.

'Oh, you won't know them. I wrote them myself,' she said, and then seeing the incredulous look that passed between us, she shrugged. 'That's why Sir Edgar Randall brought me back from Africa on his ship HMS *Rose*. He is a member of The Royal Niger Company, who were securing treaties after my people had been in a long, tough civil war. I was in an orphanage – my family died in the war – where Sir Edgar's young wife visited, and she was impressed when I quickly learnt French from her as well as English. She adopted me and I was to call her Mama. But she herself didn't survive the journey back to England.'

I felt my mouth begin to drop open and forced it shut. There was me thinking the journey from London to Brighton was quite the adventure. There was me missing my mother when Temitayo had lost two.

Before I could say anything Charlie cut in. 'So you are a war survivor?' he said.

'I suppose so, but I don't remember much. All I've been told is that I was found in a cave in a town called Imesi-ile, with a group of children hiding from gunfire. The older children who were with me told the missionaries that my people were Ekiti and my whole family was dead. I seemed about three years old and all I would say was "Temi". So they called me Temitayo. Then at the orphanage Lady Randall named me Mary.'

'So which country was that?' said Charlie.

Temitayo shrugged. 'Lady Randall said the people I came from didn't have countries, but kingdoms instead. After the war, the British wanted to put them all together.'

'Is there anything you do remember?' I said, wondering if I should ask. But Temitayo's head dipped to the side.

'From before the orphanage? Maybe. I sometimes think I remember a man whose hands smelt of hot dust, and who had a low laugh. I remember sweet food, soft – it was probably yam I've found out since – and a woman's voice singing. Then the cave was so dark and other children cried when gunfire echoed. It sounded like *ki-ri-ji kir-ri-ji kir-ri-ji.*'

Both Charlie and I were silent for a moment.

Temitayo shrugged, with a small smile. 'I was so young. I don't remember the orphanage very well either, just stiff white sheets, and I didn't like the tight clothes at first. We prayed a lot. I was only around five when Sir Edgar brought me to England.'

'But you don't live with Sir Edgar now?' said Charlie. He had pulled off his boots and socks and was rolling up the bottom of his trousers.

'No. Mrs Heap was his governess and now she looks after me. I am expected to' – she paused as if finding the right words – 'display . . . my achievements at society occasions every few months. Sir Edgar is quite proud of me.'

'I think he should be, if you can speak both Greek and Latin. And you know a lot about animals too,' I said, surprising myself by stating this bold opinion. Temitayo smiled.

'I like to read, that's all. Really, Sir Edgar credits his young wife for everything I do,' she looked around as if about to say something she shouldn't, then lowered her voice. 'But I have been alive for fourteen years and I only knew her for one of them.'

I nodded. I wondered about my mother. Was she proud of me because she'd taught me, or for myself . . . ? I wasn't sure if I could tell, or if there was a difference.

'Is Sir Edgar . . . nice?' I asked, thinking I sounded childish.

Temitayo grinned. 'I'm always told he's very kind to

me, and he's certainly never seemed unkind. He doesn't really know me, I suppose. But Mrs Heap does, and she's probably had quite enough of me!'

'She seems quite fond of you to me,' said Charlie. 'Trust me, I know what it looks like when someone has had quite enough of a person.' He pointed at himself and rolled his eyes. I could only manage the smallest laugh.

Temitayo's story was such a sad one. I couldn't imagine living with someone who wasn't my family, whose care of me was a paid position. I glanced over at her, but she only looked thoughtful as she sorted the stones into a brown pile and a grey one. She might not want people feeling sorry for her, but still I laid my hand on top of hers, which was curled round a pebble, and gave it a quick squeeze without meeting her eye.

When she continued there was a smile in her voice, 'But have you ever seen the likes of that octopus? I'm going to write about it in my diary right now so I can remember it when I need some excitement. Which is quite often, as you can imagine.' She drew out her lady-like little book and leant over it, one hand writing, the other hand cupped around the page, a glimpse of her tongue appearing at the side of her mouth.

Charlie drew out a larger leather notebook from his waistcoat pocket. 'Yes,' he said, licking the end of his pencil, 'I'm going to jot a few notes myself.'

I felt my small sketchbook in the pocket inside my skirt, self-conscious. I imagined sketching those octopus tentacles, the curved lines, the rows of suckers . . . I couldn't. I wouldn't know where to start. Flowers and ribbons, feathers and bases of hats – that was what I knew. I saw how Temitayo shielded her work from view. Maybe if I . . . no. I just couldn't. Anyway, I should probably get back, as I needed to apologize properly to Mr Lee. I'd caused a lot of trouble on my first day here; a rare animal had been hurt and a man had lost his job. None of this would have happened if Mother was here.

I drew up my knees and rested my chin on them. Charlie looked up, slipping his notebook back in his pocket.

'It's not your fault the octopus started escaping, you know,' he said. 'Old Bickerstaff agreed to your suggestion. He even tried to make out it was his own idea.'

I shrugged, although I did feel a little better.

'And he threatens to relieve Uncle Henry of his position every time he visits, so don't fret about that – the captain is mostly hot air.'

His bare toes wiggled in the sand. I tried not to think of Gerald and the octopus tangled up together, the blue blood.

'Are you coming for a paddle then, city girl? Bet you've never felt the sand between your toes before. I always like to get my feet wet, it helps me think,' he said.

'Mrs Heap says the very thought of it gives her a head cold,' said Temitayo, 'and in April, I'm inclined to agree with her.'

I laughed. Not a chance I was taking my boots off, but I walked down on the sand with Charlie, leaving Temitayo busy writing, sitting on the dry pebbles. I crouched and ran my fingers through the sand, cold, gritty, silky. The grooves I had made flooded with water. I drew a wavy line with my finger, swooping around to form a long snake-like shape, with two rows of dots. A tentacle.

'What are you drawing?' called Charlie, hopping from foot to foot in a couple of inches of freezing water on the shoreline.

I pretended not to hear him. Were the octopuses safely in the tank now?

The lines I'd drawn were already filling, blurring. I scuffed them with my feet, and picked up a stone with a hole, peering through it at the bare-footed boy.

BRIGHTON AQUARIUM

Captain Eustace Bickerstaff, explorer and manager, announces the displays for the summer season.

Magnificent British sharks, fine seahorses, aquatic animals from the far reaches of the globe, graceful sea stars, fascinating turtles and the famous seal enclosure.

Coming soon and never seen before: rare gargantuan devil-fish.

Situated on the promenade in easy reach of pier, bathing machines and all manner of seaside attractions. Ruggles Terrace Tearooms above the aquarium terrace serves the finest cakes and pastries.

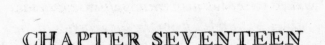

CHAPTER SEVENTEEN

The next day passed slowly. I sat at a table at the terrace cafe, feeling out of place as Aunt Bets chatted to customers, served tea and cakes and wiped tables. Neither Charlie nor Temitayo appeared. Mr Lee had been there at breakfast but didn't stay long and had his head deep in his notes. I somehow couldn't gather the courage to ask him about the octopus, still feeling guilty that it had been my idea to put a hole in the barrel.

I flicked through the magazines Mother had left for me. *Myra's Journal of Dress and Fashion*, *Weldon's Ladies Journal* ... often the colour plates inside first appeared in *Les Modes Parisiennes* so Mother loved me to study and copy them, adding my own twists to the designs. Aunt Bets had said I could stay home; she had made some biscuit dough and suggested I cut out shapes and bake them in the range, but I was too afraid of doing something wrong. She also recommended I explore the seafront or pier, but I knew Mother would disapprove of me wandering around alone.

So I waited.

I waited for Mother to send her forwarding address, to tell us she had arrived safely in Paris.

I waited to see my new friends again. I waited to see the octopus.

At teatime, every table was full and Aunt Bets looked flushed, jolly, but definitely a little overworked. I rested my chin on my hand and looked out to sea.

A square of folded white material landed on the table in front of me. I looked up. Aunt Bets raised her eyebrows, and I realized what she had given me. An apron. My cheeks grew hot. What would Mother say? She hired a charwoman to come in twice a week at home for cleaning, and didn't like me to do anything towards keeping house. But I couldn't just sit looking at magazines for weeks.

'I couldn't . . . I mean, you wouldn't want me . . . I don't know how,' I said.

Aunt Bets rested a hand on my shoulder. 'You're a

smart and capable girl, our Vin. These practical sorts of things you learn as you go. I'll be here and put you right, but only if you need it. Get doing!'

Was that really the way? Mother always insisted things were done right, or not at all. No half measures. So many times I'd started a sketch again from scratch because one line was wrong.

Get doing.

I stood, fastening the apron with shaking hands and flashing Aunt Bets a weak smile as she directed me to a table where the people were leaving.

At first I worried about breaking the china, or forgetting orders, so concentrated on clearing the tables. I watched the way Aunt Bets served the tea and cakes. With a few encouraging nods from her I was soon serving as well. When I splashed a drop of tea dregs on an elderly lady's skirt she yelped, 'Watch yourself' and my face felt on fire. I froze, mumbling an apology with a curtsey, and she simply turned back to her cake with a tut.

Aunt Bets swept by me and I expected her to scold me, but she just said, 'See – just get doing. You're doing fine and will be more careful next time.'

As the teatime crowd dwindled, Temitayo arrived and rushed straight over to me, a huge grin on her face. Today she wore a different little boater hat with cerise ribbons. I thought even Mother would be rather impressed by its jaunty angle. She slipped her arm into mine and I felt embarrassed of my tea-stained apron.

'You're allowed to work in the tea shop? Oh, lucky you. You must hear so many interesting conversations.'

I wasn't sure what to say to that; I'd been far too worried about dropping something to eavesdrop.

'Have you been back downstairs to the aquarium?' she said.

'Well – no. Not yet.'

Temitayo tipped her head to one side.

'I think I need to apologize properly to Mr Lee and . . .' I trailed off. And what?

'Well – you don't,' said Temitayo, 'but it's a good enough excuse.'

Aunt Bets told me she didn't need me any more, and I headed down the stairs with my new friend.

We rushed past the tanks, in search of Mr Lee, the blue-green light dim. The biggest tank was covered with black fabric, tacked firmly to the wooden frame.

'How annoying, I am *dying* to see them,' said Temitayo.

Mr Lee was nowhere obvious, but next to the octopus tank, which was pride of place midway down the gallery, there were two doors.

One displayed a plaque saying *Private* and the second said *Reading Room*.

Temitayo knocked on the reading-room door and pushed it open. The boxy space housed six tables and was lined with books, the one in the corner with a brass plaque saying 'reserved' piled high with papers. This room didn't say 'no ladies', but it smelt of tobacco and leather and walking in uninvited felt strange. Mr Lee was poring over a huge book, and then another head popped up.

'Charlie – you're here!' I said.

'And you are very observant,' said Charlie.

'I suspect she is,' said Mr Lee. 'In fact, all three of you are.'

His hair stood on end and I soon saw why, as he sat and immediately ran both hands through it, frowning at his papers.

I could do this. I cleared my throat. He looked up, his eyes unfocused for a moment, then smiled.

'Mr Lee, I am truly sorry about what happened yesterday,' I said as clearly as I could.

'Oh, don't think on it,' he said. 'Gerald wasn't quite suited to the position. I need my keepers to be . . . calmer in a crisis.'

'It was Bickerstaff that was the problem,' said Charlie, dark eyebrows forming a deep V.

'I won't comment on that. It's wise not to bite the hand that feeds us,' said Mr Lee.

'Are the new animals . . . recovering?' I said.

'The octopus tank is covered to allow them to acclimatize. Sorry – excuse me, I am trying to record what happened yesterday, but my drawings seem to get worse year by year.'

I peered over at his work, sorry to see it really was quite poor. He was pressing far too hard, the lines strong and dark, the octopus tentacles flat, desperately in need of contrast and shading.

'I'm going to give Vinnie and Temitayo a tour of the aquarium if that's all right with you, Uncle,' said Charlie.

Mr Lee rubbed his fingers through his curls so they stood on end, and bit the end of his pencil.

'Of course, of course,' he said, 'enjoy yourselves.'

'We will.' Charlie gave me and Temitayo a sly grin.

CHAPTER EIGHTEEN

Charlie closed the door of the reading room behind him and beckoned us over to the first of the doors, marked *Private*. He glanced around the gallery. One small family was on their way out and two couples were at the far end. No one was looking at us.

He pushed open the door to a dark passage. I looked at Temitayo and she gave a shrug. We followed Charlie inside.

'You are now behind the scenes in the aquarium,' whispered Charlie, his back to the door.

'Are we allowed here?' I said, looking around at the rough brick walls in the half-light.

'Well, Charlie did say he was going to give us a tour of the aquarium, and I didn't hear his uncle say anywhere we *couldn't* go,' said Temitayo.

'Exactly,' said Charlie, teeth gleaming in the dim light, 'and you want to see the octopus, don't you? Just don't touch anything or Uncle will have my guts for garters.'

I hitched up my skirt, following Charlie, Temitayo behind me, down a dank brick passageway that seemed to be built into the aquarium wall. We splashed through hidden puddles on the rough floor and I felt the damp seep through my buttoned ankle boots.

On the left was the glass that must be the back of the tanks. There were no plaques to tell me what I was looking at this time. I was startled by a large flat spotted fish darting from the sand as we passed, and the British sharks still circled as if they were unable to stop. Gas lights were positioned above each tank to shine into the water, and we kept to the shadows behind them. It was like an adventure story, something out of a penny dreadful and definitely not a place Mother would think was suitable for me. The air was stuffy and thick and warm, although my clothes felt cold against my skin as they soaked up the moisture.

'Does this passage lead anywhere? I mean, is there another way out?' said Temitayo.

'Not any more,' said Charlie. 'At the far end it joins

with what used to be an old smugglers' tunnel.'

'So could we go right through to the beach from here?' I said.

'Oh no. Uncle told me it's walled off and unsafe due to rockfalls,' said Charlie. 'Don't go getting any ideas. I'd end up with a thick ear if we went that far.'

'Would Mr Lee punish you like that?' said Temitayo.

'Of course not. But my father might if Uncle Henry sent me home.'

We continued on, past a boxy little fish with bulbous eyes and a tank of giant snails stuck to the glass, until we reached the largest tank. The gas lamps were low and Charlie turned them up to join the hiss of the other lamps along the corridor. But the interior of the tank was still darker, probably due to the fabric curtain on the other side.

'Uncle Henry says no tapping on the glass, no noise,' said Charlie.

I moved along until I found a gap in the seaweed and peered in.

The thick glass was amazingly clear. Smooth round pebbles covered the base of the tank, grey, tan, black and deep orange in colour, many mottled in a combination.

I scanned the water. A large common crab like any you might see at market scuttled from one side to the other, waking another just like it. Where were the octopuses?

'Are the creatures inside that temple?' I said, peering into the sculpture on the bottom of the tank. It was a big model, the size of a side table with windows in the top and sides.

Charlie pressed all his top teeth into his bottom lip as if unable to contain himself.

'They are far too big for that, surely,' said Temitayo.

'Watch and wait,' said Charlie.

I watched and waited until my eyes watered. I wondered if Charlie was playing a trick on us, because the creature I'd seen yesterday, sliding from the barrel and wrapped around the keeper, clearly was *not* in this tank.

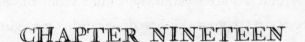

CHAPTER NINETEEN

All three of us stared into the empty tank, then at the same moment Temitayo and I turned back to Charlie with narrowed eyes.

'You'll need to be more patient than that,' whispered Charlie.

Temitayo tapped her notebook with her fingers and I heard her silk skirts rustle as she fidgeted. Finally something caught my eye. Was there a shift in the tank, or were my eyes just starting to water? No . . . it was like the stones themselves were blurring. I peered closer, both hands against the glass. Maybe it was the stuffy tunnel making me dizzy, because I was starting to feel I wanted to get out.

No. There. Right there in the middle of the tank, the stones were not stones . . . a shape flickered.

'Look!' I pointed and it came into focus.

It had to be the octopus but it was quite unlike the tentacled beast I remembered. Bands of deep red and silvery white travelled over its mass, mesmerizing. It squatted at the bottom of the tank. A . . . lump, but a lump of impossible colour. A lump that had now opened a large silvery half-globe of an eye, a black bar across the middle of it. Now its colours faded to a soft grey, the eye closed and it crept – or slithered? We didn't see a glimpse of those snaking arms – across the tank floor into the corner, where it wedged itself.

Temitayo gasped. My nose touched the glass. It was so huge, maybe the size of all four of the puffy pillows plus the eiderdown that Mother had on her four-poster bed back at home, all bundled up into a grey squishy pile, as if I'd imagined the vibrant striped-red pattern.

'It changes colour so cleverly,' I said, 'it can disappear.'

'Uncle says it is the most splendid example of disguise he's seen,' said Charlie, 'particularly as the animal is so huge.'

'How often does it put on a display like that?' said Temitayo.

'Only for a few minutes at a time,' said Charlie. 'I was

helping Uncle make observations earlier but it became quite a bore. I'm glad you saw it.'

'Now it looks like eel jelly, two days old,' said Temitayo.

'Well, you might not be looking your best if you'd been stuck in a barrel for a month then had your arm almost hacked off,' said Charlie.

'Was it badly injured?' I said; that tinge of guilt again.

'Uncle can't tell yet; he says it's best for us not to interfere.' He mimicked Mr Lee's voice: '*Come now, Charlie, be patient, a new animal needs peace and time to adjust and this one will also need time to heal as well.*'

'Your uncle is kind, though,' I said.

'Yes, he is,' said Charlie, 'but being patient is so tedious. Apparently, no veterinarian would have the expertise to treat an animal like this.'

'Is that its food?' asked Temitayo, pointing to the base of the tank.

A number of titbits lay there; I recognized sprats, eels, mussels. All dead. Some living sprats flittered dolefully back and forth in the huge tank.

'Do you think it could be . . . dying?' I couldn't keep the horror from my voice, even though I didn't know why I was suddenly so attached to this animal. It truly was the most ugly and frightening creature I'd ever seen. It was also the most fascinating.

'Where is the other one? That one wasn't also injured, was it?' said Temitayo.

Charlie gave a low whistle. 'Not exactly injured – well, I suppose you could call it that . . .'

Temitayo and I looked at each other.

'What do you mean?' I said.

'Did they make a mistake and there was only one animal in the barrel after all?' said Temitayo.

Charlie sounded quite gleeful. 'Rather a big mistake on all accounts – at least, I'm sure the octopus who was murdered and eaten thought so.'

I gasped and Charlie grinned.

'Eaten? Eaten by what?'

There were only two creatures in that barrel and one had been eaten? I snatched my hand away from where I had spread it on the glass, imagining the enclosed dark space of the barrel, tentacles writhing, fighting, and I felt sweat bead on my forehead.

Temitayo shook her head, irritated. 'Oh, Charlie. These events are part of nature, you know.'

'Ah, but this story will get the crowds in. This is perfect. Not two animals but one. Our devil-fish is also a' – he paused for effect – 'cannibal.'

'Devoured one of its own kind, a prisoner of circumstance,' whispered Temitayo.

I glared at her – I wasn't sure there was any need to

encourage Charlie and his grim imaginings – but she continued to stare at the octopus. An image formed in my mind. Sixteen tentacles intertwined, the darkness of the barrel, those rippling bands of red and white travelling over one body; the other smaller, pale, trying to make itself shrink, invisible. But it had no chance; there was nowhere to hide.

What was wrong with me? This was quite ghoulish. Mother would be horrified.

I shook my head as if trying to jiggle the images free, but my thumb circled against my forefinger, yearning for pencil and paper. I had to draw it when I had some time alone. Nobody needed to know.

CHAPTER TWENTY

Charlie pushed through the door and we followed him back into the underwater light of the gallery. He headed back to join Mr Lee in the reading room, shooting me and Temitayo a last mischievous grin over his shoulder.

Up on the terrace Temitayo joined her guardian at her usual table. Where had I put my apron? I would see if Aunt Bets needed any help and then—

I stopped still.

A man was talking to Aunt Bets at the counter. Bowler hat pushed low, narrow cane swinging impatiently, although he was smiling.

Mr Jedders.

I recalled Mother's determination to leave. At night, with no warning. Her face as she dragged me to the floor of the carriage to avoid him seeing us.

Her words – *I let him go . . . disgruntled . . . too big for his boots . . . trust me.*

Her white knuckles as she'd gripped the long hatpin.

What was Mr Jedders doing here?

'Ah, here she is. Vinnie,' said Aunt Bets, calling me over, but already examining the expression on my face and narrowing her eyes.

Mr Jedders turned, and met my gaze with a boyish grin. 'Ah, looks like the sea air suits you, Miss Lavinia,' he said.

I moved a little closer to Aunt Bets. The smile on Mr Jedders' face faded a touch. He pulled a pained expression.

'I wondered if your aunt here had a forwarding address for your mother,' he said, 'but sadly our talented Mrs Fyfe is keeping her whereabouts quite the mystery.'

I needed to say something. The newspaper had said Mother was in Paris so he must know that much. I spoke slowly but there was a wobble in my voice.

'Mother is in Paris, that's all we know, Mr Jedders.'

His eyes gripped mine for a moment and I looked down at the floor.

'Sorry we can't help you, sir,' said Aunt Bets, 'but could

I pass on a message when we hear from my cousin?'

'No need, it was merely concerning some business matters I need her decision on.'

I couldn't help but frown. He was lying. Mother had said he wasn't working with her any more.

Aunt Bets glanced at me, then stepped forward and slightly in front of me, her voice firm. 'I'll be sure to pass on your enquiry. Now can I fetch you some refreshment before you are on your way, Mr Jedders?'

'No, I must get on, but thank you. A quite charming establishment you have here,' he said. 'Do keep well, Miss Lavinia.' Mr Jedders turned on his heel and marched across the terrace, cane swinging.

Whisk tap, whisk tap.

Aunt Bets waited until he had disappeared and then we both leant over the terrace to follow his bowler hat and the whip of his cane, across the front of the aquarium and away from the sea.

'I'm thinking that fellow isn't your mother's most prized employee?' said Aunt Bets.

I shrugged. 'She said she had to let him go, that he was "too big for his boots". She hid from him on the train.'

'Oh,' said Aunt Bets, frowning, 'that doesn't sound at all like Rosamund.'

I didn't say anything. She was right; it wasn't like Mother at all.

THE SECOND HEART

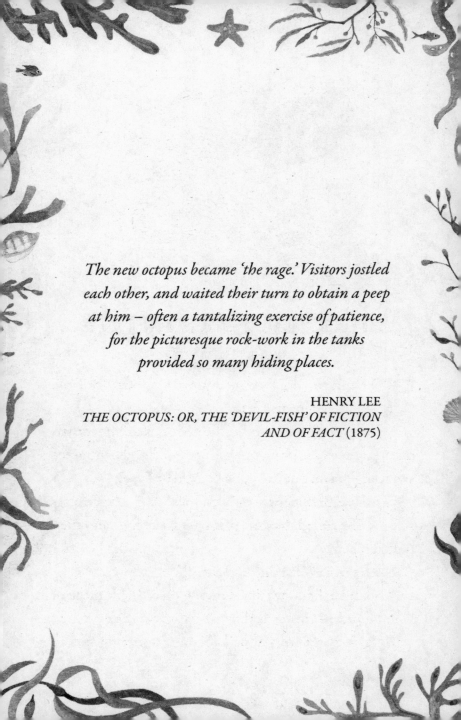

*The new octopus became 'the rage.' Visitors jostled
each other, and waited their turn to obtain a peep
at him – often a tantalizing exercise of patience,
for the picturesque rock-work in the tanks
provided so many hiding places.*

HENRY LEE
*THE OCTOPUS: OR, THE 'DEVIL-FISH' OF FICTION
AND OF FACT* (1875)

CHAPTER TWENTY-ONE

Temitayo and I stepped on to the boards of the pier, arm in arm.

Some of the gaps between the planks were wider than others, and when I caught a glimpse of the churning sea sweeping in and out below us I gave a little yelp.

'Thousands of people walk on these slats, it's perfectly safe . . .' She tested the next plank with her foot and then pulled me on.

'Aren't you even a tiny bit scared?' I said.

'Of course I am, we are standing on a flimsy piece of wood hundreds of yards above the sea,' she said.

I giggled and we skipped forward, minding not to

tread on the bigger gaps.

Hovering seagulls floated on air and the beach stretched in either direction. Below us, the aquarium clock tower was still clear, and I could make out the tables on the terrace and the figure of Aunt Bets. I was glad she wasn't far away.

'So come on then, who was that dashing young man talking to you and your aunt?' she said.

I pulled a face. 'Oh, just someone who used to work for my mother. He's looking for her.'

I could feel Temitayo's eyes on the side of my face.

'You don't know where she is?' she said.

I shook my head. 'And if we did, we wouldn't share it with him,' I said.

'Oh. Very intriguing,' she said, shuffling closer to me.

I smiled at her tone. 'Not really. Mr Jedders just doesn't work for Mother any more, so he doesn't need to know our business.'

'Quite right,' said Temitayo.

She asked more about Mother's business, and what I did in the shop.

'So do you have any designs I can see?'

My smaller sketchbook was in the pocket of my skirts. I hesitated. Temitayo was silent. I'd only ever shown Mother and the customers my drawings.

'It's fine if you would rather not . . .'

I drew out the sketchbook and handed it to her quickly, before I could change my mind.

Temitayo flicked through. 'These are so good, Vinnie! The shading, it's like they jump off the page. You are a real artist . . . but are they all of – hats?'

I shrugged. 'Yes. I draw the hat designs for our milliners, Fyfe's.'

'Yes, but do you have another book, with things you *like* to draw? You know, for fun?'

Suddenly I wanted to lie and say, *Yes, but I had left it back in London.* But why would I lie to Temitayo?

I was struck by a memory, of being much younger, sitting in the parlour of a grand house while Mother fitted a lady and her daughter with their towering head-wear. There had been a parrot in a cage, bright red with a multicoloured tail. It had a beady eye, strong black claws and bald patches on its head and breast. I watched it slowly grip a feather, its eye on me, then pull and pull, until the skin was drawn up, and finally the feather was plucked free, leaving a tiny bead of blood. Both appalled and fascinated, I found my hand closing over the sketch-book in my pocket. As Mother talked and admired and the lady preened in the mirror, I had sat in front of the parrot cage, drawing the animal, lost completely in the lines. When I looked up, Mother's face was cross. She must have been calling me and I hadn't heard.

'Lavinia? Lavinia, listen to me, child. Whatever are you doing?' she said.

The lady clutched her throat. 'What a gruesome drawing. And from a child so young.' She stepped back as though I were something she had just trodden in.

I looked down at what I'd drawn. It was exactly what I had seen, the parrot in the act of plucking its own feather. Its eye seemed to stare right at me. I thought it a good likeness but covered it with my hand.

'I do apologize on behalf of my daughter, she is but eight years old, with much to learn,' said Mother.

'Vinnie?' Temitayo's voice broke through the memory.

'Just hats,' I said, 'that's what I draw.'

The wind was wild on the pier, surrounded by sea. I had taken to tying my hair in a plait, but now it whipped free, the ribbon snatched by the breeze. I tried to catch the scrap of lilac satin, but it was gone. My hair blew free, tangling around my head. I staggered over to where a row of benches were, along the middle of the pier with a glass screen to shelter them from the wind.

We sat down. I was dismayed to find a lump in my throat.

'What's wrong?' said Temitayo.

For some reason I couldn't speak, but the wind chased a tear from my eye. I felt Temitayo's fingers around mine. The curious kindness in her expression helped the words gush out.

'It sounds so silly, but Mother always did my hair for me, and I don't know how to do it, and . . . I don't know where she is, Temitayo. I've never been away from her before for a day in my life.'

I felt tears burning behind my eyes, and my nose burnt when I tried to sniff them back. Temitayo didn't even remember her real mother, what right did I have to tears?

'I know I am very lucky, but . . .'

I covered my face with my hands and felt my fingers become wet. When the sobs subsided, I looked up to see Temitayo's eyes were kind as I wiped my face with a hanky.

'Adults are often telling me I am lucky,' she said. 'But I'd rather make my own luck, I think.'

We both watched a seagull pecking at a twist of sweet paper caught in the pier railings.

'Shall I plait your hair for you?' she said, her fingers already running through it as I nodded. She made a deft plait and tugged a ribbon free from her little hat to tie it with. 'Mrs Heap despairs of my hair – she'd like to do all these braided styles she sees in the magazines for when I visit Sir Edgar, but doesn't understand that those are not designed for my tight curls. In the end I figured out how to twist and pin it myself, so my hat sits just right.'

I nodded, impressed Temitayo had styled her own round chignon, because it really did balance the straw boaters she wore at just the right angle.

'And it never even blows around in the wind,' I said. We smiled at each other.

'Ah – I almost forgot, I brought you this. It's one of Mr Lee's pamphlets, I have already read it.'

I blinked, willing the letters to stay still on the page.

Aquarium notes. The octopus: or, The 'devil-fish' of fiction and of fact.

I opened the book to a bookplate with a picture in black ink: a ship with the arms of a giant octopus entwined around it, heavily cross-hatched and dark.

'Thank you.'

We stood and for the first time I took Temitayo's arm rather than her taking mine.

When Aunt and I went to bed that evening, I slipped a box of matches in my pocket. Feeling guilty, when she had wished me goodnight and closed the door I re-lit the candle and sat up in bed, leaning close to the flame as I opened my sketchbook. I would start on the back page as if it were the first. The ever-moving arms of an octopus were nothing like ribbons, flowers and hats, but if I didn't try here – in the quiet, on my own – I would never dare to try at all. Closing my eyes, I took myself back to the aquarium, to the passage behind the tanks, how I had stared until I saw something.

An eye.

A huge silvery circle with a black bar through the centre.

I began sketching and when I had finished the eye, pleased that the shading showed how it bulged from that soft strange flesh, the likeness spread across the page, almost without me meaning it to. Without the octopus there to copy, I remembered the plates in Mr Lee's book. My imagination took flight under the candle flicker, which reminded me of the flashes of colour across the octopus' body. I returned to the images I'd thought of outside the tank, and drew the inside of the barrel as I imagined it, the eight tentacles stretching out towards their smaller companion, bundled tight in the corner. I shaded in darkness all around, as though the animals were aglow.

I awoke the next morning in the predawn light to Aunt Bets beside the bed, head tilted to one side, looking at my sketchbook. I must have fallen asleep drawing.

'That's really very good, our Vinnie,' she said. 'Can I show it to Mr Lee today? He is always complaining about his lack of drawing skills, and this could help him.'

I didn't know what to say. It was just a rough sketch by candlelight.

'I'll—' I paused, looking up at Aunt Bets, her cotton sleeping cap still on her head. Could I really do this? If it helped Mr Lee . . . I did still feel guilty about the trouble I'd caused when Bickerstaff was there.

'I'll make a copy for him today,' I said.

CHAPTER TWENTY-TWO

I cleared the last of the breakfast tables and leant on the terrace balustrades, staring out to sea. It was always moving, even when calm like today, and the rhythmic sweep of it created the gentlest of roars. A powerful beast, softly snoring. And underneath that surface were all the animals that were now below me in the aquarium. The terrace tea shop was quiet. I couldn't believe a week had passed already and we had heard nothing from Mother.

It was just after we'd cleared up from breakfast. At home I would just be waking.

Good morning, dear heart.

Good morning, Mama.

I was quickly getting used to the routine of living with Aunt Bets, even growing to enjoy riding on the back of her bicycle, but day by day I grew more worried about Mother. How could she not have sent a forwarding address, not a note, nothing at all? At first I knew she'd be travelling and then settling into wherever she was, but she'd have time enough now, because surely the first thing she would think of was me, just as the first thing I thought of was her, every day. It didn't seem possible that she was all right. But Aunt Bets didn't seem concerned; she thought Mother had just got in with the fashionable crowd in Paris and lost track of time. She said a week wasn't so very long.

What Aunt didn't understand was that Mother had always included me in everything before, even when I was a tiny child. When she had company – usually fashionable customers she had become friendly with – I was never sent to bed but would fall asleep on a cushion by her feet, my lullaby the tinkle of laughter and chink of glasses. At market I helped carry her bags; on fair weekends we would walk together in the parks. And I was by her side nearly all of the time at the milliners shop.

How could she have forgotten me now?

I tried to shake the thought free, running my hands over the crisp material of my new dress. Aunt had used the money Mother had left to buy me three cotton dresses, much more practical for spring and for helping in the tea shop. Each had matching bloomers for cycling. Aunt Bets hadn't cared what colours I chose and wasn't going to choose for me like Mother always did, and at first I'd felt frustrated.

'Does this suit me?' I said, holding up a fine yellow check. Mother always said that I looked sallow in yellow; I wondered if Aunt Bets agreed.

'If you like it, it suits you. Buy it,' she said.

I loved Aunt Bets, but I sometimes grew a bit weary of her 'get doing' attitude. But how could she know that Mother chose everything for me? Could that be true? No – there must be some things I chose for myself. If there was I couldn't think of them; it must be because I was becoming flustered staring at the bolts of stripes, checks, florals, with no idea of what *I* thought suited me.

'I'll bet you could happily choose colours for your hat designs,' said Aunt Bets. 'Just think of it like that. I'm going over the road, I'll be back in ten minutes.'

So she really wasn't going to help me. But she was right. Mother trusted me with the hat designs, even if she made tweaks of her own.

I narrowed my eyes and picked out what I thought I liked. The only thing I was sure of was a short summer cape in rich lilac with a jaunty orange-and-black check.

I'd heard Mother say that a good headpiece could turn into a signature style. I thought of the way Temitayo always wore her little boaters tipped at an angle and decided this cape would be my . . . thing. It fastened high so would keep the spring breezes out, and wasn't so long that it would tangle in Aunt Bets' bicycle wheels. Then I chose three bolts of fabric for dresses: black-and-white print, a plain lilac and one with a pale-orange stripe that seemed to go with my new cape.

I had flushed, imagining what Mother might say about my choices. I'd never worn such simple, practical fabrics. At least she'd be pleased there was no yellow.

I sighed and leant my head against my hand, elbows on the balustrade. The sea glittered in amber sunlight. It would be May in a few days and the sea breeze had dropped today, so it had been the warmest day yet.

Mr Lee had greatly admired the copy of the drawing of the octopus I'd given him but I wasn't sure if he was just polite, sorry for me because he knew Mother hadn't been in contact. Still, when the terrace was quiet and the aquarium nearly empty, I had taken to making sketches of the sea creatures. I'd enjoyed adding vivid yellow to the seahorses, and picking out the gleam of the light on the sea lions' glossy bodies as they lounged on the rocks. But no matter where I was in the aquarium, with the circling sharks, or the horned faces of the turtles, I was aware of the octopus tank, still shrouded in black. I longed to see those tentacles unfurl in the water, but the octopus was still not moving, not eating, and I'd begun to lose hope that it would ever recover.

Aunt Bets patted my arm affectionately, wiping her hands on a towel.

'It's uncommon warm, and quiet. I'm going to close for an hour,' she said.

I spun around. Aunt Bets never closed and for a moment I thought she must be ill. But she gave me a mischievous sort of look as she whipped off her apron. She held open a cloth bag. Some sort of clothing? I reached in and pulled a garment out. It was thin cotton and had a sailor collar, but was not a dress; instead, it finished in short bloomers.

I gasped.

'Yes, yes, the water will still be nithering cold, but you won't believe how refreshing,' said Aunt Bets, laughing at the look of horror on my face. 'You don't have to go in, but I'm going to.'

As we strode along the promenade, past the entrance to Palace Pier and towards West Pier, I was forced to skip to keep up with Aunt Bets. The better weather meant more tourists and the line of the promenade curved ahead of us, dotted with people like ants running along a windowsill. But the beach itself was almost empty and lined with blue-painted bathing machines. Half-hut and half-cart, these wooden boxes were dwarfed by their huge wheels. I couldn't believe we were going to go inside one and get into the sea . . . no. I couldn't imagine it, even as we got closer. All those creatures in the aquarium came from the sea that stretched ahead of us, so vast, it made us and everything on land seem so poor and flimsy in comparison.

'This is the men's bathing beach,' said Aunt Bets. 'The ladies' is just the other side.'

She finally stopped at a booth on the promenade painted in blue-and-white stripes, with the lettering *Professor Cowell's Ladies' Baths*. Below it a row of bathing machines stretched along the beach, maybe twenty of them, all out of the water, up on the pebbles.

'Hello there, Gerty,' said Aunt Bets to the lady in the booth.

'First day of the season,' said the lady, 'I can always rely on Bets. And who is this?'

Aunt Bets introduced me to Gerty as she paid and we followed two women – dressed in blue-striped mob caps to match the bathing machines – down the slope of stones to the nearest hut, which the women tilted back with two poles and wheeled towards the shoreline.

'Will you be needing a dipper, madam?' said one

of the women.

I felt my eyes widen. I'd seen dippers on one of the funny postcards Aunt Bets had sent me. They did exactly what their name suggested: they picked up bathers who couldn't swim and dipped them in the water, like an apple was dipped in toffee.

CHAPTER TWENTY-THREE

'Oh, Vinnie, your face!' said Aunt Bets, and to the bathing hut attendant, 'No dipper needed, thank you. Just take us into the shallows.'

She pulled me by the hand up a set of steps that the woman lowered. We were still on the dry stones, but the cart wheels were in the water. I stared out across the blue-grey expanse, trying to remember the plaques and which animals came from English shores. The eels, crabs, some of the . . . sharks? Mr Lee had told me that the animals were more afraid of us than we were of them, but that didn't seem very reassuring right now. But what would it feel like? No – I had no intention of going in. Really, it would be more sensible anyway for me to watch Aunt Bets, ready to call for help if she needed it.

The inside of the hut smelt of fresh paint and damp wood and had two benches, one along each wall plus a couple of shelves and a whole row of hooks above it. The other end had another door. With the doors pulled shut the only light came from the little gratings up near the roof. It reminded me of the barrel and the octopus inside.

Aunt Bets hung up four towels and passed me the bathing suit.

'Quick,' said Aunt Bets, unhooking the front of her dress and hauling it over her head. 'They are waiting for us to get changed, then they'll take us out a bit further.'

Her eyes glittered in excitement. I gulped. Deeper? But Aunt Bets was already pulling on her bathing suit, her back to me, and I didn't want to disappoint her, even if I wasn't going to touch the water. So I did the same, quickly undressing, hanging up my clothes and slipping into the bloomers and short dress.

I'd never worn anything so revealing in my life and I found myself giggling. Aunt Bets gathered up my plait and popped on a mob cap in a navy to match my costume.

'Unless you want to put your head under?' she said.

I shook my head so hard the cap nearly fell off. 'I'm not sure I want to put any of me under,' I said.

'Then you don't have to, of course,' said Aunt Bets. 'I'm impressed you came down here at all.'

I frowned at that. Did Aunt really think me so timid? I supposed she must. I supposed I was.

Aunt Bets shot me an excited smile. She knocked three times on the door that led to the beach and the whole hut began to move. I squealed, wobbled and plopped down on the bench.

'Not too far—' The hut creaked and the wheels rumbled. I imagined the water beneath the boards.

'All right,' said Aunt Bets and opened the door at the back. I gasped. The whole beach could see her.

'Just wave when you are ready, ma'am?' said the voice of the attendant. Aunt Bets closed that door and opened the one at the other end of the machine. The opening framed a spectacular view: the sea glittering and calm, the sun scattering a shining path across it, leading straight to us. Aunt Bets took my hand again and led me out on to another wide ladder. The air hit my bare legs and I sat on the top tread as my aunt stepped down the rest of the steps, and right into the sea. The depth was only midway up her body and I released a sigh of relief. She gasped as she dipped her shoulders and then laughed out loud. Her bathing suit billowed out around her.

'It's absolutely bitter,' she said between sharp breaths, as if she was telling me the most wonderful news.

'And you seem to love it,' I said, clutching my knees and shivering at the thought.

She began to stretch out her arms, swimming in circles. 'I started bathing during my first summer in the tea shop. It gets mighty hot up there and this is just the tonic. But then I found it a tonic on cooler days too. You can just dip your toes, if you want to,' she said. 'You'll know what I mean then.'

I gave her a dubious look but arched one of my bare feet – which looked very small and milk-pale – so just the tip of my big toe touched the water. I had expected it to be like ice, and it was cold, almost cold enough to bite, but not quite.

And I found myself stepping on to the next step so both my feet were submerged up to the ankles. Submerged in the actual sea.

'Ooooo,' I said with a gasp, but the lap of the water was gentle and the sun warm. The feeling was coming back to my feet and I wiggled my toes, watching them through the water. In the sea. I'd go down just one more step, that would still be below my knees, would barely wet my bathing suit—

I scarcely knew what had happened before it had. One foot slipped on the step, my hand grappled for the railing and missed, and I pitched forward, the dark-blue water eager to meet me. My breath was ripped from my chest, cold stung like needles, water in my ears, my eyes, my mouth . . . then arms holding me tight, holding me up.

'All right, all right, I've got you. Just reach down with your feet,' said Aunt Bets' voice.

She was there. I clutched her arms. I wasn't going to drown, I wasn't going to drown, *I wasn't going to drown.* At last my mind believed it and I coughed and spluttered and heaved in painful breaths as my feet found the stones and I could finally come back to myself. I was in the water up to my armpits.

I slowed my breath; the cold had numbed me. My lip trembled, and I felt I might sob with relief, but instead found myself laughing.

I was in the *sea*.

I had longed so much to see it. Now I was in it!

Aunt Bets started to let go of my shoulders but I grasped her hand. My chin trembled with shivers, but I smiled, feeling completely, utterly and almost a little too much . . . alive.

I scrambled up the steps into the bathing machine, careful not to slip again, pushed through the door, grabbed the towel and wrapped it around me. It was warm and dark. I'd been in the sea, all of me, but all was strangely . . . well.

Aunt Bets soon joined me, helping to dry my hair.

'Well, our Vinnie, you do have hidden depths,' she said.

'Doesn't mean I want to be *in* the depths,' I said and we both laughed.

She hugged me and I was glad of the warmth, but more so of her whispered words into the top of my head. *'Proud of you.'*

CHAPTER TWENTY-FOUR

My sea swim had left me more awake than I'd felt since I arrived in Brighton. The light seemed a shade of bright lemon, the air tingling fresh. My wet plait dripped down the front of my dress. When Aunt Bets grinned at me, the smiles I gave back were real rather than polite. We'd shared something completely unexpected together.

We were walking so fast – Aunt Bets definitely walked faster than Mother – that we started to catch up with a boy dressed in oversized rubber boots and a woollen hat. He carried a zinc bucket which was clearly heavy, as he passed it from hand to hand.

'Is that Charlie?' said Aunt Bets. 'Whatever are *you* doing out in the fresh air? You and Mr Lee have become quite the hermits.'

Charlie turned. 'I met the fishing boats. Mr Lee reckoned our octopus might like some fresh oysters,' he said, offering up his bucket which was filled with ridged brown shells, giving away their contents with pearly flashes through the water.

'Your devil-fish eats better than we do,' said Aunt Bets.

'Right now it doesn't eat at all,' said Charlie. 'This is just about the only thing we haven't tried. And we had word from old Bickerstaff today – he wants to know how his new conquest has been received. So we've had to remove the covering at the front of the tank and hope for the best.'

Aunt Bets was suddenly quiet. I wondered what would happen if the aquarium didn't get more visitors, how that would affect her tea shop.

I followed Charlie down to the octopus tank. It was now filling with other small sea creatures – the live foods that had been added to tempt the octopus to eat – and it was populated by crabs, shrimp, even a rather magnificent lobster, yet the octopus had barely moved from the corner and as far as Mr Lee or Charlie could tell, hadn't eaten a morsel. I shuddered to think about the other octopus that it had eaten; maybe it was still quite satisfied from that? It remained a pinkish-grey colour, tentacles folded beneath like a lady with her skirts tucked up. The tube at the side of its neck – the siphon – opened and closed gently, showing it was still breathing the water, still alive. Mr Lee hadn't even been able to get a look at the injured tentacle. I spread my fingers against the glass. *Come on, strange one. Eat something.*

This time I passed more confidently through the door marked *Private* and into the damp corridor behind the tanks.

Charlie pulled out a stepladder and climbed up to unlock the top of the tank, and before I'd realized what he was doing he turned the brass latch.

'Is that a good idea, shouldn't Mr Lee—'

'It's fine, Vinnie, I have plenty of experience feeding the animals.'

I decided not to argue but took a step back.

The octopus was curled against the back corner as usual. A strut ran all the way along the top of the tank and the top pane of glass flipped down on brass hinges. It left a space large enough for a man to climb through and for all the aquarium furnishings to be lifted in.

Charlie produced a small hammer from his pocket and prised open a couple of the oyster shells, then threw them in the tank near the mound of the octopus. He raised his eyebrows at me and we both sucked in our lips as we watched. The noise of the pumps and bubbling water was loud back here, but I was sure I could hear Charlie's pocket watch ticking. Ticking. And still the octopus didn't move. Its funnel stirred gently, in and out, and as it did, the rest of its body swayed slightly.

Charlie's shoulders slumped as he climbed down the ladder and took the rest of the bucket of oysters. He tipped it into the middle of the tank. The iridescent glints of their shells reminded me of the pearl necklace Mother had tucked into her dress in the train carriage.

Had it come from an oyster like this? It was hard to imagine one so big.

'Look what I've done,' he said, as the shells tumbled over the temple model in the middle, almost covering it. 'Now visitors can't even see the one interesting thing there is to see.'

He started back down the ladder and I felt a burst of desperation. We couldn't give up on the octopus – it had been hurt because of my idea. I fumbled for something that might help. The octopus was injured, sick. I remembered Mother had employed the charwoman to sit with me when I had a fever, trying to help me sip broth. But it was only when Mother came up from the milliners and laid her cool hand on my forehead that I had felt strong enough to take a sip.

'Could you, I mean, have you . . . touched it?' I said. 'Fed it yourself? In case it's sick and too weak to move, to reach the food?'

I immediately felt silly. This wasn't a runt puppy or abandoned kitten; it was practically a sea monster.

But Charlie turned to me, eyes wide. 'You might just have something there, Vinnie. We need to think like an octopus,' he said, 'which is not going to be easy as they have brains in their legs, but that is beside the point.'

I'd seen this in Mr Lee's pamphlet but couldn't really take it in. Possibly nine brains and definitely three hearts. I'd spelt out that part even more slowly than usual, thinking I must be reading it wrong.

'Mr Lee says we're not to disturb the animal in any way – of course Bickerstaff suggested we prod it with a pole – but it isn't as if the poor beast has been given the best introduction to humans, is it? Octopuses are sensitive and clever' – he was talking to himself now as he took off his hat, jacket and waistcoat and hung them on a hook on the wall behind him – 'so maybe it is time to show him we are not *all* inclined to whack him one.'

Charlie rolled up his shirt sleeves and reached for a hook on a pole that was propped up by the tank. 'Vinnie, please hold the ladder firmly, won't you?' he said.

My eyes widened. 'Are you going to climb in – I mean, you can't . . .'

But Charlie was already on the top rung.

What had I done now?

CHAPTER TWENTY-FIVE

I gripped the ladder with both hands and pressed my foot against the bottom rung as Charlie climbed. I remembered that snake-like arm curving out of the barrel, searching, then clinging, the scream of the keeper, the blue-black blood. If Charlie needed help there was only me. Where was Mr Lee? How long would it take for me to run upstairs and fetch Aunt Bets?

'I think you should wait for Mr Lee, I can get him. Charlie!'

I watched in horror as he posted his top half through the opening so only his legs were outside the tank. His boots creaked as he rose up on tiptoes.

'Remember how it went for that keeper? I didn't mean you to – please don't.'

I took a firmer grip on the ladder and a deep breath, picturing the octopus suddenly unfurling the full length of its arms to reach for my friend. It wouldn't only get Charlie; it could easily reach me as well. I wanted to step away, my imagination running wild with images of tentacles circling necks, but Charlie needed me to hold the ladder.

This had been my idea. Again.

I watched in horrified fascination as Charlie's bare arm descended through the water, his skin pale and dead-looking, his arm distorted by the water so it seemed a lot longer than it should. He leant over further, and his fingers stretched only a few inches away now from the grey-jelly bulk of the octopus. I shuddered, narrowing my eyes.

'I can't reach him, so I'll waft the water to try and gain his attention,' he said, voice muffled through the glass.

Charlie began to wave his hand back and forth. The ladder rocked, weeds in the tank swayed, and the octopus itself moved a little too; then gradually one arm drifted free and the whole animal arose from its resting place, adrift in the waves that now slopped back and forth across the tank. The octopus remained a sickly grey but finally I saw the circular suckers on the inside of its arms, those two lines of pale lilac rings as the tentacles unfurled and drifted upwards.

It must be dead after all, the movement only due to the movement of the water. I was stunned at even the thought of it having died, of it having been killed by its fight with the keeper, even though it shouldn't really be a surprise if this was the case; it hadn't moved in a week. Then I started back, and the ladder trembled. Charlie was still as a statue, his arm in the tank like marble.

Something drifted from the octopus along the bed of the tank.

Something pale and huge but detached completely from the main body of the octopus.

It took me a moment to spot the suckers. These were not lilac but a deeper grey than his body and ragged rather than smooth. But it *was* one of the octopus' arms.

And then I understood. It was the damaged arm, colourless and tatty, and it now lay stretched out on the base of the tank like a white eel, a monster from some penny sheet.

'It's . . . fallen off,' I gasped. Suddenly I feared the whole animal was going to come apart and disintegrate arm by arm in front of my eyes.

'Great Scott! Uncle Henry wrote about this,' said Charlie, now bobbing with excitement.

What was he so excited about? The octopus still

hadn't moved and had been sitting curled up on its own rotting limb.

'Mr Lee wrote about what? Charlie! You are rocking the ladder, keep still.'

I peered through the glass.

One crab – ironically it was supposed be there for the octopus to eat – leapt into action and raced across the tank floor to the dead octopus arm, pincered off a chunk of the lifeless flesh and stuffed it into its trapdoor mouth.

The octopus started to spread, tentacles unspooling like ribbons, the top part of each one thick and muscular, the ends spindly and delicate.

This idea had worked! Charlie being so close, the movement of the water . . . something had changed, because the gigantic creature drifted up. Dapples of white and slate grey flashed across its skin as it got closer to Charlie peering down at it through the surface of the water. Its tentacles now spread wide, it seemed to have grown to twice the size. My drawing hadn't captured this, not well enough.

I stepped back. The destroyed arm, still being steadily devoured by a gang of crabs in the corner, had been replaced! By a tiny arm, identical in every way except size. It was the strangest of sights, and almost as creepy in its own way as the dead arm. It nestled like a baby being guarded by seven huge brothers and sisters.

'Look – has it . . . it's grown another arm?' I shuddered. It was too other-worldly.

'Will you look at that? This is in Uncle's pamphlet – what do they call it? Something like regeneration? Genesis means beginning . . . *regenesis* – that's it.'

The ladder rocked as Charlie bounced around in excitement. The octopus floated up closer to the surface of the water, where Charlie was still leaning over.

'Charlie, get down. Shut the tank—'

'I'm trying,' he said, then more urgently, 'Vinnie! Help me, it's my buckle—'

Charlie wriggled, his belt buckle caught in the hooked catch of the tank.

The octopus' seven remaining large arms were now seemingly on different missions. Two investigated the temple sculpture, winding through the windows; another three stretched long, so long, *too* long, all the way to the far end of the tank, and stuck to the glass, exploring, and moving steadily back towards Charlie.

And it was too awkward for Charlie to reach the buckle. He was well and truly stuck.

CHAPTER TWENTY-SIX

'Move over, I'm coming up to help you.'

Charlie shifted to the side of the ladder, still frantically jiggling his belt – he couldn't see what he was doing with the top half of his body trapped in the tank. The ladder wobbled, unbalanced until I started to climb, pinning it with my weight.

'Keep *still*.'

One hand gripping the rim of the tank, I unhooked the buckle and he slid his body back through. I'd have expected more relief but his eyes still clung to the octopus.

'Wait, Vinnie. You have to look properly. Not

through the glass.' He shifted on the ladder so there was room for me to perch a couple of rungs up.

Despite my fear and the wobbling ladder, I peeked over the rim of the glass. Charlie already had his head back in, and I gripped a bunch of fabric at the back of his shirt, both to stay steady and to stop him going any closer.

The octopus' sack-like head was only just below the surface of the water. If I curled into a ball, I reckoned its head would be as big as I was. Its eye pinged open, like molten metal with a bar of black through the middle, like a window into utter strangeness, like it was a pocket watch swung by a street hypnotist. I couldn't look away. Its expression was more intelligent than any cat or dog, yet somehow even less like a human. Its legs slid over the glass as it stared at me.

Then with no warning, the octopus swivelled its siphon tube and shot an almighty plume of water clear out of the tank directly into Charlie's face.

I caught Charlie by the shirt as he staggered back, and then almost fell myself as I felt a cool, soft touch at my hand on the rim of the tank. Charlie stumbled down the ladder, then grabbed the pole with the hook on the end. That slight pressure on my hand, the gleam of the wet skin, flickering red and spots of darker red, shifted across my knuckles. Waves of battling instincts – to snatch my arm away and run, or stay completely still. I was waiting for pain, but all I felt was a cool, soft weight.

'Wait,' I whispered. 'It's – touching me.'

'What? Oh my—'

'Shhhhhh!'

Then the tentacle slipped from my hand and glided back across the glass.

Charlie guided the hook into the latch and slammed the panel closed. 'Are you all right? Did it . . .'

I stared at my hand. Slightly damp, not marked, not slimy, not hurt, just trembling.

'No – I'm . . . fine,' I said. 'It was . . . gentle.'

'To you maybe! How am I drenched and you are totally dry? I get blasted and you get to . . . hold hands?' Charlie's red hair hung over his eyes in wet strands and water dripped from the end of his nose.

'Our octopus has excellent aim.' I giggled.

Charlie grabbed a hank of hair and wrung it out, and then we were both laughing so hard I had to clutch my stomach.

Finally I wiped my eyes.

'We need to tell Uncle,' said Charlie.

'Are you going to tell him everything?' I said.

'Oh no, I don't think he needs to know it *all*. Like me trapped in the tank, or you shaking hands with his devil-fish – do you?'

I shook my head. I couldn't imagine the full story of what had just happened would go down well with Mr Lee. I probably wasn't even supposed to be here.

'You'd better dry off a little,' I said.

He grabbed his waistcoat and used it to rub his hair before putting it on again along with his jacket. Most of his wet shirt was covered at least. He took a cap from his pocket and pulled it down low. 'There. Good enough. When Uncle sees our octopus is finally on the move he won't even notice.'

We left the passageway and Charlie headed straight towards the reading room.

The creature was now clinging with three arms to the temple and taking the oysters one by one to feed them underneath to its hidden mouth. I'd not been able to believe that part when I'd seen it in Mr Lee's pamphlet. It looked a bit like a parrot's beak and it didn't seem at all likely that such a soft, flowing animal had something like that, hidden beneath.

Now I saw it must be true, because the octopus definitely had something sharp under the web of skin that joined the tops of its arms together, as it was now making short work of the oysters, cracking and crunching.

Maybe what the animal had needed was contact. I held the hand it had touched in my other hand. I wasn't likely to experience something like that ever again. My blood seemed loud in my veins.

The octopus neatly flipped out the shells one by one until quite a pile grew in front of the sunken galleon. As it did so its colour settled into a deep red, its head – which I remembered was actually called the mantle – rose high above its eyes and it reminded me of a tall hat, like one the bishop had worn on one of the rare Sunday trips to church I'd made with Mother. It threaded its arms between the miniature pillars. I watched, enthralled, as more and more of its bulk disappeared, squeezed improbably between the miniature Greek-style balustrades. It gathered its arms back up, each holding an oyster shell, so it looked like a ball of flesh studded with the iridescent shells, mostly hidden.

Circling the temple, it really was like a sea monster. An image sprang into my mind. 'What if we made a shelter for him that looks like a ship?' I muttered to myself.

'That is a tremendous idea – he could wrap his arms around it, and would look like that picture of the kraken in Uncle Henry's pamphlet.' Charlie was back, grinning at me.

Maybe not all of my ideas were completely terrible after all.

I looked down at my hand where the octopus had touched me, even though I knew there was no mark, and I realized for the first time that I was beginning to think of the octopus not as an 'it', but a 'he'.

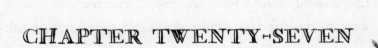

CHAPTER TWENTY-SEVEN

As soon as I reached the top stair to the tea terrace, Aunt Bets beckoned me over.

'There you are. Pop to the grocers on the corner and fetch me a pound of granulated sugar, will you? I've completely run out.' She lowered her voice and handed me some coins. 'I blame it on Mrs Heap and her friends – you can stand a spoon up in their tea.'

The grocers was only at the corner of the main road. I could just about see it in the distance from the terrace, and I'd been there with Aunt Bets on the bicycle to fetch a delivery of dried fruit. I'd just been touched by a gigantic octopus; I refused to be afraid of such a simple task. On my own. It was *fine*.

Aunt Bets was already heading back to the counter. She glanced over her shoulder with a look that clearly said *get doing*.

I pushed open the door to the grocers and the bell rang, jangling over my head on a metal spring until the door closed by itself. The shop was dim inside compared to the bright sunlight, and there were no other customers. Dark wood shelves lined every wall, packed with everything from tinned food to soap. I guessed the grocer must be out the back. I turned to survey the items on the shelves – scrubbing brushes, tooth powder, sacks of potatoes and flour – then I jumped back, as the bell rang again. A young man in a bowler hat stepped in.

Mr Jedders.

I stumbled back, startled.

'Miss Lavinia, how nice to see you. You are looking well,' he said. The black cane swung and came to a tapping halt on the floor in front of him. *Whisk tap.*

I gave him a nod, my heart starting a thudding dance in my chest. Why was he here? He lived in London, and Aunt Bets already told him . . .

'It's been eight days since your mother left. She has obviously sent you a forwarding address by now?' he said, leaning forward, both hands on the engraved handle of his cane.

I glanced over my shoulder. The grocer still wasn't back.

'Oh, the owner will just be a few minutes. He found a boy pilfering in the stock cupboard, just as I was passing.' He smiled, showing his small neat teeth.

I took a deep breath. 'Mr Jedders, if my mother wanted to contact you, I am sure she would have sent word to you directly,' I said, proud that my voice had come out firm and clear.

The young man's handsome face seemed to change, the skin growing tighter over his bones, eyes pale and piercing. Then his charming lopsided smile was back. 'As you know, Mrs Fyfe left in rather a hurry and we do have some ongoing business,' he said.

I shook my head.

'Lavinia, you must be reasonable. Your mother and I had a little . . . misunderstanding . . . my fault entirely, and I need to apologize to her. You know me, I've been a loyal and trustworthy assistant to her for a number of years.'

Where was the grocer?

'I don't *know* her address,' I said, and this time I couldn't keep the tremble from my voice.

Mr Jedders stepped towards me. I swallowed, stumbling back until my spine pressed against the counter.

His voice was just above a whisper. 'Little Miss Lavinia, please don't treat me like a fool. Mrs Fyfe barely lets you out of her sight. I *will* find out where she is. But it would be so much easier if you would simply tell me.'

Finally the grocer appeared behind the counter, red-faced, chest heaving beneath his brown overalls. I released a sigh of relief.

'I must thank you, sir,' panted the grocer. 'Three of my most expensive ivory pipes that child had snatched!'

'At your service, sir. We can't allow ragamuffins to get away with such thievery,' said Mr Jedders. 'A happy coincidence I was just passing.'

'Indeed. Strange thing was the child was so quick to give them back, and with such remorse. I've never known that in a thief. I wasn't even inclined to give him a thrashing, just a clip round the ear,' said the grocer, mopping his brow with a handkerchief.

Mr Jedders tipped his hat. 'Hope to see you again soon, Miss Lavinia,' he said, then turned to the grocer. 'Pleased to make your acquaintance, sir.'

The grocer fetched me the bag of sugar as Mr Jedders left.

'If we had more fine young men like that, the world would be a better place,' he said, nodding towards the door where the bell was still gently swinging.

CHAPTER TWENTY-EIGHT

The walk back to the aquarium was a long and frightening one; for a split second every man with a cane or a hat was Mr Jedders.

My mind raced as I strode along the street, eyes searching. Could Mr Jedders really have been as threatening as he seemed? I knew I was quite timid – certainly compared to Temitayo and Charlie – so could I have been imagining his tone?

I will find out where she is.

No. I was not imagining it. I needed to warn Mother he was looking for her, but how could I do that when I didn't even know where she was?

Back at the aquarium, I told Aunt Bets everything and couldn't help a few tears escaping as I sat near the counter sipping sweet tea with shaking hands. I wiped the tears away angrily. It made me look young and scared and made Aunt Bets look so sorry for me, and I didn't want any of those things.

'I've got this horrible, *horrible* feeling about Mama, Aunt Bets.' I took a big gulp of tea to force back a sob. 'We need to find her before he does.'

'I don't honestly know how,' she replied. 'I could contact the police, but Rosamund is a grown woman who told us she was going abroad, so I can't see what they will do.'

What could I say? Aunt Bets was right. But I was now convinced something was wrong.

'Let's just make sure you are always with someone. For the time being,' said Aunt Bets, 'although it sounds like you were very clear in what you said, so hopefully he's got the message.'

She came round from behind the counter and hugged me, so my cheek pressed into her apron. I breathed in flour and cinnamon and felt a tiny bit better.

I stuck close to Aunt Bets for the rest of that day, but the twist of fear in my stomach didn't go away. I needed to know where my mother was before Mr Jedders found out.

When Mr Lee arrived for breakfast, with Charlie, his satchel overflowing with papers, I felt like I'd been thrown a lifeline. Charlie wanted to be a journalist and journalists were supposed to find things out, weren't they? I'd get him on his own and explain the whole situation.

I always helped Aunt Bets at breakfast – the one guaranteed busy time of the day – and I took over their teas, but before I could say a word Charlie slammed a paper down, rattling the table.

'Will you just look at this!' he said, jabbing at an article with his finger.

I blinked, unable to believe what I was seeing.

My artwork – my sketch of the two octopuses entwined together in the darkness of the barrel. The drawing I'd done in bed by the light of a candle, right there – in a printed newspaper.

'How?' I blurted.

I plopped down on a chair next to him and pulled the article around to look. My lines looked better in a real newspaper. I still couldn't believe it.

'Uncle Henry showed it to me, and we agreed how uncommonly good it was, so I sent it off with my article. I knew you wouldn't mind.'

'Charlie,' said Mr Lee, 'you cannot send off an artist's work without permission, no matter how *uncommonly good* it is. I do apologize on his behalf, Vinnie. I fear I am far too lenient with him.'

'I don't mind,' I said, still feeling a little dazed.

'What's doing?' said Aunt Bets.

Charlie gleefully explained, and I dared not look at Aunt Bets.

I felt a squeeze on my shoulder. 'This is absolutely excellent, Vinnie. You must draw more if this is what you enjoy – get doing. As soon as the rush is over, you could go down to the aquarium ...'

'Yes! I will furnish you with a table, or an easel, whatever you prefer,' said Mr Lee.

I opened my mouth to protest, but then closed it and smiled instead. My drawing in a newspaper?

Mr Lee ate quickly and soon Charlie and I were alone.

The article was in such tiny print. I traced it with my finger, trying not to mouth the words and feeling a flush on my cheeks that they would surely all notice.

'Here – read it aloud if you want and I'll fill in any longer words,' said Charlie.

I hesitated. But when I began to read, I found I knew more of the words than I thought and Charlie didn't let me struggle with the ones I didn't.

BLOODTHIRSTY GIANT DEVIL-FISH TO TERRORIZE BRIGHTON

But never fear, it is not the popular medicinal waters of Brighton beach resort that are haunted by this gruesome animal.

The story began in the deep Atlantic when intrepid collector and aquarium manager, Captain Bickerstaff, netted two octopuses – uncommonly huge for their species – almost capsizing the fishing boat that captured them.

Still entwined in each other's arms, these beasts finally reached Brighton Grand Aquarium to reveal a shocking truth. Only one octopus remained in its wooden prison.

The giant octopus of Brighton Aquarium is a cannibal and the barrel was filled with blue blood, the only trace left of its smaller travelling companion.

CHAPTER TWENTY-NINE

'This is marvellous, Charlie,' I said. 'You are so clever. I can barely read it, and you actually wrote it! This is sure to get some visitors...' I saw his face and trailed off.

'I didn't write it,' he said, his voice very flat.

'Oh. But...?'

'It was... someone else. One of the keepers must have spoken to a journalist because Uncle says it has nothing to do with him. I worked so hard on that piece. But they still used your sketch, I'm pleased to say,' he said.

I scanned his face to see if he really was pleased or if he was being bitter, but there was no trace of a sneer.

'I must accept the competitive world of journalism,' he said, 'and this article has a quite different style to mine, which must be more suited.' He seemed to brighten.

'And you *are* just starting out,' I said.

'Yes . . . I am only fourteen. But you're only twelve and your first sketch is in a national paper! I think that deserves cake,' he said.

I fetched him a large end-piece of Battenberg cake, then swallowed, unsure how to approach what I had to say next. I pulled my chair closer to his and scanned carefully around. I'd done this many times since my confrontation with Mr Jedders.

I lowered my voice. 'My mother hasn't been in contact and it's been ten days. It's like she's just disappeared. And this Mr Jedders, the assistant that she used to work with, followed me to the grocers' – I chose my words carefully – '*demanding* to know where she is. There's something going on and it involves him. I know it.'

Charlie brandished his notebook, eyes bright. 'Right. Tell me the address of the milliners, and everything you know about this demanding ex-employee Mr Jedders,' he said.

That didn't take long. I could describe him, but had no idea where he lived or anything about his people. I just didn't know him that well at all.

'Do you think you could draw him?'

I drew out my sketchpad. Everything about Mr Jedders came alive on the page, his thin *whisk-tap* cane, the pale curls around his ear, his brown bowler hat pulled low.

But I could see that it wasn't enough to go on. I suddenly felt like crying.

'Something else might come to you,' said Charlie. 'Any small thing could be useful, anything that caught your eye, or made you wonder.'

I gazed out to the sea. Today it had white froth dancing across the surface and the sound of the waves was like a hiss. Trouble was, I had never paid a lot of attention to Mr Jedders. I pictured him arriving at the milliners. He would greet Mother, he would flatter any customers that happened to be in the shop. Then Mother would send him on an errand or delivery.

Delivery. A memory sprang into my mind, something that had seemed strange at the time.

'Has anything arrived for me today?'

Mother looked up from her ledger, using her pen to point to a box in the corner.

'Mr Jedders had parcels delivered to the shop a few times. Just for him, not for the milliners or Mother,' I said.

Charlie sat forward, all his attention on me. 'Could

you remember any exact dates that one of these parcels arrived?' he said.

At first I shook my head; of course I wouldn't be able to – but then I recalled we had left London on the 20th April and Mr Jedders had definitely received a package the day before. It was a large trunk and Mother had frowned and spoken quietly to him about it. I hadn't heard what she'd said but had guessed she was telling him not to have such bulky personal parcels delivered to the shop.

'He received one on the nineteenth of April.' I shrugged, unable to see how that could be in the least bit helpful, but Charlie slapped a hand on the table.

'This could be a start, Vinnie,' he said. 'I'm overdue a visit to my brothers in London. Didn't I tell you they both work in the post office? I am going to do my best to find where those parcels came from.'

CHAPTER THIRTY

'I hope you don't mind me setting you up here?' said Mr Lee. He indicated a seat and small folding desk for me as promised. A new, larger sketchbook with high-quality paper was already there.

I glanced at the two families gazing into the tank.

'Won't I be in the way?' I whispered.

'Certainly not,' said Mr Lee. 'We've had a surge in visitors and I'm sure that's down to the article and particularly your excellent artwork.'

I swallowed and Mr Lee smiled, then turned to answer a child's question.

The blank page of my sketchbook suddenly seemed

like a white expanse impossible to cross. Like a frozen sea, and if I drew, my lines would become cracks, and I'd be sure to fall in. Did the sea freeze? I was becoming so much more ... fanciful since coming to Brighton. I never used to think like this in London with Mother, where things were fixed and certain. Now I was sketching animals, my artwork was published in an actual newspaper, and next I'd be drawing in front of tourists? When I sketched designs in front of the customers at the milliners, I was never alone for a moment; Mother was there directing me.

I looked up, and the octopus unfurled a huge tentacle right opposite me. It clung to the glass and I saw every one of those amazing circular suckers in such detail. I drew one circle, then the next, the suckers expanding into rows, like stepping stones across that white sea of a page.

I was glad when Mr Lee stayed with me, standing to the side of the octopus tank so he could talk to visitors, telling them facts about the animal. The octopus only stayed still long enough for me to finish the tentacle study. Then he shot from one side of the tank to the other, body shaped like an arrow, and I quickly flipped the page to capture this shape before he curled inside the temple. Another page. When he grasped the wooden galleon Mr Lee had organized and explored and wrestled with it with only two arms while the others fed oysters into his mouth, I looked up from the page to realize a small crowd had gathered around the tank.

'Is he fighting with a pirate ship?' said a small boy at the front.

'It looks like it, doesn't it?' said Mr Lee.

Colours sped across the octopus, brick red, with dots of purple that spread and joined until the whole beast was indigo with striped arms, then suddenly he flashed back to the same colour as the wooden ship he held. The crowd 'oohed' and 'aahed'.

'Show your colours!' said Mr Lee. 'That's what they used to call out to ships to find out if they were pirates, and our devil-fish certainly knows how to show his.'

The octopus settled and the crowd wandered off. I finished the row of suckers on the sketch, focusing so hard on the fine ribbing that splayed out from the centre of each one, that the world around me disappeared.

'You really are so talented.'

I jumped, dropping my pencil. I recognized that voice. 'Temitayo,' I said with a wide smile.

I stood and found myself drawn into a quick embrace.

She held up a book with French writing on the back: *Vingt Mille Lieues Sous Les Mers.*

I knew *vingt* meant twenty; Mother had taught me to count to twenty in French when I was very young and then I would recite the numbers to applause from her friends.

'*Twenty Thousand Leagues Under the Sea*. You should read it, it's been translated into English. It's quite old now, I bet Mr Lee has read it,' said Temitayo, talking to me as naturally as if we had already been mid-conversation.

'Mr Lee had a similar picture in his booklet about sea monsters,' I said.

'But it isn't as good as this, is it?' said Temitayo, opening up the book at a page in the middle to show me the cut-out article with my drawing. 'This is really good, Vinnie – you are clearly going to be an artist.'

I shrugged. 'More of a designer. In the milliners.'

She frowned. 'There's definitely more to you than hats. The first time you draw the octopus it's published! But . . . you don't seem terribly excited.'

'I'm just worried about my mother,' I said. I quickly told her about Mr Jedders cornering me in the shop.

'What an arrogant, bullish man!' she said. 'How dare he scare you that way? I'm going to be sticking with you now, Vinnie. If he harasses you again, he will have us both to contend with.'

I was glad to hear Temitayo say this and gave her arm a squeeze. I remembered that she had been preparing to visit her guardian. 'How was your visit? Did you remember everything – the song and the verses?' I said.

'Word-perfect, of course.' She drew back her shoulders and tipped up her nose. I laughed. Then she became more serious. 'But ... well, I suppose it was perfectly fine,' she said.

I gave her a questioning look as it clearly wasn't perfectly fine.

'Thing is, I'm not a little child any more, Vinnie. They used to coo at me, touch my hair, marvel that a child from Africa could speak such good English, even though they knew I was brought here very young, so what else am I supposed to speak?'

'Did you mind? When they touched your hair?' I said.

'Not when I was small, but lately I have had to try hard not to flinch away,' she said. 'This time was different. They didn't touch; instead they stared, they clapped politely, but they were quieter. They said things like "quite the young lady now".'

I pulled a face.

'Exactly, Vinnie! And some of the young ladies there seemed the same age as me. I couldn't imagine they would ever be expected to ... perform as I was. Sir Edgar asked me if I would like to attend finishing school in Switzerland when I'm old enough. What was I supposed to say to that? They are just waiting for me to be old enough and *finished* enough to marry, and then they won't have to think of me any more.'

'I feel like you might have a different plan?' I said, and surprised myself by continuing. 'You are good at so many things, Temitayo. If there is more to me than hats, there must be more to you than finishing school.'

Temitayo's eyes were very dark, and when they met mine they seemed to be looking right through me as she nodded. Then she was focusing over my shoulder into the octopus tank, and her eyebrows shot up.

'What?' I said.

'Do not move,' she said. 'Am I seeing what I think I am seeing?'

I'd turned to talk to Temitayo, so my shoulder leant against the glass of the tank. I now followed her gaze to where the octopus was pressed against the glass right by me, arms slowly exploring in all directions.

'I know the creature can change colour to blend in, but this – this really is quite the spectacle!'

I remained still as Temitayo ducked to peer closer, and then I saw it myself. I saw what she meant and gasped. The bulbous head of the octopus and the tops of the arms closest to me were the strangest colour and pattern; at first I thought I must be imagining it. Other gasps joined my own, as the visitors saw what we were seeing and their exclamation became a chorus that called every person in the gallery to the octopus.

By Jove, am I seeing things? Impossible.

Quite miraculous.

Temitayo and I had something in common with the octopus. There was more to all of us than it first seemed. Because a moment ago the octopus had been mainly cobalt blue, a beautiful deep colour. Now the blue was blooming patches of lilac – the cobalt deepening almost to black and the lilac forming squares. A grid. Flashing lines of orange . . .

The octopus was exactly the same colour and pattern as my cape, pressed up on the other side of the glass.

A lilac check.

CHAPTER THIRTY-ONE

'Whenever you are ready, Vinnie,' Mr Lee said, crouching a little to talk to the youngest member of a family of visitors, who looked about five years old. 'You see, our octopus here likes Vinnie best of all and that's why he will only mimic her cape.'

'Why?' said the little girl.

Mr Lee dropped his voice to a stage whisper. 'Well – I think clever animals often like children better than grown-ups, don't you?'

The little girl nodded shyly, then her mouth formed an 'O' that was soon echoed by her older brother and parents as they gazed over my shoulder. The octopus was on the move.

I stood now by the glass, and watched the octopus' bulbous head extrude from the top of the temple and a single arm dart towards the glass. An octopus had three hearts but I often wondered if he also had eyes in his arms. I pressed my shoulder to the glass and watched his suckers slide across, then all at once he darted from the temple and met me at the glass, his whole body opposite me, flashing red, pink, lilac, white, brown, deep purple, then the pattern of the cape coming into view.

After I had first shown Mr Lee what the octopus could do, we had experimented. But if I wasn't wearing the cape, the creature would swim to the glass in his customary brick red, browns, oranges and indigo, would flash white, on and off, and then swim away, seemingly disappointed in me. Mr Lee and I tried holding up materials in a multitude of different patterns, but the octopus showed no interest and we hadn't seen him recreate this copying trick with anyone else.

But it was enough. I looked at the amazed faces of the family as they stared at the lilac check of the cape spreading up one, then two of the octopus' arms.

The octopus was a true spectacle and Aunt Bets said the best thing I could do to help her was to encourage more visitors into the aquarium, so I had spent the day helping Mr Lee demonstrate and sketching in between.

Finally the last visitors left up the steps, into the sunlight. When Mr Lee went over to the sea lions to direct the keepers who were cleaning out, I was glad to have the subterranean world to myself.

Charlie had said he would stay with his brother for a few days but the time was passing slowly and my worries grew, winding up tight, like a spinning top about to be released. Could Mr Jedders somehow have discovered Charlie was trying to find out information about him?

What if Charlie didn't come back? What if he disappeared like Mother? I realized with dread that's how I thought of her now. Gone. I couldn't imagine her sweeping along the streets of a strange city. I couldn't imagine her doing anything at all, other than being back beside me.

The octopus unfurled an arm across the glass and seemed to stare right at me with one eye.

The door to the gallery slammed. Red hair sprouting from beneath a cap that fell over his eyes, those long legs that seemed too big for his body. Charlie. My whole body slumped in relief.

'Ah, I knew you'd be here. Mrs Ruggles has a fresh batch of cheese scones that might interest Uncle,' said Charlie, wiping crumbs from his mouth. 'I obviously tested them already.'

Mr Lee strode over from the end of the gallery and

clapped Charlie on the back. 'Charlie, my boy. How are your brothers?'

'Oh, quite boring really,' said Charlie with a shrug. 'I'm going to take a stroll on the promenade,' he said, raising his eyebrows at me, 'stretch my legs after the journey.'

'I might come with you,' I said.

'Good idea,' said Mr Lee, reaching into his pocket and pulling out some coins which he handed to Charlie. 'Treat yourselves to a twist of cockles and I'll tell Aunt Bets where you are.'

CHAPTER THIRTY-TWO

I didn't say a word to Charlie until we were out of the aquarium and walking along the promenade.

'So – did you . . .'

'Hold on. Forget cockles – that's what we're after,' said Charlie, 'and then I'll tell you.'

He pointed to a hand-drawn cart with two large silver-domed lids, surrounded by people. I caught a glimpse of the sign, glossy white painted on blue: *Capaldi's Famous Ices. Cream Ice.*

I opened my mouth to refuse but then snapped it closed. I'd always looked longingly at these barrows in London, surrounded by children licking their chops, but

Mother said the penny licks – the little glasses which the scoops of coloured ice were served in – were unsanitary and anyway, a lady didn't eat in public. But this was the seaside and I'd never tasted cream ice.

Charlie was already in the queue and arrived back with two large shells with a scoop of creamy pale cream ice in each, and two smaller shells, presumably to eat them with. I took one from him, the cold through the shell making my fingertips tingle. We walked down the steps from the promenade to the beach and found a rock to sit on.

'Did you find anything out?' I said, trying not to sound impatient that he was making me wait.

''Course I did. I'm going to be an investigative journalist.'

I dipped the smaller shell into the cream ice, which was already starting to melt, sitting in a pool in the shell like an island. It was sweet and creamy. I wasn't sure if it was wonderful or too much.

'I have an address those parcels were sent from; it's in Camden. I don't think there's any way this Mr Jedders could live there – my brother says it's a respectable enough area, but a rough street. Still – I have an address.'

Charlie held out a slip of paper. I took it.

9, Litcham Street
Kentish Town
London

'Thank you,' I mumbled. Suddenly the cream ice seemed far too sickly and I laid the shell on the pebbles as I read the address. What was I going to do with it? I didn't even know where Kentish Town was, which suggested it wasn't somewhere I'd ever been or where Fyfe's customers came from. I imagined telling Aunt Bets that I needed to go to London for this reason; she just wouldn't allow it.

'You eating that?' said Charlie, already scraping his cream-ice shell clean.

I shook my head and Charlie tucked into mine as well.

'I'll go with you. I've got it figured out. We can say we are taking a trip to the London Aquarium to see their new specimens to report back for Mr Lee.'

It took a few moments for this to sink in. 'You'll go with me? On the ... train? You've only just come back.'

He grinned. 'There's something about this fellow Jedders, I know it . . . a good journalist goes by gut instinct. Let's go and see what's in Litcham Street. We have to start somewhere.'

'Yes. Yes. Let's go,' I said. I didn't like the thought of any of it, but the thought of continuing to do nothing about Mother disappearing, about Mr Jedders cornering me, demanding . . . I liked that thought much less.

9 Litcham Street.

This was a plan.

Charlie had now finished my cream ice as well. There was a blob on his chin and I rubbed my own chin to show him. He swiped it off with a grin and then we ran down the steps and across the pebbles. Aunt Bets had bought me some sturdy flat boots and it was now easy to keep up with Charlie. He fetched a rusty tin can from the shoreline and started throwing stones at it. He cursed when his stones kept missing, and when my first pebble hit the metal with a satisfying clang we both laughed.

THE MURDEROUS MIRACLE MONSTER OF THE SEA

The cannibal octopus of Brighton initially terrified us with its culinary exploits, devouring its companion during its journey halfway across the ocean to our shores. But the surprises continue.

The gigantic creature seemed gravely injured in its murderous endeavour, and indeed one of its eight appendages became detached from its others. With the advantage of having seven other tentacles, it was hoped that the octopus could survive in this way, but it wasn't expected that it could grow its own arm back!

But that is indeed what happened, as a miniature replica of the lost limb is now growing in its place.

The devil-fish is now attuned to the environment provided at the Brighton Aquarium, and fortunate visitors may witness it in full display of changing colour, one of the only creatures on the planet that can do so.

CHAPTER THIRTY-THREE

Charlie threw the newspaper down on the train seat next to him, sending up a cloud of dust.

'It has to be the same writer from the last article. I've asked at the paper and this journalist is anonymous,' he said, his bottom lip sticking out.

'Do you think someone is copying your article?' I said, gently.

'No, no, no. It's quite different from mine. Only the actual news is the same,' he said. 'I contacted the newspaper and they said the writer had submitted the piece before I did.'

'Where from?'

'Anonymous again,' he said, and passed the paper back to me.

I glanced again at my drawing. This time I had known Charlie would send it so I'd taken my time and was fully proud of it. But I folded the paper.

'It's fine for you to look at it, Vinnie. If my work was published, I'd probably never stop looking at it.'

'Not if – when,' I said.

He gave me a weak smile.

We didn't speak for the final part of the journey that led us to London Bridge station. It was only the second time I'd been on the train but Charlie was very confident with the tickets since he was from a railway family; he'd been able to quite easily persuade Aunt Bets I would be safe with him.

Thoughts of Mother crowded my mind. When the post had arrived that morning at Aunt Bets' cottage I'd been waiting, startling the postman as I flung open the door, willing today to be the day Mother sent her address. I needed her. But there was nothing, so here we were, on our way to Litcham Street.

I'd forgotten the smells of London, first the hot metal steam and nose-tickling coal smoke of the train, then without the constant Brighton breeze, all the smells of vast numbers of people melded together: woollen clothes, leather bags, face powder and cologne. As we followed the stream of passengers through the station, I stopped myself hanging on to Charlie's sleeve more than once. He wasn't my mother. But the last time I was in the city I had been with her, and I felt suddenly vulnerable. I had expected it to feel more like home.

I tried to square my shoulders. I was Lavinia Fyfe, born and bred here. I was also Vinnie – who dipped in the sea, who was learning to ride a bicycle, who had new friends, who drew an octopus and had it published in the newspaper. London should feel less scary to me, not more. But as I stuck close to Charlie, weaving through the crowds, I missed Mother's reassuring presence more than I had since the first day she left.

We took a stagecoach directly from the station to the address on the slip of paper. My heart started to lift. This part of the city looked quite proper, long straight rows of four-storey terraced houses, not so different from the houses of Grosvenor Square – maybe a little narrower, but the men were in suits, the women starched-looking and respectable.

The coach pulled to a halt and Charlie and I tumbled out. He spoke with the coach driver.

'Can't take you any further, guv,' he said. 'Litcham's there, next block off Weedington Road.'

He looked me up and down, lingering on my cape with a raise of his eyebrows. I was wearing my lilac check one – it felt like a sort of good-luck talisman now the octopus liked it so much. I hadn't even thought that something a lot plainer might be more fitting; Brighton was a tourist town and people wore jaunty colours.

'God bless, miss,' he said grimly, and with a whip of the horses, the stagecoach trundled off up the rutted road.

Charlie and I shrugged and followed the man's directions, past the tall houses, dodging a pair of nannies pushing giant wheeled prams containing babies in white ruffled bonnets. We reached the first turning and stopped dead.

'This can't be Litcham Street,' I said.

Charlie pointed up at the sign on the wall.

I stared along the street. It was only slightly narrower, but the walls of the houses were dirty. Ragged children slouched in doorways and washing flapped on lines criss-crossing the entire street from one side to the other, dimming the sunlight. The smell was intense, eye-watering. Mr Jedders had always looked so dapper, suited to Grosvenor Square with its scattering of respectable tailors, drapers and Fyfe's millinery. Could Charlie and his brother have got this completely wrong?

'Right. Well. Let's not hang around,' said Charlie. I didn't reply as we rushed along the centre of the street, avoiding the murky water in the gutters. I breathed through my mouth to avoid the stench.

'I've read about these suburban slums,' whispered Charlie. 'One minute you're in a respectable neighbourhood, but the next road over . . .'

'Should we check the address?' I said, skipping to the side as a ragged boy tipped out a pot right there on the street. It wasn't fair that these people had to live like this.

'Definitely not,' said Charlie out of the side of his mouth. 'Head high, shoulders back; in places like this you need to look like you know where you are going.'

When we arrived at the address, Charlie and I looked upwards at the dark sooty windows and stained brickwork.

'What shall we say?' I said, overwhelmed by the grim surroundings.

Charlie didn't reply. We really hadn't thought this through. I frowned and then an idea pinged into my head. I reached into Charlie's satchel, brought out his notebook before he could stop me and put on a sweet smile.

'Mr Jedders left this in the tailors on Weedington Road where he has business. We need to return it in person.'

A slow smile spread across Charlie's face. 'You're a lot bolder than I thought, Vin. If he's in, we say we've made a mistake and will wait on Weedington Road.'

I felt anything but bold and there were a lot of flaws in this plan.

'And then what?'

Charlie didn't answer; he was already knocking smartly at the door.

CHAPTER THIRTY-FOUR

Number 9 Litcham Street was the right address.

But Mr Jedders wasn't in, and the gruff woman who opened the door wasn't keen on letting us through.

'This must be delivered personally. It's business,' said Charlie importantly. He put a foot in the door and reached out to pull me in behind him.

'Many thanks. Up here, is it?' he said, pointing up a flight of narrow stairs.

The woman placed both hands on her hips. 'He won't like this,' she muttered.

'I shall accept all blame, ma'am,' said Charlie. 'Just a delivery and we'll be gone.'

She directed us to the top floor and we made our way up the dirtiest, dingiest flight of stairs I'd ever seen, passing people huddled on the treads. Our footsteps creaked on the soft wood. Each floor was made up of narrow branching corridors and doors that seemed impossibly close together. Outside some were rag-rug doormats.

Both the apartment in Grosvenor Square and Aunt Bets' cottage were a similar size. Two bedrooms, parlour, scullery. Ours had an indoor toilet and Aunt Bets' had an outside closet. By the distance between these doors I guessed these were one-room homes, with the water a pump outside in the street somewhere and goodness knows about the toilet. It certainly smelt like some had used the corridors for just this purpose.

Charlie leant close to whisper, 'These would once have been decent houses for a family and servants, but now they might have two entire families living in one room that was meant to be a bedroom.'

I couldn't imagine it, and my mind instead flicked to the first day we'd seen the octopus, the barrel containing its massive bulk, legs tangled in far too tight a space, imprisoned. Finally we reached what I thought must be the top flight of stairs, that led to a trapdoor above us. An attic. Charlie and I exchanged a look, and I'm sure my eyes were as wide as his, but I'm not sure mine had the same sparkle. Charlie seemed to be . . . enjoying this?

He pushed against the wood but it was locked from the inside. A narrow frame of light shone around the trapdoor and I saw shadows pass it. He gave it three smart raps. There were people up there, moving. The floorboards above us creaked and a sprinkle of dust was caught in the light. Charlie knocked again. More shifting. Charlie looked at me and shrugged. He pressed his mouth up to the gap.

'Important delivery for Mr Jedders,' he called, so loudly I stumbled back.

We waited. More movement above. Then finally the trapdoor opened a crack. A girl's voice.

'You can't come up 'ere. Private property,' she said. 'Pass your delivery up, I'll see 'e gets it.'

I was suddenly swept with misgivings. What in the world could a place like this tell us about my mother?

Then a smell drifted down to me, a smell I knew. Fabric. The hot crisp smell of cloth being sliced with the sharpest of shears or the most delicate of scissors.

Mama!

All my missing her, all my disbelief that she had left me, my fear when we hadn't heard from her, surged up. She must be here – something had happened for her to be in a place like this; I couldn't think what but I wasn't waiting any longer to find out. Without thinking about what I was doing I rushed past Charlie and pushed both hands against the trapdoor. There was a cry of surprise, a kerfuffle and a thud as the trapdoor flew open, and I scrambled through it, Charlie right behind me, gripping my elbow.

The girl I must have knocked over sprang to her feet and started towards us, but I stepped away from the trapdoor as my eyes flicked over the long room. More girls, many girls crammed in rows along trestle tables, working, their sewing held still in their hands as they stared at us. All had their hair tied back in smudged kerchiefs and some wore handkerchiefs across their mouths and fingerless gloves despite the heat. The humid air was thick with metallic-tasting dust. I scanned each face for Mother, although I already knew she couldn't be here. Why would she be somewhere like this?

The girl who we had knocked over took hold of my arm and some of the other girls stood up now. The first girl hissed at them, but I couldn't make out any words as my ears were filled with a rhythmic rushing sound. I shrugged out of the girl's grip and strode along the narrow passage towards the end of the room, hung with dripping curtains. I ducked around them to where three huge coppers stood, many times the size of the one Aunt Bets had shown me in the tiny scullery in her terraced cottage, although lately the tea shop had been doing so well she'd been able to send our clothes out for laundering.

The girls turning sticks in the dark water stopped and stared, arms bare and wet, and . . . green.

This wasn't a laundry.

And Mother wasn't here.

Disappointment and relief crushed my chest and it was only then I noticed. Layered over the other smells was a scent of garlic. Everything – every bolt of swaying silk, every handmade flower, every hand-rolled ribbon that spilt from baskets in the centre of the workbenches – was bright emerald green. One of the most fashionable colours we were always asked for; Mother said it was so difficult to get hold of at the right price.

Also known as Paris Green.

CHAPTER THIRTY-FIVE

I tried to make sense of what I was seeing. I'd never given any thought to where the supplies for the milliners came from, and as I took in the girls' lowered faces, the handkerchiefs tied across their mouths and noses, the gloves, the cramped conditions and the thick air, I wondered if all the components of the hats we made could come from places like this. This garret was a world away from the cool order of our milliners; it was . . . hellish.

I walked back to Charlie who was now in an intense discussion with the girl, who had clearly realized there was no package to be delivered. But the discussion was only heated on her side; Charlie was calmly writing in his notebook.

'So when was the last time you saw Mistress Fyfe of Fyfe's Milliners?' he said.

'I already told you, I never seen her. I just heard of her when I worked for my other place. Everyone in this business knew her, but she's long gone. Paris, I 'eard.'

Charlie opened his mouth for another question but the girl poked an angry finger at his shoulder.

'You ain't with the peelers so you got no right asking so many questions. You need to leave. Jedders don't have visitors.'

'Mr Jedders used to work for Mistress Fyfe—'

'Yes,' the girl sighed, tapping her head, 'but he can't work for her when she's in Paris, can he? So he is running this place. And if he finds out anyone has been here . . .'

I could see now that the girl was not only angry but frightened. Her hands shook and I swallowed, wondering what she was afraid of. I cleared my throat. What would Aunt Bets say to this girl? She was straight-talking and honest but always kind – to everyone.

'I'm sorry, miss. This is my fault. I'm Mistress Fyfe's daughter, Vinnie. My mother is missing and I'm so worried about her.'

I was surprised to hear a catch in my voice, hot tears at the corners of my eyes.

The rustle of the room fell quiet. Then a girl called out from the worktable. 'He won't be back for another hour, Ruth, let the child speak.'

'I'm Vinnie Fyfe,' I said. 'I promise Mr Jedders won't know we've been here. We don't want him to know.'

Charlie grunted but I ignored him.

I held out my hand and the girl looked at it for a moment, then took it. Her hand was hot, damp and roughened, but I squeezed it tight.

'Ruth,' she said, and quickly dropped my hand. I resisted the temptation to rudely wipe my fingers on my skirts.

'Thank you for talking to us, Ruth,' I said; now I had her attention I didn't know where to start. 'So Mr Jedders doesn't talk of my mother?'

The girl gave a sharp laugh and shook her head, arms now folded across her stomach.

Someone coughed and immediately muffled the sound.

'Mr Jedders don't *talk* to us girls. Sorry, miss, you ain't going to 'ave no luck 'ere,' she said with a sharp chuckle.

My initial bravery was now fading and disappointment cut off my words. If they didn't know anything, then what was the point of this whole journey? Mr Jedders might have set up this dreadful workshop, but that wasn't our business. My eyes flicked to where

Charlie was crouched talking quietly to one of the girls further down the workbench near the coppers. She was holding out her hands and he was inspecting them.

Ruth followed my gaze and then sprang into action, racing over to them. I followed.

'Martha! Turn round!' she hissed. 'Get on with your quota, or I'll tell 'im we need someone else.'

The girl twisted on her bench and grasped at Ruth's skirt, and I noted the hands Charlie had been inspecting. They were a sickly colour and bandaged, but old blood soaked through the rags. Her narrow face was shockingly young, maybe younger than me, scabs on her lips, wide eyes filling. 'Oh, you wouldn't, Ruth, I know you wouldn't, not with Ma being how she is—'

'Cut the waterworks, put your gloves back on and do the work,' said Ruth, her voice low but not unkind.

Martha nodded quickly, already ducked back to the pile of green ribbons she was hemming.

'Now you must leave. Please,' said Ruth.

Charlie lowered his voice. 'This is not right. These girls are not well, you can't work in these conditions. It could be the dye, the green dye you are using. I read an article, health warnings. This place is full of it, you can smell it like garlic in the air, a mix of copper and arsenic rumoured to cause—' He took Ruth's hand and held it up. 'You too have a green tinge to your nails—'

'Don't you touch me, boy!' Ruth snatched back her hand. 'Don't you think we know?'

Charlie's face drained of colour as the girl lowered her voice.

'We've all already seen how this can end.'

CHAPTER THIRTY-SIX

The coughing started up again and one of the girls was fed water from a clay bottle by the others either side of her, in between bouts of hacking into a handkerchief.

I swallowed. 'Does Mr Jedders actually *know* that this work is making you so . . . ill?'

The answer was obvious – how could he not see? – but I couldn't believe he could knowingly be involved in this. Ruth looked me up and down and I felt embarrassed by my lilac cape, like my clothes were especially designed to make the girls in this place look even more shabby. I was sure she would snap at me, but she blew out a long breath. She didn't sound angry any more, just tired.

'Did my grandma's gaffer in the cotton mill know that littl'uns were lucky if they didn't lose a leg? Did the owners of the match factories know that girls were losing their faces to the phossy jaw?' Ruth was now shaking, her face bright red. The girl behind coughed again. 'They all know. Everyone bleeding *knows*. He didn't even pay for the coffin!'

Coffin?

Both Charlie and I fell into a dark unbelieving silence. I knew that factories were an unhealthy place to work. I felt young, foolish, stupid, and every time the girl coughed I flinched.

'But the match girls revolted, they formed a union,' said Charlie. 'No one should suffer like this any more. If the newspapers were to hear of it . . .'

Ruth's glare was as cold as her voice. 'Ah, so that's your game, with your fancy threads and your letters. If the newspapers hear of it, we'll be gone for opening our gobs, for letting you in, and don't you think there'll be others queuing to take our places? No unions here. Ain't no workers' strike could make a blind bit of difference. We complain . . . we find a new position. Ain't no safety in numbers in a place like this.'

'But there are labour laws—'

She interrupted him with a laugh. 'Listen, boy. If you breathe a word then Martha's five brothers and sisters she feeds will be on your conscience. Along with me own sick da and brother. Half of this room will be dying in the workhouse with their families – and this place will still be doing the same thing somewhere else with different girls. But what happens to us . . . will be on you.'

I saw Charlie swallow.

'We won't say anything, I promise,' I said, gabbling, horrified by the trouble we could have caused them, already sick and in pain, but my mind raced. 'We . . . will find a way to help. We could bring medicine for—'

'No medicine cures being poor. Only thing you can do for us is forget you were ever here at all. We don't need nothing from you 'cept the silence you just promised.'

The girl who had been coughing was now hunched, back at work, skeletal fingers in threadbare fingerless gloves sewing a green glossy ruffle like hundreds I'd seen in the milliners. Hundreds I'd drawn. Could they all come from places like . . . this? I had never even thought about it. I needed to tell Mother. The girls knew her name, but she couldn't know them, know about this. The kerchief around the girl's head had come loose – she had large bald patches in her dark-red hair. She saw me looking and pulled the material forward to cover it, shooting me a withering glare. My cheeks burned in shame.

Ruth's eyes held mine then flicked to Charlie. 'And you? Do we have your word?'

I realized my hand was gripping Charlie's sleeve but I didn't let go. A silence fell over the whole workshop and I realized all the girls were listening. Waiting. Fearful that if Charlie reported this place they would lose their livelihood.

'Yes,' he mumbled.

Then there was a commotion, the girls whispering to each other, getting back to work. A girl ran to Ruth and hissed in her ear.

''E's back. 'Ee's on the stairs.'

CHAPTER THIRTY-SEVEN

Ruth grabbed Charlie and me by our collars and we were forced to run with her to the far end of the workshop. She pushed us behind the curtains of hanging freshly dyed fabric, and we crouched, one of us behind each of the dyeing barrels as the girls stirring the foamy deep green mixture continued their job as if we weren't there.

The trapdoor creaked open and I recognized the *whisk tap* of Jedders' cane. *Whisk . . . tap, whisk . . . tap.* He was walking slowly, the cane tap louder as he came nearer. I curled myself tightly, pressing my face into my knees. I'd opened the door to this man many times; his cheery 'Morning, ladies,' had rung out through the milliners, and the younger women had often whispered how he was quite the dandy as they blushed behind their fans. Could this really be the same man? The *whisk tap* stopped and I didn't dare move, but then I had to know where he was; he could be glaring down on us right now. I turned my head just a fraction and there were his black polished boots and the metal tip of the cane, only a few inches in front of the barrel.

The moment stretched out, like a swing at the point of turning, hanging motionless. A man who was capable of scaring these girls, of making them so ill – dying – what would he do to me and Charlie?

He sniffed and turned, the *whisk tap* growing fainter. I breathed out carefully, straining to hear the trapdoor open and close, telling us we were safe. But that sound didn't come.

The slap of wet cloth against the side of the barrel drowned out any noise from the girls at the benches. There had been a desk at the far end near the trapdoor and I hoped Jedders was sitting there now, far away from us.

The thick garlicky stench was strong and sour down here so close to the vats of the toxic dye, and I held a handkerchief to my mouth. It was a lace-edged white one Mother had given me for my last birthday and my stomach clenched in embarrassment when I saw one of the dye girls glance at it sideways. She wiped the sweat off her face with a dirty kerchief tied around her neck. The corner had once been hand-embroidered with flowers but the stitches had come undone, a hole left in their place.

More minutes passed, my legs cramped and I was forced to come out of a crouch and sit on the floor damp with green dye. Charlie did the same, clutching his cap in a white-knuckled hand.

Finally more footsteps coming towards us, no cane this time.

'Ruth, line up the girls. Inspection,' he said. It was strange to hear that drawl, that voice that pretended to be better bred than it really was, here in this godforsaken place.

More movement. The girls who had been stirring the barrels looked at each other and one chewed on her lip as they dried their hands on their green-stained aprons. They pushed through the curtains to join the others. I met Charlie's eyes, but he looked as terrified as I did.

'Next,' said Jedders.

I peered cautiously around the barrel to find a tiny gap between the draped fabric, where it bunched on the floor. I craned down and if I angled myself right I could see feet, the back of Jedders' boots and then other feet facing him. Boots with repair patches and holes in the toes. Every now and again a set of dirty bare toes.

'Next,' said Jedders, and that pair of feet stepped aside. This continued on, one girl after another stopping in front of the man for a short while, then stepping aside.

Then a longer pause. 'I warned you last time, we'll have blood on the merchandise. You'll have to go. See her out, Ruth.'

CHAPTER THIRTY-EIGHT

I covered my mouth. *Blood on the merchandise?* I presumed when Jedders had said inspection that he was checking the quality of their work. He was not. He was checking their hands, their hair maybe. Jedders was checking for signs of the poisoning.

'No sir, please,' said the girl's voice, her bare feet unmoving, small toes curled into the floor.

'Off you go, you know the rules,' said Jedders. None of the feet moved. A sound of soft sobbing.

'I'll take on Martha's quota while her hands heal, sir,' said Ruth's voice, low and calm. 'Every bit of it will get done.'

'So you can work more quickly than you are currently working? Is that true, girls?'

Silence from Ruth, silence from the girls.

'Are you under the impression that my decisions are up for negotiation?'

'No, sir, of course not, sir—'

Swish, whump.

The sound of the cane whipping through the air and meeting its target. I stifled a gasp. A cry of pain and the barefoot girl stumbled backwards, collapsing into a pile of rags.

'Get rid of her,' he said.

Mr Jedders stepped aside and continued to inspect, calling out, 'Next, Next', more quickly and more harshly. Someone helped the sobbing girl to her feet and a minute later I heard the trapdoor slam. The rest of the inspection continued. No other girls were let go.

Finally there was only one pair of feet in front of Jedders. Brown boots recently mended. The way the cheap, worn leather had been so carefully polished squeezed my heart.

'Ruth,' he said.

'Sir.'

'Do you think I enjoy these inspections?'

A pause. 'No, sir.'

Jedders chuckled. His cane tapped against the floor.

'Well, it is not for the likes of you to presume what I enjoy and what I don't, but it turns out you are correct.'

Another pause.

'It is bad enough that I am reduced to spending even a moment in this hell-hole, and I do not expect insubordination!' His voice rose, booming, terrifying and strangely high-pitched on the last word.

'I am sorry, sir,' said Ruth.

'Hold out your hands,' he said.

I glanced at Charlie. His face was a sickly greenish colour, nothing to do with the dyed curtains filtering the light.

Swish, thwack.

Swish, thwack.

Swish, thwack.

My heart thumped in my head. The first three times the cane must have struck Ruth's hands, her feet remained rooted to the floor and I heard nothing, but the next three times Jedders' boots rose at the heel and then slammed down in time with the swing of the cane. Ruth whimpered and then finally collapsed to her knees, curling herself around her hands.

Silence.

'And, Ruth, I do not expect to see girls here without boots. We will maintain respectable standards. This is for letting them slip.'

Swish, whump.

The cane landed one more time, this time on what I hoped was Ruth's back, because maybe that was better than it being her head.

'I'll be back tomorrow. Work hard, girls, and you might find an extra penny in your wages. Also . . . pigs might fly.'

He chuckled as the trapdoor slammed.

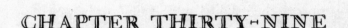

CHAPTER THIRTY-NINE

For a few moments after Jedders left, Charlie and I dared not move. The workshop was silent. Then the girls working at the dyeing barrels appeared and I stood, peeking behind the curtain.

'He's gone,' said one of the girls in a flat voice as she stirred the paddle around the vat.

Charlie stood next to me. 'We need to leave. Now.'

The workroom was silent aside from the rustle of the material through fingers, of the work being done. Just as Mr Jedders had directed.

One of the other girls was wrapping Ruth's hands. The older girl met our eyes as she passed and I would have expected her to look angry or sad, or in pain . . . but her eyes were empty, her face expressionless. I had never wanted to get away from a place so much in my life – my legs were desperate to run, my mind to forget. But one phrase of what Ruth had said before Jedders' visit stuck in my mind. I had to know.

'You said he didn't pay for the . . . coffin.'

Ruth's glare gripped mine, scornful, and her voice was low. 'Ah, but lil' Agnes died in our other *premises*, so that's all forgotten now. We don't speak of it, do we, girls? We've 'ad a lovely fresh start. And Jedders ain't employing any more of the real littl'uns. So all must be well.'

'I am sincerely sorry to hear this. When was your move of premises, Ruth?' said Charlie.

Ruth waved her hand. 'About a month? But what does it matter to you? 'Ave you not seen and heard enough? Go. And keep your mouths shut.'

My heart galloped in my chest as we raced from the building and that hellish workshop, terrified we would bump into Jedders, terrified he would know we had found this place and could cause those poor girls more wretchedness. Charlie was silent, his gaze fixed as we retraced our journey down the street, soot-blackened walls seeming to lean in on us, the ceiling of washing lines like strings of ragged ghosts. My breath only started to slow when we were out of Litcham Street. The people on the next street were ordinary to me; they made me feel safer.

But Mr Jedders had looked ordinary too.

Nothing was safe. Because it was becoming clearer now. Jedders' last murderous workshop had closed just before we left for Brighton. Mother must have found out what he was doing somehow, and he must have threatened her. I wished she had told me, explained.

The man my mother had trusted and then fallen out with was . . . evil. And desperate to find her. And Mother was missing, and what if something bad had already happened to her? I didn't know what to say to Charlie, didn't even know what to think about what we'd just witnessed.

Charlie spun around. 'You should never have promised what you did to that girl. Never,' he said.

I stopped, taken aback by the force of his anger. Out of everything we'd seen, Charlie was angry at *me*? What had I promised? I thought back to my words to Ruth. I stood by them.

'Of course we can't report that place, not if those girls rely on it for their livelihood . . . you heard what she said.'

'You don't understand a thing, Vinnie. If no one reports what is happening there, then nothing will ever change for people like her.'

He went on to tell me about other factories, the brick-works with the killer dust, the cotton mills with their lung-rotting damp. He described the grim phossy jaw, how a face could fall apart, and I was desperate not to hear any more. I thought about our cotton clothing, how I struck a match every evening to light the gas lamp or a candle, and felt sick.

Then I remembered how Charlie had scribbled in his notebook, how his eyes glinted as he looked at the girls' hands, and my shame was replaced by anger.

'I admit I don't know a lot, Charlie. But I did see you were excited to hear a ghoulish story. You're just annoyed you can't write it,' I said. I regretted it the moment the words left my mouth. Charlie's lips trembled and it took him a moment to gather himself.

'What is the point of journalism, of newspapers, of any writing if it doesn't tell the truth about things that are wrong? If the truth was reported it might be worse for *those* girls, but better for thousands of others. When the truth is printed, laws can change. But you don't see that, do you?'

We started to walk again, his steps clipped and shoulders hunched. We could just leave that horrible place, but those girls couldn't, and how many other people were trapped in similar situations? Had I been wrong to promise to keep quiet? I rubbed my forehead and thought of Ruth and Martha. The girl with the red hair. Lil' Agnes, a smaller girl I'd never seen, that no one would see again.

'I understand, Charlie. But you gave your word you wouldn't say anything to anyone as well, so I don't see why you are blaming me,' I said.

Charlie dragged in a deep breath through his nose. 'So childish promises are more important than changing things for all the other people made ill by their work?'

I shook my head, exasperated.

'Those girls told us not to tell. It's their lives. Isn't it their decision?' I said, my voice barely above a whisper.

He didn't reply.

I couldn't get it straight in my head, what was the right thing to do. We fell into tense silence and Charlie flagged a stagecoach to take us to the station.

We travelled in silence. Hundreds of times I opened my mouth to say something to Charlie, but he did not lift his head from his newspapers until we reached Brighton.

CHAPTER FORTY

I turned the key in the lock on the cottage door, Temitayo behind me. This was the first time I'd been at Aunt Bets' house without Aunt Bets. It had been her idea. When I had hugged her tight she had probably presumed I was missing Mother after visiting London, and I hadn't told her different. She'd suggested baking always cheered her up and the next moment Temitayo was there, thrilled to have a chance to do something she'd never done before. I'd been glad to be swept along.

'It smells delicious in here,' said Temitayo as we hung up our capes and hats, 'let's cook up a storm.'

Temitayo was so enthusiastic about the baking, wielding

a wooden spoon like a sword, swamped by Aunt Bets' apron, with a dash of flour on her nose, that I had managed to hold back the story and the tears until the two trays of petits fours – heavily decorated with almonds, candied fruits and angelica – were in the oven and the air was thick with the scent of baking biscuits.

Temitayo sat me down on the kitchen stool and handed me a fresh handkerchief when mine was soaked through. When I saw the embroidery in the corner I remembered the girl stirring the barrel full of poison and gave a little moan.

'Now are you going to tell me what on earth has happened?'

I shook my head. 'I can't,' I said, and allowed the sobs to take over.

Ten minutes later the little biscuits were out of the oven and I was able to draw a whole breath without hiccupping. I needed to work out how the workshop was related to Mother. I needed to find her more urgently than ever. If she knew about those girls, about the death of lil' Agnes . . . or maybe Mother had already tried to help them and failed. But with Charlie so furious with me, how was I going to figure out what to do next by myself?

I looked at Temitayo and her deep-brown eyes were warm and kind, and very clever.

I swallowed. 'You can't say anything to anyone.'

Temitayo was a good listener, and after I finished telling her about what we had seen, she didn't comment right away. Then she told me she had heard about the workers' revolts and factory strikes, but didn't seem to have any more answers than I did when it came to what to do about either the girls, Jedders or my mother. I asked her not to talk about it again with Charlie and we cleared up in silence. Finally Temitayo spoke slowly.

'I'm going to have a good think, Vinnie,' she said, 'but this is a true conundrum . . . and a serious one. But you aren't alone, I'm here.'

When we removed the tray from the oven Temitayo declared this batch of petits fours were slightly over-cooked and we should bake another batch. We sat side by side at the kitchen table, which was strewn with flour, the air tasting of sugar, our fingers sticky from the candied peel.

'Let's have a decorating competition,' she said. 'Two minutes to make the best-decorated petit four in the country.'

I laughed, glad of the distraction. 'I accept the challenge. Go!'

My hands sped, and soon the petit four in front of me had an almond at the top then rows of tiny bits of peel splaying out beneath.

'And stop,' said Temitayo.

I stared at Temitayo's muddled creation and suddenly made sense of it – a top hat of raisins, rosy cheeks from half cherries and a curved moustache from candied orange peel.

'Not Captain Bickerstaff?' I said, covering my mouth to stop the giggles. 'Temitayo, you are bad.'

'And you've got octopuses on the brain,' said Temitayo, 'but you can even make bits of peel look like art. You win.'

We had finished the rest of the batch and put it in the oven when I heard the door open and voices in the hallway. I tensed.

'It's just your aunt and Mrs Heap,' said Temitayo, her floury hand warm on my wrist. My heart slowed.

'All this mess for a batch of petits fours!' said Aunt Bets, hands on her hips, but a smile on her lips.

'The best petits fours ever, though,' said Temitayo.

'Oh, Mary, whatever next,' said Mrs Heap, covering her mouth. 'The very state of it, the very state of you!'

Temitayo's smile dropped a little.

'Always best to clear up as you go,' said Mrs Heap, eyes crinkling. She bustled in and hung her cape on the back of the door. 'Do you have a spare apron, chick? I was a kitchen maid when I was the same age as these girls, in service up at Randall's manor – oh, a lifetime ago now. Old Mrs Randall took me on as nurse to little Sir

Edgar, but I always missed my stool by the kitchen fire and gruff old Cook taught me to bake. I was rather good with pastry.'

Temitayo and I grinned at each other in surprise.

'Well, now we have four pairs of hands, I think we can take on the challenge of a Black Forest gateau, don't you?' said Aunt Bets.

It was evening by the time Temitayo and Mrs Heap left, the gateau baked, assembled and some generous slices eaten at the kitchen table with hot tea.

We finished clearing up together and I became desperate to tell Aunt Bets what I'd seen, but I couldn't betray the girls.

'Being back in London reminded me so much of Mother,' I said, to explain my obvious upset. 'I'm so worried about her.'

She gave me a crisp, tight hug then held me by the shoulders at arm's length. 'I know you are. So today I went to the police station to explain the situation and they said they will contact their colleagues, the gendarmes in Paris, to see if they can find her. But you know what I think: Rosie will just be busy making new contacts, she'll be completely fine.'

I nodded. If we could just find Mother then everything would be better.

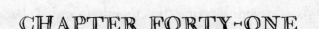

CHAPTER FORTY-ONE

I had a restless night, tossing and turning in bed until the sheets tangled around me like giant tentacles. I was up and dressed before it was light and for the first time it was me who woke Aunt Bets rather than the other way round.

Mr Lee and Charlie were already at the aquarium when we arrived and all the keepers, who were usually behind the scenes, were there too, peering into the tanks. Charlie rushed over to me.

'Vinnie! He's gone. He's completely disappeared!' he said.

'Who has?' I said, confused.

'The octopus, of course. Vanished.'

Was he joking? The octopus was always hiding, that was his . . . thing. I met Charlie's eyes carefully. I'd been worried he was still angry, and I didn't want to argue about the girls again.

The octopus had tricked us this way before, last time hiding in a shadowy corner, the mottled patches that crossed his body perfectly mimicking the drifting weed. I rushed over and pressed my nose against the tank, peering into the dark shadows behind the seaweed then across the bottom of the tank. I spread my cape against the glass, expecting a snaking arm to join me. Nothing.

'But he can't be *gone*,' I said. 'He can't open the latch from the inside.'

'The latch is still closed,' said Mr Lee, joining us. 'I've used the pole to search the entire tank. Charlie even leant right in.'

'And he didn't squirt me, and he loves to do that to me, and all the keepers. So he definitely isn't there.'

'And with Captain Bickerstaff due any day after reading about how popular he'd become.'

I didn't know what to say. It was like a magic trick, the closed tank, the vanishing beast. Aside from anything else, the octopus was simply too huge to be hiding anywhere else unnoticed, even with his most clever disguise.

I pressed both palms against the octopus tank and leant closer so my check cape was against the glass again, closing my eyes and willing him to simply appear as he had before.

When I opened my eyes I noticed a strange movement in the next tank. The spider crabs. All three of the huge creatures were there, two of them tangled together, the other in a corner, legs tucked underneath itself. They were fearsome to look at, so of course they were a visitor favourite, with their giant spiny red backs, beady black eyes on stalks, and impossibly long jointed legs. They'd only been moved to the tank next to the octopus two days before, for something else to fascinate the crowds when it was busy and they had to wait to get close to the octopus.

There was something wrong in the spider crabs tank. I peered at the jumble of bodies and legs. One of the armoured pink legs . . . drifted. The crabs usually moved in a slightly jerky but determined way, and if they were at rest they tucked their legs beneath them. They didn't drift like that. Not ever. The water in this tank was murkier than the others, fragments floating.

These three crabs were not at rest. Well, I supposed you might say they were in their final rest. Because the safe haven of the crabs' tank had been an illusion. Underneath a huge armoured shell, the size of a dinner platter,

I spotted the unmistakeable lilac circle of an octopus sucker. With a slight shift, he transformed that giveaway patch of arm to match the rest of him, reddish and spiked in texture, a perfect copy of the colour and texture of the crabs' shells.

'There you are!' I said to myself, feeling the grin spread across my face. I took a moment to admire the miracle of him, the octopus who used his own body as artwork. Then, louder, I called out: 'I found him!'

CHAPTER FORTY-TWO

'Are you all right behind here, Vinnie?' said Mr Lee as he led us through the door marked *Private* and into the passageway behind the tanks. 'It is rather dank and dark, I'm afraid.'

Charlie raised his eyebrows at me. I nodded, miming the turn of a key on my lips.

'Quite all right, Mr Lee, thank you.'

I wasn't going to tell Mr Lee that I'd already been here with Charlie. Twice. I released a long breath and allowed myself a smile. The octopus was found – although it was still a mystery how he got into the tank next door – and Charlie didn't seem to be annoyed with me, although I still needed to talk to him properly.

'Our devil-fish created a better illusion than Pepper's Ghost!' said Charlie.

Mr Lee turned and gave me an exasperated look.

'Oh – piffle! You must have heard of Pepper's Ghost,' said Charlie. 'You either, Vinnie?'

'I think I have heard the name, maybe from the ladies in the milliners.'

'*The True History of Pepper's Ghost* by John Henry Pepper. He uses mirrors, glass and clever lighting to create a ghost that could float through a crowd. It looks so real, I've seen it. It's the same illusion as the Headless Woman you see at fairground shows.'

Mr Lee propped the ladder up, shaking his head.

'Neither of you have seen it?' said Charlie. 'You do need to live a little.'

I had asked to visit the fair when I was younger but Mother said it was common and dirty.

'Pepper's Ghost, eh, I shall look it up. Might make a good name for our octopus.'

'Pepper?' I said, thinking it sounded more like the name for a small black dog.

'Ghost,' said Charlie. 'Yes! We shall call him Ghost. After all, he does seem to have passed clean through a wall.'

Mr Lee opened the top panel of the crab tank and

attempted to gently shift the octopus with a pole mounted with a sponge which they used for cleaning the inside of the glass. Charlie and I held the ladder and it shook with his efforts.

The octopus wasn't budging, flashing a triumphant scarlet red, then purple, then lilac. Now he had been discovered, he had enclosed most of himself inside the two crab shells like a clam and there didn't seem to be any dislodging him. But I couldn't keep the smile from my face and despite Mr Lee's mutterings, he was delighted too. Ghost was the right name for our eight-armed friend. We still had no idea how he had got into the next-door tank, but we definitely knew he hadn't been a polite house guest, killing and devouring all three crabs and then hiding behind their empty shells.

Mr Lee said it was impossible that this animal – an invertebrate with a body of muscular jelly about as far from human as it was possible to be – could have deliberately hidden himself this way. It showed too much intelligence by far. But he didn't sound like he believed that and nor did I. And now that Ghost had been found his tentacles rolled out one by one, took hold of the leg of the crab, breaking it free of the unfortunate body, and fed it through a gap between the two shells.

'It's like he's taunting us,' I said.

Mr Lee drew himself back through the open pane but

before he could turn, a fountain of water squirted out of the opening, soaking Mr Lee and Charlie but somehow missing me.

Laughter erupted from me without warning. I was still giggling as Mr Lee closed and secured the tank and climbed down the ladder, his curls stuck to his whiskers, and then I found I couldn't stop laughing until there were tears in my eyes.

'Are you quite all right, Vinnie?' said Mr Lee as I took the handkerchief from my sleeve and wiped my eyes. At the sight of his concerned expression I suddenly felt that maybe I was not really all right at all. Flashes of the hunched girls in that steamy garret, Martha's hands, the green dye poisoning them. What had the previous workshop been like? The one where a little girl died, that closed just before we left London. Just before Mother disappeared. I tried to swallow down the lump in my throat.

'Just tired,' I said.

'Of course you are.' Mr Lee patted my arm. 'Train travel exhausts me. Charlie told me all about the London Aquarium. But seems they don't have anything as magnificent or mysterious as our Ghost.'

We both turned back to the spider crab tank.

'Well I never—'

Before Mr Lee could finish I stepped sideways to the

octopus tank and there was Ghost, back in his own tank. How? He'd done his trick again, right there in front of us, and we hadn't seen. Bold as brass, gripping his latest wooden galleon like a kraken. A very greedy beast, head round and bulbous, arms swaying in the water to their own tune. His silver eyes were wide open, watching me through their rectangular slits. For a shivery moment I thought he must be enchanted after all, supernatural like the creatures of myth.

I pressed my shoulder to the glass and the octopus slowly unfurled an arm. As it suctioned the glass opposite me it bloomed into the lilac check of my cape once again.

'Yes – I saw what you did, Ghost. Very clever,' I said.

We watched for a moment as the lilac check spread up Ghost's arm to his head, flashed white a few times, then he was back to his triumphant red.

'Vinnie the octopus tamer,' said Mr Lee.

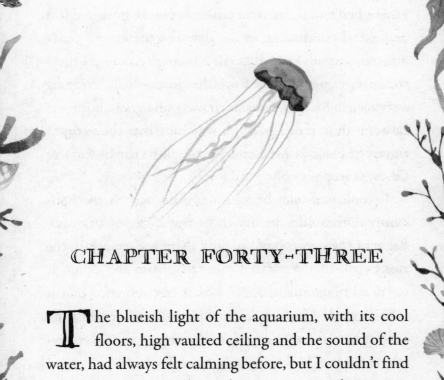

CHAPTER FORTY-THREE

The blueish light of the aquarium, with its cool floors, high vaulted ceiling and the sound of the water, had always felt calming before, but I couldn't find peace there now. Where the aquarium ceilings were vaulted, the workshop had been low-ceilinged; the air here was always cool, in contrast to that stinking toxic heat. I was surrounded by creatures of the sea, trapped in beautiful prisons, but with everything they needed provided for them. Yet those girls were imprisoned just the same, in a hell of Jedders' making, which was slowly killing them. I had shortened Mr Jedders to Jedders in my mind. He was no gentleman, no mister. We had to do something. But what?

I sighed and focused on Ghost as I sat in my usual seat and sketched, shading in the detail of the empty crabs' armour that now rested at the base of their tank. I drew the octopus peering out from the closed shells, gripping a crab leg in his arm. My sketch was quite grisly, but I was rather proud of it. I was also watching that the octopus stayed in place as Mr Lee tried to get to the bottom of Ghost's escape act once and for all.

It took one man being up to his chest in the half-emptied crab tank before there was a cry of triumph. Right at the very top of the tank there was a crack in the stonework that separated one tank from the other. It seemed impossibly small, but Mr Lee confirmed that if Ghost's beak – hidden under his head and beneath the canopy of his arms – could fit, then there was no reason why the rest of his body could not follow.

The hole was filled as Ghost remained on his temple throne, arms gently swaying. I wondered if Ghost knew what they were doing because he didn't seem to react, but his arms swayed through the water in such a way, like snakes, that I felt sure he was sensing with them, maybe not seeing but something else.

As I packed up my drawing things Charlie arrived, walking briskly across the gallery floor. I wished I still had my pencil in my hand, something to do, a reason not to look directly at him, because we'd not spoken yet about what we had seen in the workshop.

With Mr Lee and the attendants in the corridor the other side of the tank, Charlie and I were alone in the gallery. I rolled back my shoulders. Charlie might know a lot more than me about most things, but I wasn't going to let him persuade me that sacrificing those girls for the greater good was the right thing to do.

I looked at Ghost so I could avoid looking at Charlie, and the octopus turned pale yellow, no pattern, just two horns rising either side of his mantle. I'd noticed pale colours showed he wasn't comfortable; he'd flash that colour when people tapped at the glass just before he curled into the back corner. But he was still sat spread on top of his temple like a lord. Could he somehow tell how I was feeling? No. I shook my head at myself but continued to watch Ghost as Charlie stood behind me. It was still before opening time, no visitors yet.

'I'm sorry, Vinnie,' he said, very quietly. 'What we saw in Litcham Street . . . Great Scott, it made me angry – but I shouldn't have taken that out on you.'

I turned to meet his eyes and saw that he really did look sorry. In fact, there were dark smudges beneath his red-rimmed eyes, and I felt any lingering thoughts of being cross about how he'd spoken to me melt away.

'It made me angry too. But even more sad,' I said.

There had to be something we could do for those girls, to stop Jedders, and find Mother and how she was connected to it all. But if there was, neither Charlie nor I could think of it. If only the answers could unexpectedly appear like the octopus had.

Charlie scuffed the toe of his boot against the edge of a floor tile.

'I thought you'd be writing your next story to go with this.' I pointed at my picture. 'It's absolutely impossible anyone else could know about this one.'

Charlie smiled. 'You're right, Vinnie, I need to get my scoop.'

DASTARDLY DEVIL-FISH'S GHOSTLY FEAST

Once again, we urge you to make a visit to the newest addition to the underwater menagerie of Brighton Grand Aquarium.

The giant octopus was already making quite a name for itself due to its size and ability to change colour, but its latest capers might just shoot it to sea creature stardom.

When attendants found the tank empty they could not believe an animal this size had escaped. Could this magnificent and valuable beast have been stolen? But they had been wrong-footed by this cunning creature.

One of the octopus' skills is to squeeze through the smallest of gaps and in this way it managed to squeeze through an improbable crack and enter the neighbouring tank, where it, under the cover of night, devoured the occupants. This was no mean feat as the unfortunate victims were a family of large spike-shelled spider crabs, the shells of which this soft-bodied predator proceeded to wear like grisly armour.

The devil-fish has now been named Ghost in homage to the grand illusion known as Pepper's Ghost, although the creature is a true marvel, with no smoke or mirrors required.

A visit to this octopus named Ghost might also find you in the company of a marvellous young artist who against all odds seems to have befriended the ravenous beast, which even changes colour to match her clothing. To see it is to believe it!

CHAPTER FORTY-FOUR

The next few days were hot for May. Crowds flocked from the promenade into the cool water-lit gallery to visit the devil-fish Ghost and other wonders of the ocean, and then headed up for refreshments on the breezy terrace in droves. Aunt was busy enough that she had employed a girl to help, so I could be downstairs in the aquarium.

I pressed my hand and forehead against the cool glass. It was even stuffy down here, in the gallery, sat at my desk, sketching. Definitely too warm for my checked cape, yet I wore it anyway as seeing Ghost react to it excited even the hottest families with the tiredest children.

Ghost was even more entertaining than usual today, darting from one side of the tank to the other, arms streaming behind him, head sharpened to a point. The octopus was mainly deep indigo with the occasional bloom of his normal brick red. It was an unusual colour for him and one I associated with him being irritated; he would turn very dark with flickers of white that felt like a warning. He seemed intent on finding something, collecting shells and the largest stones into a pile at one side of the tank and then moving them to the other.

'It has to be one of the keepers, that's the only possible answer,' said Charlie, startling me as he shoved the newspaper under my nose, a little downhearted again as his own writing had not been published. 'They were the only others who knew about this.'

'Hold on,' I said, as I closed my sketchbook, protecting my drawing from the newspaper print. Mr Lee had asked me to draw Ghost how he was behaving today, as he was particularly lively, shooting back and forth like an arrow.

I scanned over the article, eyes lingering on my drawing. Ghost looked positively malevolent peering out from the closed shells, waving a crab leg as if in triumph.

'Your drawing is excellent as always. Uncle Henry told me he thinks you are getting better and better,' Charlie said.

'Thank you,' I said. 'But I'm sure your writing was excellent too. So is it just that some of your words have been changed? Could the newspaper have done it?'

'No – this is written by someone completely different, and their style – I'm sure it is the same writer as the other pieces. I feel like someone is in my head, Vinnie, and it's starting to give me the collywobbles.'

'What is it doing?' interrupted a young man with a spindly moustache, peering into the tank.

I didn't know. I hadn't seen Ghost behave quite like this before, especially not during the daytime when he'd spread across the glass or perch on the temple, rising to crush one of the wooden galleons to get to the hidden treats inside, but mainly saving his main activity for the evening. He shot from one corner to the opposite, crisscrossing the tank, smooshing his tentacles against the surface every time he met it before rebounding off.

'Look, he's using the shells like armour, or a disguise, just like it says in the paper,' said an older man with great authority, pointing over Charlie's shoulder at the newspaper.

Charlie huffed, clearly not wishing to be reminded of the article again. 'I'm going to treat myself to a slice of Mrs Ruggles' best Battenberg.'

Ghost had stopped shooting from one end of the tank to the other, and picked up a bundle of shells with half of his arms while two arms explored the temple and another two, including the shortened one from the injury, slid across the glass opposite me and flickered brightest red.

I fixed the view in my mind. The angle was perfect, showing how Ghost's arms operated independently, and I opened my pad on a new page. I was quickly absorbed in my sketch, blocking out the sound of the people around me and disappearing into the world of Ghost through my pencil and paper. I watched bemused as he carefully piled the oyster and crab shells around the base of the temple and then reached one arm over to the weed growing at the back of the tank and plucked a frond. He tore it into pieces and it floated around the tank.

When the visitors headed off to enjoy the evening cool, Mr Lee arrived.

'This behaviour is interesting. He wouldn't allow the boys to clean the shells out earlier. He squirted Thomas so hard, poor lad lost his cap.'

I laughed.

Mr Lee frowned into the tank. I stood and joined him. Ghost was inside the temple and drawing oyster shells around the outside. He had dragged a terracotta bottle and the wooden galleon into the same area and filled some of the holes with the weed he'd picked earlier.

'Look, he's disguising his den. They do this in the

wild when they are vulnerable to predators.' Mr Lee scratched his chin. 'I hope the crowds are not getting to him. It's a balance because we want the visitors to get a good view, but welfare . . .'

'Maybe he thinks the spider crabs' relatives will come back to take revenge,' I say.

Mr Lee shook his head but smiled.

And then Ghost disappeared. Inside the temple he blew out a cloud of debris and cleared the bottom and then sucked his entire body and head inside. His arms curled through the windows and outside. I rested my cape against the tank. Ghost ran his arm across the glass and there was a hint of lilac check before he pulled that arm in too.

'Vinnie, there you are,' Aunt Bets called across the gallery, flustered. I was surprised; she rarely came down into the aquarium. 'Hello, Henry. There was a messenger boy here, Vin. He wouldn't say who he came from but said only you must open this.' She handed me a letter with my name printed in plain capitals on the front: *MISS LAVINIA R. E. FYFE.* PRIVATE.

My heart leapt as I ran my finger over the ink. Who would call me that? Who else knew my middle names were that of my mother and Aunt Bets? But it was the curl at the base of the F that confirmed it – I would know that handwriting anywhere.

Mother. Finally.

I clutched the letter to my chest and to my dismay, tears spilt from my eyes before I could blink them back.

THE THIRD
HEART

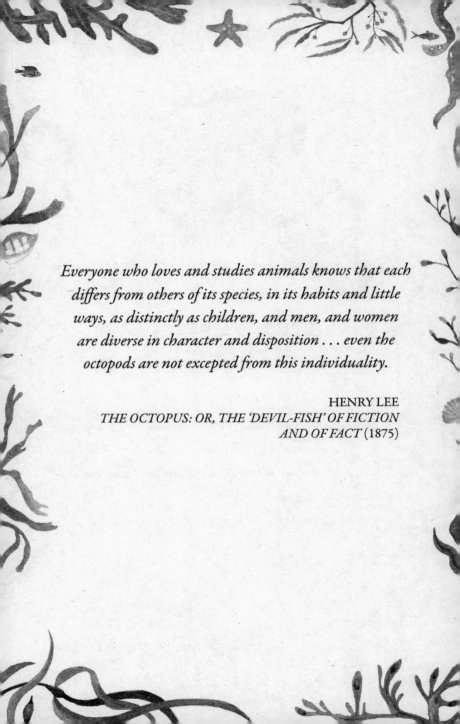

Everyone who loves and studies animals knows that each differs from others of its species, in its habits and little ways, as distinctly as children, and men, and women are diverse in character and disposition . . . even the octopods are not excepted from this individuality.

HENRY LEE
THE OCTOPUS: OR, THE 'DEVIL-FISH' OF FICTION AND OF FACT (1875)

CHAPTER FORTY-FIVE

Dear Lavinia,

Come to the boarding house below immediately and ask for Mrs Jane Hill. Read this alone. Destroy this note, show no one. Come alone. Please ensure you are not being followed.

29 Rock Place
Brighton
M

Brighton?

Mother had sent this message from Brighton? But she

was in Paris. And the warning about being followed? Did she know Jedders had been here too? None of this made any sense.

'Did the boy say where it had come from?' I said.

'He didn't say anything.' Aunt Bets tilted her head to one side but didn't question me. She hadn't recognized Mother's writing; they didn't write to each other. 'Here – sit down, our Vinnie. Take some sweet tea.'

She guided me to the chair behind the counter of the tea shop, where I reread the note with shaking hands. I needed to go. I needed to see Mother, now. But first I must pull myself together. I closed my eyes and forced in some deep breaths. I couldn't think straight.

Mother couldn't be in Brighton, but it was definitely her handwriting. I stood, wiped my eyes again and looked up to see Aunt Bets with her arms folded.

'Something strange has been going on with you. You're worried, so I'm worried. Let me help,' she said and her eyes were so clear and honest and kind, my tears started again. I brushed them away angrily and made a decision in that moment.

Read this alone. Show no one. It was the first time I had ever disobeyed a direct request from my mother.

I handed Aunt Bets the note. When she had finished I tucked it in the back of my pocket sketchbook, deep in my skirts. When my sketchbook wasn't on my person, I slept with it under my pillow. It would be as safe there as burning it.

Ten minutes later Aunt Bets was securing her bicycle with a chain and padlock outside what looked like a guest house. This couldn't be right; Mother couldn't be so close. The street was one of grand four-storey townhouses, all painted white with tall bay windows on the ground floor.

Before I could say anything Aunt Bets knocked at the door. I was taken back to standing outside 9 Litcham Street in Kentish Town. I wished I could go back to how I had been then, when I didn't know what was happening inside.

A cheerful woman opened the door.

'We are here to see Mrs Jane Hill,' said Aunt Bets quietly.

The lady frowned. 'Mrs Hill left a message. Only Lavinia Fyfe is permitted. Sorry, ducky, our guest left clear instructions...' Recognition flickered over her face as she looked at Aunt Bets. 'Oh, it's yourself, from the terrace tea shop. I send all my guests down to you. Best tea and cake in Brighton town.'

'That is so kind of you,' said Aunt Bets.

'What have you got in today, I might treat myself later,' said the lady with a delicate lick of her lips.

'Fresh scones, a fine ginger cake, Madeira . . . but please, Mrs Hill is a relative, and Vinnie here is my niece, I can't let her go up alone.'

The lady hadn't taken much persuading and now we stood outside a door with a brass plaque with a number eight. I knocked.

'Come in,' came a faint voice.

At first I thought my mind was playing tricks on me. The woman in the bed simply looked like my mother, it couldn't actually be her. But they were her eyes, sparkling blue, her chestnut hair in one thick plait over her shoulder, a grass-green silk robe over one of her fine lawn nightgowns. She was pale, her cheeks hollow – I'd never seen Mother like this. Her hands were crossed on top of the covers. I stepped forward like an automaton.

'Lavinia, dear heart. Come,' she said, her voice quieter and with a strange creak to it, but hers all the same.

I ran to her and collapsed on to the bed, my face buried in her chest as she stroked my hair. I felt sobs rise up and swallowed them down, for this was no time to feel sorry for myself – Mother was clearly sick, very sick. Something hard pressed against my cheek. The huge pearl she'd showed me in the train carriage was still around her neck.

'Rosamund, are you ill? Were you taken ill in Paris?' said Aunt Bets, now standing at the door of the room.

'I have not been well, dearest, and I did not wish you to see me this way. Look how it is distressing you,' she said to me. To my dismay her eyes pooled with tears and she held a lace handkerchief to her mouth and gave a sharp cough.

'Is it the consumption?' I said, unable to keep the horror from my voice. 'Mother, why are you in a guest house? I'm old enough to take care of you. Have you seen a doctor?'

'A nasty bout of influenza hit me the moment I left you. It is very contagious and I had no wish to spread it.'

I couldn't take it in. Mother had been here, ill, just walking distance from the aquarium, for a month?

'Vinnie has been so worried, Rosie,' said Aunt Bets, perching on the opposite side of the bed. 'Is this the right place to recover from serious illness? Who is looking after you?'

'I hired a nurse, of course, Elizabeth, of which I no longer have need. Just a few more days of rest and recuperation. I am capable of taking care of myself, dear cousin. And yes, Lavinia, a doctor saw me too. There is really no need to worry. As you know, I have a very strong constitution.'

I opened my mouth but no words came.

'Oh, Lavinia, do close your mouth dear, are you a girl or a fish? You can't have picked that habit up from dear

Elizabeth,' said Mother, flashing a weak smile. Mother was here! This was the Mother I knew. And she said she was getting better. 'You know how important appearances are, Lavinia. My image is everything – my customers might never think of me the same again knowing I had had a nasty infectious illness. They equate Fyfe's with vitality, with perfection. They imagine me in Paris, mixing with the best of the best.'

'But you could have written, even if you didn't—'

'I really was far too unwell, dear heart,' she said. 'I am much stronger now.'

'Well, that is good news,' said Aunt Bets, a little abruptly. 'I shall tell the police to stop the search. They have the French gendarmes looking for you.'

Mother gave Aunt Bets a sharp look. 'I appreciate the concern, Elizabeth, but what a dreadful fuss. It's been a month, that's all.'

I saw Aunt Bets' jaw tighten. 'Now, Rosamund, I'm very sorry you've been unwell, but please explain why this Mr Jedders has been so desperate to find you. He has quite frightened Vinnie.'

I hadn't expected Aunt Bets to say this and looked from her to Mother and back again.

CHAPTER FORTY-SIX

Mother coughed again, resting her head back on the pillow.

'Oh, you know male pride, cousin, that is all. Jedders suffers from it more than most. He is desperate to have his old position back. He'll just have to accept it.'

I could see Aunt Bets was not convinced. 'It does seem very desperate to have somehow tracked Vinnie down here.'

'I wouldn't put anything past Jedders; he is a sharp one, unwilling to accept no for an answer.'

Aunt Bets held up a hand. 'Look, Rosie, be truthful

please. Do you need help? Do you owe this Jedders money?'

'Oh, Elizabeth, for pity's sake. I owe that man nothing. Everything he has had was down to me, to my ideas . . . and Lavinia's designs, of course. I have taken only what is ours, what is Fyfe's, and he will now need to make his own way.'

Mother closed her eyes for a moment. Were we tiring her too much?

So Mother didn't know about the workshop as I had thought. I had somehow persuaded myself that Mother had found out about the workshop and knew about the death of little Agnes. That we had left London because Jedders knew she knew and wanted to silence her. Mother had always told me not to let my imagination run wild. I should have listened.

Silence hung in the air. If Mother didn't know about the workshop, I needed to tell them both what Charlie and I had seen, about those poor girls. But Mother coughed again and looked so pale. I helped her take a sip of water.

'Thank you, dear heart,' she said with a weak smile.

How could I tell her about Jedders, about the workshop, about him following me when she had been so sick and was still recovering?

'Mother is still not quite herself, Lavinia. Tell me all

about your time here, dear heart, it will cheer me. I have seen nothing of Brighton but these four walls and I have missed you so.'

What I wanted to do was tell her what Jedders was really like, what Charlie and I had seen, but instead I sat on Mother's bed and described my life in Brighton. I told her about Mr Lee and Charlie, and about Ghost and his antics, about going behind the tanks in the aquarium. I wondered if she might disapprove, but she listened avidly.

Finally I drew out my pocket sketchbook, a little nervous.

Mother took the book from me and browsed the pages, nodding at the new hat designs in the front.

'Oh, clever heart, these will do quite nicely.' A page fell open at the back and she blinked. 'Gracious, Lavinia, whatever is this? It is quite unsettling. Did one of your new friends draw it?'

My cheeks burnt. 'No, Mother, I drew them. That's Ghost, the octopus.'

Mother shuddered and snapped the book shut, and I was suddenly glad she hadn't seen the newspaper clippings of my drawing I had slid into the back.

I changed the subject and told her about how I'd made a friend in Temitayo, how clever she was, and how much I liked her, but she frowned.

'Brought from Africa as an infant you say. Like that Sarah Forbes Bonetta, the Queen's god-daughter? That girl was quite the talk of London society for a time.' She lowered her voice. 'I heard she was a wilful miss.'

I wasn't sure what to say to that. What did this Sarah have to do with Temitayo, just because they both came from Africa?

'Isn't wilful just another word for independent-minded?' said Aunt Bets. She had been hovering by the door, giving me time to see Mother.

I swallowed. 'Well, I don't know about this Sarah, but Temitayo is so bright and lively, Mother, you would like her.'

Mother's lips pressed together. 'Bright and lively is very well, but grace and gratitude are more important in some *situations*.'

I wasn't quite sure what to say to that. Mother had closed her eyes, her head tilted to one side. I squeezed her hands and she sighed, eyelids fluttering.

'That is probably enough for today, Lavinia. The doctor did warn me over-exertion could set back my recovery.' Mother opened her eyes and beckoned me back to her, holding me tight so her lips were close to my ear. 'Soon I will be well enough for Paris,' she said. 'You need to be ready.'

She reached out to cup my cheek and I sighed. I'd

missed her so much. I felt small and young and comforted. All would be well.

Mother pressed her handkerchief to her mouth once again and gripped my hand so tight it almost hurt. 'Don't tell anyone about my illness or being here, Lavinia, nor you, Elizabeth. Not a soul. Word must not get out – I will not stand the shame of my weakness being known. You must swear this on my life.'

Her eyes were so wide and glittering I could not bring myself to argue, and even found myself promising.

'And you, Elizabeth?'

'As you wish,' said Aunt Bets, 'but I am sure your customers would think more kindly than you imagine. And this isn't to do with you not wanting this Mr Jedders to find you? Because I am quite happy to help you contact the police . . .'

Mother reached out her hand to Aunt Bets. 'No, no, cousin. Mr Jedders hasn't actually done anything, has he? You are very knowledgeable in the world of cake and tea, I am sure, but the higher echelons of society think differently. It is not so long since the young prince himself succumbed to the Russian flu and Parliament was closed. Customers truly do not need to be reminded of this. There is always such a stain of contagion left after illness. And I certainly don't need any doings with the police. The scandal of it!'

Aunt Bets' smile became fixed but she still bent to kiss Mother's cheek. 'So you being here is nothing to do with that Mr Jedders man?'

'Oh, Elizabeth, I've already explained this to you. Mr Jedders is a very persistent man, but I hardly think he can have given me the influenza, do you?' she said, patting Aunt Bets' hand. 'Now sit back, dear heart, and let me look at you.'

Mother scanned me up and down. I had pinned my hair out of the way when I dressed that morning as it was a windy day. I wore the check cape and the orange-striped dress.

'Dear me, Lavinia, you are quite gaudy.' Mother sighed back on her pillow. 'Thank you, Elizabeth, it is so kind of you to come, and of course to look after Lavinia so well. Now I feel quite exhausted. Please wait for me to send for you before you come again.'

Aunt Bets planted her hands on her hips. 'I should think we must come back tomorrow with some nourishing soup and cake, you look quite thin ...'

'Rest is more important, the doctor was quite clear about that. You will hear from me very soon. In the meantime, not a word to anyone, as word will spread.'

I didn't want to leave Mother but I smiled, because a wave of pure relief was breaking over all of my confused feelings as she closed her eyes, her hand reaching for the pearl around her neck as if to check it was there.

Mother was here. She would get fully better and then help me sort all of this out.

CHAPTER FORTY-SEVEN

The next two days passed far too slowly as I waited for Mother to send for me again.

Aunt Bets clearly still found it very strange that her cousin was in secret convalescence in a guest house just a few streets away, but I thought I could make sense of it now. Mother had always cared for appearances and reputation, but I'd never noticed how much before living with Aunt Bets and spending time with my new friends. And the way she had always kept me so close was more unusual than I had realized. She was a very protective mother.

I'd taken to wearing my slim-toed boots again. My

feet needed to get used to them, as the workaday boots Aunt Bets had bought me weren't going to fly in the fashionable streets of Paris.

On the third day nothing seemed to be going right. It was hot and still and very busy at the tea rooms. A boy had bumped into me when I was clearing one of the tables and sent my tray flying, breaking a very fine teapot. He had helped me clear up the mess and Aunt Bets said it didn't matter – but it put me out of sorts and I felt like I should help her the whole day to make up for it, rather than spending my usual afternoon in the cooler aquarium.

It seemed an age before I could finally sit down with an elderflower cordial. We'd found Mother, yet I was still waiting. The girls in the workshop were still in danger. And now I had a further worry, because Ghost had continued with his strange behaviour, sitting still atop the temple, surrounded by a barricade of shells.

Charlie appeared, eyes bright and cheeks flushed, and I hoped he'd come to fetch me because Ghost was on the move, but instead he slapped a newspaper down in front of me. Another article about the octopus? I understood Charlie's frustration, I did, but my mind was spinning from seeing Mother. I wanted to tell Charlie, but she had said to tell no one.

'Vinnie, are you even looking?' he said. 'Here, let me read it to you, I need to take it in, anyway.'

DOES PARIS GREEN COME AT TOO CRUEL A PRICE?

Since this publication last wrote about some of the more sinister side effects of certain clothing manufacturing practices, some more reputable factories have discontinued using the most toxic substances, namely the copper oxide and arsenic present to make that most vibrant and fashionable pigment, Paris Green.

It would be hoped that the fashionable crowd would spurn this colour, but since the risk to the wearer is negligible, the scarcity of the shade due to safety concerns has only served to push prices to never-seen-before levels. Meaning Paris Green is quickly becoming a sign of the elite.

But would the society lady be so desperate to run her soft hands over green silks, or accessorize with verdant flowers, if she could see the scabrous hands that had made them?

With huge profits to be made, the manufacture of this pigment has been pushed underground, making the workers' conditions even more pitiful. Back-street dyers, like the workshop this publication recently discovered in a dingy top floor of a slum tenement, are unventilated pits of despair and desperation, where girls as young as eleven hide the pustulating sores on their hands and the green tinge in their pallor from cruel and unscrupulous managers.

My heart drummed.

Charlie had said he wasn't going to write it.

And now he was reading it as if he'd totally forgotten his promise.

He'd broken his word to the girls in the workshop.

He'd broken his word to me.

Disappointment throbbed through me, a burning kind of sadness adding to the despair I already felt for the girls.

I didn't know what to say to Charlie so I stared back down at the newspaper, and I realized that he hadn't written where the workshop was; he hadn't mentioned any of the girls' names. He hadn't mentioned the death of lil' Agnes.

So there was that. But my cheeks were still hot with the betrayal. With the thought of how easily those girls could be turned out and into the workhouse. Even if this article didn't cause it.

'I know!' said Charlie. 'That's exactly how I must have looked when I first read it. How could he possibly have found this out? It's like the man's inside my head.'

It took a moment for what he said to sink in, for my anger had been so quick.

'You didn't write this one, either?' I said.

'Of course I blasted well didn't, Vinnie,' he said and then flushed. 'I apologize for my cursing, but I did give my word that I would not.'

I nodded. 'You did. And I'm sorry I doubted you.'

I let my anger drain away as I cleared the table.

'For pity's sake, sit down,' he said. 'Someone is spying on us, Vin.'

'What about one of the girls themselves, could they have written this?' I said, and then seeing his expression, I continued, 'There are charity schools who teach letters, or maybe orphanages, and that Ruth seemed clever.'

Saying her name took me back to the workshop. I'd rather accept we had a spy than remember the sound of Jedders' cane against her hands.

'Is it the same person who wrote the other articles?'

'I was going to check that, try to see if they have the same style. Do you have those clippings with you?'

I nodded, reaching into the folds of my skirts for my pocket sketchbook. My fingers scrambled for the smooth, familiar cover. My fingers found nothing. I stood, reaching my hand in again. Only my pencil was in the pocket.

'It's gone. It's gone from my pocket,' I said. 'There's no hole. I don't understand.'

'Oh well, probably dropped when you were cycling. Uncle Henry will have copies of those articles.'

Despite the heat a cold feeling crept down my neck. The sketchbook couldn't have fallen out. The pocket was deep. I had definitely put it in there this morning. When could it have possibly—

I gasped and the words came rushing out. 'There was a boy, he bumped into me, I dropped the tray, the teapot broke, he and his brother both helped me clear up ...'

'The oldest pickpocket trick in the book; they make out they are helping and when you're distracted, those slippery little fingers have the watch off your wrist. Or the sketchbook from your pocket,' said Charlie.

'But what would they want with my sketchbook ...' The cold feeling at my neck spread to gooseflesh across my forearms.

Mother's guest house. The address. It was in the back of the sketchbook. I remembered when Jedders had cornered me, the grocer conveniently chasing a thief at that very moment.

Jedders had hired a pickpocket.

Mother.

The tap of a stick on the terrace made me spin around.

I must be seeing things in the evening light with its reaching shadows.

Because there – out of her sick bed and here on the terrace as if I had conjured her – was Mother, herself.

CHAPTER FORTY-EIGHT

'Mama!' I almost knocked my chair right over in my hurry to go to her.

It had been only three days since I saw my mother in bed, an invalid. And now she was fully dressed in a deep pink dress and the straw bonnet hiding her face wasn't her style at all. In the shadow of the rim her face was sharp, but colour bloomed bright in her cheeks. Her eyes darted around the terrace taking it all in. I wondered if she could be delirious and glanced around for Aunt Bets but she must have been behind the counter.

Charlie had also stood and remained standing, awkward.

'Mama! Are you well enough – can I fetch – what do you—'

'Please don't fuss, Lavinia. And no searching around for that cousin of mine either, I am here to see you, my dear heart.' Her silk-gloved hand gripped mine and I was suddenly conscious that if my skin was rough it would snag the delicate material. 'Now can we talk down in your aquarium, dear heart, for the sun is quite blinding up here,' she said.

'Of course, Mama, but—'

Mother looked over her shoulder yet again. 'We'll talk in a moment, dear heart,' she said. 'Lead the way.'

My head spun. Mother had recovered so much in just three days, but seemed even less herself, her shoulders hunched, eyes darting around the terrace from beneath the bonnet.

'But, Mother, you are surely not well enough?'

Mother barely leant on my arm as we walked so briskly down the stairs – the cane tapping – I was fearful she would fall. When we passed a group of visitors on their way out, Mother turned quickly to the wall as if to inspect one of the carved friezes. She still didn't want anyone to see her, so why come to such a public place rather than sending for me? I thought again of the stolen sketchbook, the address.

'Mama, has Mr Jedders . . .'

'Shush now,' said Mother.

One of the keepers stopped us at the door to the gallery – the group must have been the last visitors of the day. Mother looked to the floor, hunching further and leaning on her cane.

'I just need to see Mr Lee,' I said to the man with as much confidence as I could manage.

The keepers were all used to me by now and let me through at all hours. I wondered if he would question who Mother was, but he simply raised his hat.

I led her to the chair in front of Ghost's tank, the one I usually used for sketching. I noticed how he still wasn't moving, spread over the temple, surrounded by shells stuck to the tentacles he had wrapped around him.

'Your visit was such a tonic I have found myself quite revived and am set for Paris, Lavinia. I will send for you very soon, dear heart, but it is best I get settled first.'

My heart dropped. She'd come here to say goodbye? She was going to leave me again? Last time I had felt so hopeless, all I could do was obey her, but I had to have some say in this. I made my voice firm.

'No, Mama. I insist on coming with you. You haven't been well, you need me there.'

She peered out from beneath the bonnet, darting glances at the door. 'Let's not talk about this now. Show me the wonderful things you've seen? What about this behind-the-scenes passage you mentioned?' she said.

Her changes in conversation were making my brain whirl. She was ill, she was better, she was here, she was leaving, and now she wanted an aquarium tour?

'The passage, dear heart? Is it through one of these doors?'

'Oh, it's very damp and dark, Mama – I don't think—'

'Where does it lead, Lavinia?'

Again, my mind was whirling. 'Erm . . . it joins to a smugglers' tunnel.'

Her cane rested against the glass and caught my eye. It was slim and black with a carved face. The smiling side faced me, but I remembered the skull on the other side without seeing it. It couldn't be.

'Is that Jedders' cane?' I blurted.

There was a beat of silence. 'Oh, Lavinia, of course it isn't.'

My gaze lingered on the cane. She was lying. She had to be lying. How could there be another cane exactly like that? But why would Mother lie . . . to me?

'Do stop fussing, dear heart, I simply want to see all of the things that have interested you. It is a rare treat to be allowed behind the scenes,' said Mother. 'Is this the door?'

CHAPTER FORTY-NINE

Despite my misgivings we entered into the tunnel. I was aware of the uneven floor and Mother's delicate shoes, but she urged me on, her hand gripping my shoulder.

Outside Ghost's tank were both the stepladder and a stool the attendants used. I insisted Mother sat down to catch her breath. Surely the damp air would be bad for her.

From this side we could see more of Ghost. His soft body was a deep throbbing red and filled the back arch of the temple. His arms folded back over it, displaying the rows of lilac suckers, fewer shells stuck to them than there were at the front. His siphon blew gently into a hole at the side of the temple. Aside from that, he was completely still.

'A beast indeed,' breathed Mother. Then she held her forehead as her lashes fluttered.

'Mother, are you unwell?' I said.

'Just a little tired. I need smelling salts, dear heart. Elizabeth will have some,' she said. 'I will wait here.'

I hesitated. That mind-whirling feeling again. I wasn't at all sure Aunt Bets would have smelling salts; I'd never seen her use them.

'But what if you faint and I'm not here?' I said.

What if Mr Lee came out of his workroom to find a stranger here?

'I won't faint if you fetch me the smelling salts, Lavinia,' she said, massaging her temples. The gas lamp behind us reflected off the glass and lit her face.

My breath caught in my throat. A thin trickle of something dark ran down Mother's cheek.

'Mother, are you hurt?' I pointed to my own cheek. 'Is that . . . blood?'

'Don't fret about that, the mirror tipped forward on its hinges as I was leaving, just a scratch.'

She reached up to touch it and her glove came away with a violent smudge of crimson. She gave an impatient sigh. Something was very wrong here. I tried to see into the shadow of her bonnet, catch a glimpse of the cut on her face again, but she was now bowed forward, in shadow.

'The smelling salts, dear heart,' she said, in the firm voice I'd obeyed my whole life.

Clutching my skirts, I rushed back along the passageway. This all linked together: the cut on her face, the too-bright way she was looking at me. Mother was feverish and delirious; maybe she had fallen and banged her head. But that didn't explain Jedders' cane. Or my missing sketchbook.

Mother was right about one thing: I really did need Aunt Bets.

I flung open the door from the passageway behind the tanks, taking one last look back at Mother, a tiny figure, lit by a pool of light from the gas lamp, in her pink dress, sitting on the stool. She was holding something in the palm of her hand, staring at it. In the dim light I caught the glow of the pearl, the heirloom she now wore around her neck. At least she was still sitting on the stool and not yet collapsed. I closed the door behind me. When I turned to face the gallery a shadow moved.

A figure stepped from behind a column.

Mr Jedders.

CHAPTER FIFTY

For a lingering moment Jedders and I stood still, opposite each other. His face was smoothly shaven, blond curls behind his ears, bowler hat pulled low, and I was suddenly back in the milliners, watching Mother open her ledger and point to something, him nodding in agreement, and I felt all of this must have been a terrible mistake.

Then he smiled and I started back. His small teeth were streaked with blood, his lip swollen, purple. Mother was bleeding, Jedders was bleeding. She had his cane . . .

Swish, thwack. Good girls.

I knew who this man really was, and my hands shook. But Jedders didn't know what Charlie and I had witnessed, so he might still want to keep up the pretence of being a respectable man.

I wanted that too, I really did.

Stay calm, I told myself, think carefully before speaking.

'Hello, Miss Lavinia,' he said with a tip of his hat. 'Don't happen to know where your dear mother is, do you?'

I shook my head, probably a little too fast, trying to keep my eyes from his mouth and the blood on his teeth. I couldn't let this man get to Mother, trapped in the tunnel and ill – I squared my shoulders.

'No idea at all?' he said, the corners of his lips curling down. 'That is a great shame.'

He looked behind me at the door in the wall and I couldn't help it – I didn't mean to, but I took a step back.

'Because it almost seems that she might be some-where close by,' he said, and then his eyes tracked down to the floor in front of the octopus tank. 'Ah, this is my cane. How very strange. I wonder how that got here.'

He picked up the cane, and I caught a glimpse of the horrid ivory carving of the face, tongue sticking out, before he swung it through the air.

Whisk . . .

The back of my neck prickled. I was babbling now. 'She isn't there, there's nothing back there, just where they feed the animals. Why don't we go upstairs? This place is closed and my aunt will be wondering where I am, she'll be down any moment . . .'

He smiled again and I tried not to look at his bloodied teeth, but when I met his eyes I saw the smile hadn't reached them, had got nowhere near in fact, because they were round, surrounded by skin so smooth it almost shone, as if they had never been wrinkled by a true smile in his life.

His voice changed, all charm gone. 'Move aside, child.'

'You can't go in there, it's private—'

'Move aside. Or I will move you.'

I stayed still. Everything inside me told me to duck around him, to run to Aunt Bets, but Mother was behind there, trapped in the tunnel, and I would never leave her.

'Have it your way.' He moved too quickly, lifting his cane with one hand, pressing the length of it against my side, as he grasped my wrist with the other hand, hauling me away from the door as easy as if I were a bag of potatoes. I gripped his hand on my wrist with both of mine, curling my fingers around his, trying to unpeel them as he pushed the door open with his cane.

Mama! There was nowhere to hide in that tunnel. What did he want from her, what would he do to her?

'Stay here or I swear you'll get a hiding,' he hissed through clenched teeth and I heard the same tone as when he'd spoken to Ruth.

I will not accept insubordination.

But this man was not in charge of me. He was not fit to be in charge of anyone.

He twisted me around by my wrist so I faced the octopus tank. Ghost didn't move from the temple, but released the shells he had been holding. His colour pulsed darkest red, then I was sure I saw the check of my cape, just for a flash followed by spots of glowing blue I'd never seen before. The octopus was always surprising, even now I saw that, when this evil man was so much stronger than I was, than Mother was—

Wait. Always surprising?

Maybe I could be surprising too.

I stopped trying to wrench Jedders' hand off me and instead gripped his wrist with both of my hands and let my knees go soft, my whole body a dead weight, clinging to him, dragging him down on one side. He hadn't wanted me to get away; now he had his wish.

'Why, you little—'

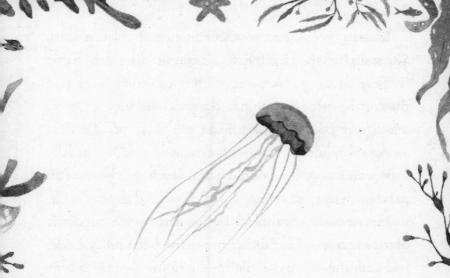

CHAPTER FIFTY-ONE

I closed my eyes tight, telling myself to hang on to Jedders no matter what he did next, feeling him try to drag my dead weight, my hands slipping on his wrist, hearing the *whisk* of the cane and cringing from the pain to come, but determined that no matter how much it hurt I would not let this man get to my Mother—

Mother. Why couldn't she hear me and Jedders? See us through the tank? I didn't want her to come, for this man to get to her, but she must have heard what was happening. Then new voices, a blur of movement.

'Vinnie? What the . . .'

'Quick!' A second voice I knew very well.

Charlie and Temitayo skidded to a halt in front of us. She snatched the zinc bucket he was holding and swung it in a wide arc, intercepting Jedders' cane before it could reach me with an almighty clang. Then another *swish* and a war cry from Charlie as he staved off the next swing of Jedders' cane with his mop. Jedders finally shook me free and I scrambled up. Temitayo's boater still perched at the perfect angle as she wielded the bucket as if keen to make another strike. Charlie wore a huge pair of rubber boots. The bucket must have been full. Charlie had been mucking out the seals and the floor was now slippery with slime.

Jedders faced my two friends as if in a crazy duel.

Then he spun around and wrapped his strong arm around my neck.

'You were right to cling on, girl,' he hissed into my ear, then raising his voice, 'Rosamund! Oh, Rosamund . . . come out now. Hide-and-seek is over. I've got Lavinia and she really wants to see her mama.'

He squeezed me tighter so my throat released a strangled gasp.

The zinc bucket shook in Temitayo's hand as her eyes met mine, horrified. Charlie panted, staring from Jedders to me and back again, clearly terrified that if he intervened again Mr Jedders would hurt me.

'Now sir, I am sure you don't want to—' said Temitayo.

Jedders ignored her, raising his voice. 'So you still want to play, Rosamund?' He spun the cane in his hand so the end pointed in my face. A tiny silver blade shot out.

It glinted. I couldn't take my eyes off it.

'I wonder if precious Miss Lavinia would be as much of an artist without her eyes,' called Mr Jedders. 'Come on, Rosamund, I'm just here to take what's owed to me. You can't keep running. You can't keep hiding.'

I didn't dare struggle, didn't dare move, the glinting edge was too close; it filled my vision, filled my world.

But it was Mr Jedders who moved, stumbling then releasing me.

'What in blazes—'

At first I couldn't make out what was happening. A dark pulsing mound of flesh, sliding, Mr Jedders flailing and falling, one leg spiralled with a huge tentacle, another tentacle around his throat—

Ghost!

Ghost's mantle followed his huge tentacles. The octopus was out of his tank, and surged through the door of the passageway into the gallery, seemingly intent on Jedders.

Then Jedders' cane, that blade, stabbing down, towards Ghost right between those silver eyes, but the screech of metal against metal as Temitayo swung the bucket again to meet it, this time sending the cane clanging to the floor. Charlie kicked it out of reach.

The octopus tentacle round Jedders' neck wound tightly, and both of his hands slipped and slid across the glossy, yielding flesh, trying to get a grip, trying to gouge, and unable to make any impression at all. The choking man kicked.

His face turned crimson then purple.

'No, Ghost!' I cried and then I was kneeling with Charlie and Temitayo, trying to help Jedders wrench a tentacle thicker than a man's arm from around his neck. My nails skated over Ghost's soft, cool flesh with no hope of releasing those powerful suckers.

If Ghost intended to kill Jedders, then Jedders was going to die.

I remembered how the keeper had hit the octopus with the rake, injuring him so badly he had then lost an arm.

If I found Jedders' cane with that tiny evil little blade, could I make Ghost let go?

Would I even try?

'Well, what have we here?' The voice came from behind but I couldn't take my eyes off the octopus, because as quickly as Ghost had grasped Jedders, his tentacle uncurled from the man's neck and slid back to join the rest of him. The massive jellied bulk of the octopus pulsed and surged, flashing blood-red and luminous blue spots, across the slimy floor. His front tentacles quested in front of him, dragging his bulk, then squeezed back through the door into the tunnel. As the octopus glided through the doorway he nearly filled it with his bulk.

Jedders collapsed back, spluttering and gasping, clawing at his neck, and as the octopus disappeared, I turned to see three police officers, domed helmets low over their eyes, buttons glinting in the light of the tank.

CHAPTER FIFTY-TWO

I skidded backwards across the slippery floor of the gallery, out of the way, as two of the policemen grasped the wheezing Mr Jedders under his armpits and hauled him to his feet.

'Enoch Jedders, you are under arrest,' said one of the officers, wrinkling his nose at the stench of seal muck that coated the man's previously dapper clothing. 'You are under arrest for running a criminally unsafe establishment. A girl of thirteen died yesterday from arsenic poisoning, and you are also suspected of involvement in a further death of a girl of eleven five weeks previous, same cause of death.'

Dead? It had to be Martha. That poor girl with her bleeding hands and green skin who Jedders had dismissed. And the younger was Agnes. I met Charlie's eyes, then Temitayo's, both wide with shock and confusion.

Martha *died*? Yesterday?

Some of the missing puzzle pieces slipped into place. Jedders must have known Martha's death would lead the police to him, so in desperation had arranged the pick-pocket to steal my sketchbook, and struck lucky, finding Mother's address. By why look for Mother instead of going on the run?

The two officers twisted Jedders' arms behind him and the third officer snapped on a pair of handcuffs.

'Rosamund Fyfe owes me,' said Jedders, his voice gravelly. 'This is on her, it's all her.'

'We will also need to—'

I couldn't hear the policeman out. Mother was still in the passage, sick, maybe in a faint. She must be, because otherwise she would have come when she heard Jedders threaten me.

I glanced at Temitayo then Charlie and gave the slightest shake of my head. They mustn't follow me. Charlie frowned but Temitayo dipped her chin and nudged him and I prayed she'd understood just to say nothing. I hitched up my skirts and ran past the men and into the tunnel. My breath seemed too loud and my footsteps echoed.

The footstool sat, empty. Mother wasn't there.

But Ghost was. Ghost was not only back in his tank, he was in exactly the same position he had been before he left, sat upon the sunken temple, tentacles curled backwards, suckers covered with oyster shells so his body was barely visible.

'Mother?' I hissed, peering into the dark.

Where was she?

The catch on Ghost's tank was undone. It was outside of the tank, so he couldn't have undone it himself. Why would Mother do that?

I used the pole hanging behind me, stepped on to the stool and twisted the loop so the bolt was across. One of Ghost's silver eyes peered from underneath a shell, the metallic glint reminding me of that tiny vicious blade on the end of Jedders' cane. Ghost had saved me. I spread my palm across the glass for just a second.

'Thank you,' I whispered.

Ghost shifted and I caught sight of something in the temple. It had been no more than a flash but I had seen clearly. Rows and rows of oval things hung from the roof of the structure like strange lanterns strung across a ceiling, or bunting for a birthday party. I peered closer. The weird shapes were about the size of my thumb.

I took another look at Ghost, not understanding

what I'd seen. Now wasn't the time to figure it out so I tucked my skirts in my waistband, glad of the cycling bloomers underneath, and ran.

I raced past the backs of the other tanks, in and out of the pools of light from the gas lamps, splashing through puddles. Voices echoed behind me until the passage curved into silence.

Finally the tanks ended, taking the light with them, but the passageway continued on. I guided myself along the brick wall into the shadows. This passage was narrow, my breath loud.

The old smugglers' tunnel. I'd just told Mother about it. She had known Jedders was coming after her and she . . . ran?

CHAPTER FIFTY-THREE

The sea pounded the beach in a steadier heartbeat than my own, which was throbbing in my ears. I'd never been in such utter darkness. I slid my hands along walls that were no longer brick but damp, crumbly chalk. Must be the smugglers' tunnel. Half running, half stumbling, I tripped over piles of rubble expecting to find Mother collapsed at every corner. Where was she?

A blue-grey light seeped into the tunnel and I sped up, emerging from the low mouth of the cave into a tussock of grass, with chalk boulders in front of it. It was still an hour or more off sunset, the sun ducking in and out of racing grey clouds.

The wind had picked up, it was high tide and the waves crashed so hard, the sea spray chilled my hot face. There was barely anyone out for an evening stroll on the promenade.

Where had Mother gone?

I scanned the beach, spotting a flash of pink pass between two of the bathing machine huts, out of sight from the promenade. I leapt down the stairs two at a time, lurching across the pebbles.

Mother was leaning against the wooden wall of the hut, peering one way up the beach, and then out to sea.

'Mama! You are safe.' I scanned her face, taken aback to find her flushed and bright-eyed. 'We are both safe now, Mama. Jedders has been arrested!'

'We are not safe, dear heart,' she murmured. 'I must hide.'

'But why? Jedders is . . .' She didn't wait for me to finish.

'They will still look for me. They didn't know I was in the tunnel but they know you were, and now you have disappeared.' She shook her head, impatient. 'If only you hadn't followed me, Lavinia.'

This wasn't fair, it wasn't.

'How could I not follow you, Mama? You've been so sick and you were fainting and in that tunnel—' I said.

I followed her round to the front of the bathing

machine. The bolt on the door was secured with a padlock. Mother whipped out her purse from her skirts. Inside was a selection of hat- and hairpins; she always had these with her. She took hold of the padlock, inserted a pin into the lock and with an expert jiggle, the lock fell to the ground. My mouth fell open as Mother – was this really my respectable mother? – pulled me into the dark of the bathing machine and closed the door.

'What is that *smell*?' whispered Mother in the dark wooden cave.

All the questions I wanted to ask Mother and she was only interested in a smell?

'Maybe seal muck? Charlie was cleaning out the seal pen, then Temitayo must have seen Jedders arrive and they both ... they saved me, they were wonderful, Mama.'

There was a long silence. Mother must be horrified that I had been in danger.

'Seal droppings? Yes. Quite fitting for Mr Jedders,' she said.

'Mama – how are you so well again?'

'I have always had a strong constitution. Complete rest for an entire month was more reviving than I could imagine.'

I felt out in the dark and found Mother's hand, cool in its silk glove. Relief cut through everything else I was feeling. Mother was recovered. But ...

'None of this makes sense to me, Mama. I know about Jedders and the workshops. And the first little girl died just before we left London. Was that why we left?'

My words seemed to sink into the sound of the waves from outside. Now for the question. The biggest question I had ever asked her.

'Mama, did you know what Jedders was doing?'

'Of course not, dear heart! Mr Jedders was angry when I refused to invest Fyfe's money in what he called "production". Sourcing materials was his job, not mine. I now realize that his workshop had to be closed – due to that poor, poor child – and that was why he was so insistent on my investment, the greedy scoundrel. It felt a very good time for the trip I'd been planning. I did not expect him to find us in Brighton.'

Production. A cold, sterile sort of word: no one would link it to the steamy, poisonous workshop, especially not someone so refined as Mother.

'I saw, Mama, it was . . . evil, and Jedders such a cruel master. The police would never believe that someone like you were involved in that place.'

'He will try to place blame on me, Lavinia,' she said. 'The law is not favourable to single women. And of course, I bought the Paris Green silks from him, with no idea where they came from. But why should the police believe that?'

It made more sense now. Mother had been duped by Jedders.

'Dear heart, I know this is incredibly unsettling for you, but there is actually something you can do for me.'

I nodded.

'You need to simply tell the police that you visited me in Brighton when I was ill in April,' she said.

I frowned into the dark. 'But that would be lying . . .'

'Simply stretching the truth. The new workshop was only set up once we left London, so if you can testify that I was ill in bed . . .'

'But can't the guest house owner, or the doctor or your nurse tell them that?'

I tried to piece together what she was saying. And then it came to me.

'You *knew* what he was doing. You *knew* he had a new workshop and the other girl died! But you didn't tell the police?'

'He threatened me. If I told anyone, he would put the blame for everything on me. The Paris Green silks, flowers, ribbons in our designs – my ladies even said I was leading a new trend for green.'

I nodded, recalling the designs I'd drawn, all green. So much green. My poor, beautiful, clever mother. It would look like she was involved, it really would.

'I'll do it. I'll tell them I visited you, Mama. I'll make them believe it.'

Mother moved closer to me, wrapped her hand round my shoulder. I threaded mine around her waist. *Rosamund Fyfe and Daughter.* Just me and Mother, always.

She whispered into my ear, 'There are things you don't understand yet, Lavinia, about the way the world works for men and for women. Younger women who do not have a husband are mistrusted. It was expected that I would remarry after your father died. If I'd had any family, it would have been forced upon me. Men believe it isn't natural for a woman to make their own way in life. They believe that they are the only ones who can succeed in business, have a head for money, or run the country. So if they see a woman prosper, without a man to guide her, that makes them very uncomfortable. They will find a way to blame me, and I can't let that happen. I will not end up in prison, or worse – the insane asylum, accused of mania.'

I took in what she had said. The horror of it.

'You aren't ill, are you, Mama?' I said, gripping her hand. 'Tell me the truth, please.'

Again that long silence, the boom of the waves like the Earth's own drum.

'I am truly sorry, Lavinia, for lying to you, but it was the only way. I needed to disappear until Jedders gave up looking for me. I needed an alibi if he persuaded the police I was involved in his scheme.'

'But why didn't you keep me with you?'

'Would that be fair? To keep you locked away as well?'

I thought of her room in the guest house. I shook my head.

'But you were so close to us . . . why did you stay in Brighton?'

She squeezed my hand very tight. 'That was a mistake, I realize now. But I simply couldn't bear to be too far from you.'

Tears sprang into my eyes. Mama had missed me, just as I had missed her.

'But you can't just run away from the police,' I whispered, suddenly remembering where we were, in a bathing machine, not so far from the police who had Jedders at the aquarium.

'I simply need time, dear heart. I will find a hospital, I will be taken ill again. The police will never know I have been here, and along with your story corroborating my illness, they will have no choice but to believe me.'

CHAPTER FIFTY-FOUR

I perched on the wooden bench in the dark of the bathing machine, silent, Mother's warm breath on my hair. Jedders – that monster of a man – was trying to frame my mother for his vile scheme, tricking her into buying so much of his green silk. I wouldn't allow her to take the blame. The words *insane asylum* rang in my head.

I thought of Aunt Bets having never been married. I thought of Temitayo's guardian, Mrs Heap, who had been married twice and didn't seem to have liked either of them. Then there was Mr Lee, who had supported my drawing, who never told Aunt Bets what to do or seemed to think he knew more than she did. But Mr Lee was just one man. How many times had I heard the ladies in the milliners say they couldn't choose a certain colour due to a comment their husband had made? Or that they had to wait for next month's allowance before ordering, because they had no money of their own.

'Everything I have ever done, I have done for you, for us, for Fyfe's, dear heart,' said Mother. 'My ambitions will one day be yours. And I am deeply sorry for having lied to you.'

But there was something she wasn't telling me, something missing in all this.

'Why did you come to the aquarium?' I said. 'You must have known Jedders would try there first.'

'Jedders found me at the hotel,' she said. 'Lord knows how, but he did.'

I knew how. The pickpocket, the note I had so stupidly left in the back of my sketchbook.

'I was foolish, I know. But how could I run again without seeing my girl first?'

I clutched her hands tight. My mind was one step slower than the story unfolding. Jedders *found* Mother at the guest house. Mother arrived at the aquarium with *his* cane. He had blood on his teeth, she had a bleeding cut too . . .

I drew in a sharp breath. 'Did he attack you, Mama?'

A noise outside the bathing huts; it sounded like it was coming from the other end of the row. Men's voices.

'That's the police,' hissed Mother.

The urge to just let the police sort this all out was still there, but Mother was right, what did I know about the way the world worked? If she didn't trust the police to get to the truth, then I shouldn't either.

The police were moving slowly, opening the huts one by one. I pictured the promenade outside; where could we hide?

No. Not both of us. To protect my mother I had to let her go. I whispered my plan to her as the voices came closer.

'Wait with Elizabeth and be ready for me to come for you,' said Mother into my ear.

She was going to find a hospital, pretend to be ill again. And with me vouching for her illness, she'd be safe from blame.

'I can distract them. Don't worry.'

'My good shrewd girl.' She took my cheeks in her hands and kissed me on the forehead.

The men's voices were so close.

This was my cue.

I slipped out of the hut, ran towards the breaking waves, then took a deep breath and plunged into the foaming sea. The waves broke up to my waist, tearing at my skirts, trying to drag my feet out from under me. I panicked, gasping at the cold. I would fall, I would drown. I remembered Aunt Bets, how she'd looked into my eyes and I'd felt the bottom, grounding me. I found the pebbles with my feet, dug in my heels. I stood firm against a wave that soaked me from head to toe, then ran back up the pebbles as it swept out.

I wanted to collapse on the dry stones but could not stop now. I needed to lead them away, away from Mother.

When I heard the police exclaiming, I fell to my knees, wailing.

'It's the Fyfe daughter. She's soaked through and in shock,' said one.

'We need to keep searching the huts.'

'Mrs Fyfe isn't here – that Jedders scoundrel wouldn't know a true word if it smacked him in his noggin.'

I trembled. Neither this nor the tears were much of a stretch for me after everything that had happened. Then I fell silent, collapsing on to the stones. When one of the policeman tapped my face, I flickered my eyelashes and moaned. Both of the policemen would be needed to carry me to safety. I felt a heavy greatcoat fall around me.

'She's in shock, best get her into the warm quick smart, before we have another injured girl on our hands.'

'Jedders says he's been attacked by an octopus! And there's me thinking I'd heard it all.'

'He is a fine storyteller. What with that and his tales of the lady stealing his takings and investing in diamonds of all things . . . a rogue and no mistake. They'll enjoy his tales in the clink.'

Mother was wrong; they did blame Jedders, not her. I stifled a smile of relief. This would all be over much more quickly than we'd thought.

As they struggled to get me up the steps to the promenade I opened my eyes just enough to see a figure dart out of the hut and leave the beach, melting into the shadows.

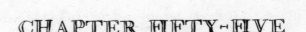

CHAPTER FIFTY-FIVE

'First may I confirm you are Lavinia Fyfe, daughter of Rosamund Fyfe, currently resident with your aunt, Elizabeth Ruggles, at Roberts Road, Brighton.'

I had stopped trembling and sat bundled in Aunt Bets' coat, hands wrapped around my second cup of sweet tea. The police had polished off almost a whole Battenberg and now the older one, who had extremely fluffy mutton-chop facial hair, spoke more calmly, note-book out, Aunt Bets by my side. I cleared my throat and answered in as strong a voice as I could manage.

'Is it correct that your mother has been residing in Brighton in some secrecy for the last month? With such success that even you, her daughter, thought she was in Paris when all along she was a short way from you?'

This is what Aunt Bets had told them. The truth.

I paused. I had to do this.

'No. I knew where she was, I knew she was ill, but she didn't want anyone to know so I kept it secret,' I said, trying not to falter, 'from everyone.'

I heard Aunt Bets draw a sharp breath next to me. I couldn't look at her; this was much more difficult than I had expected. But I had to lie to her, lie to everyone, for Mother. I was all Mother had.

'Rosamund is a very proud and determined business-woman, and she insists on keeping up appearances. It was very important to her that no one find out she was unwell,' said Aunt Bets.

'If you could just allow Miss Fyfe to answer without interruption, ma'am,' said the policeman.

'I was giving some context, as her cousin,' said Aunt Bets, her voice deceptively calm. I willed her not to argue with the policeman and make this take any longer.

'So you did not tell Miss Ruggles, your aunt, your guardian, that her cousin was ill and residing here in Brighton?'

'Mother asked me not to.'

Aunt Bets laid a hand on my arm. 'Rosamund and I have never been . . . close,' she said. 'It's no great surprise she wouldn't confide in me, only Vinnie.'

'Miss Fyfe. Is it true that you work with your mother at Fyfe's millinery in London, drawing hat designs?'

I nodded.

'And the man by the name of Mr Jedders also worked for your mother in London?'

I felt Aunt Bets' eyes on my face. 'Yes,' I said.

'What exactly did this Mr Jedders do as part of his employment?' he said.

I paused, frowning. 'Lots of things, deliveries, running errands for Mother . . .' I trailed off. 'He brought in the materials we needed. Worked with suppliers.'

Suppliers. Just as cold a word as *production*.

'Vinnie is twelve years old, officer. She can't be expected to know the ins and outs of Rosamund's business—'

'Thank you, Miss Ruggles,' said the police officer.

'So part of Mr Jedders' role was sourcing materials?'

I nodded again.

'Materials such as the Paris Green silks, ribbons and dyes that you saved for your most exclusive customers?'

Aunt Bets tutted but didn't interrupt.

'Yes,' I said.

'Did you ever see your mother bring these materials into the shop herself?' he said.

'No, never – it was Jedders' job to deal with all of

that. Mother designed the hats with me and then the materials were selected from our stock and sent out to seamstresses. Then the customers came back for fittings.'

The policeman sat back, those mutton-chop sideburns twitching.

'So tell me how you and Mr Charles Bower came to be in Litcham Street, a notorious slum row in Camden, on the first of May.'

I felt Aunt Bets' eyes burn into the side of my face, and swallowed.

At that moment Charlie rushed up to the table, notebook already in hand.

CHAPTER FIFTY-SIX

'Oh good, we need to speak to you as well, Mr Bower.'

I tried not to look at Charlie. I couldn't get him or his brothers at the post office into trouble, but one lie was leading to another. Where would it end?

Both the policeman and Aunt Bets listened in silence as I told them Charlie and I had seen Jedders by chance when we'd been in London and followed him. I wasn't good at this, I was going to ruin it all. And would Charlie be able to lie to the police? He was always blurting out his words without a thought.

'Yes – it was so very strange,' continued Charlie. 'We

were just coming out of the Royal Aquarium – have you officers been at all? I wouldn't bother, it is nowhere near as good as our own here in Brighton, we have a giant octopus you know – when Vinnie spotted this Mr Jedders outside at a newspaper stand. We hid behind a column because, you know, he'd been acting peculiarly, cornering Vinnie in the grocers, really quite unpleasant. But we decided to follow him and see what he was up to . . .'

The policeman blinked at Charlie and raised a hand to stop his stream of words.

Aunt Bets and the policeman narrowed their eyes at the same time as I nodded in agreement with Charlie.

I looked at my hands in my lap as I spilt out what happened in the workshop, Jedders' cruelty to the girls. No lies there at least.

'Oh, Vinnie, you should have told me. I would have helped you,' said Aunt Bets.

I couldn't look her in the eye, even though this part was no lie. 'The girls made us promise not to tell. It was their livelihood.'

'And yet somehow the story was leaked to the press rather than reported to the police.'

'We didn't have anything to do with that,' I said.

'No – we certainly didn't,' said Charlie.

'Martha Jones was a girl of only thirteen. Poisoned by

arsenic in that workshop. And this was the second of Mr Jedders' deadly production efforts, after the first workshop caused the death of young Agnes Evans in Southwark.' The policeman shook his head.

'So he closed this green dye workshop when the first girl died, but immediately set up another with the same risks?' said Aunt Bets.

'Men like Enoch Jedders ain't concerned about risks, madam, only profits. Turns out this particular shade of green is the talk of high society, silks in the brightest shade worth more than their weight in gold. I ask you!'

'Where is this Mr Jedders now?' asked Aunt Bets, her face pale as dough.

'In gaol, ma'am. Our colleagues are currently searching your cousin's former premises in London, and we also have a team outside who will search your tea shop premises. Plus your own residence.'

Aunt Bets and I looked at each other, now so close together we were almost sharing a chair, her warm, roughened hand clasped tight around mine.

'What are you looking for?' said Charlie.

The policeman sighed and noisily drained his cup of tea. 'Mr Jedders claims Mrs Fyfe has stolen his profits from the business and invested them in diamonds. A tall tale if ever I heard one, and one designed to delay the trial, I'm sure, but we must investigate all the same.'

'He's lying – Jedders is lying, trying to pass the blame to my mother,' I said.

'Well, we need Mrs Fyfe's statement urgently, so if she contacts you in any way, you let us know.'

'If Rosamund turns up here you can be sure we will,' said Aunt Bets. 'Now, if you are finished . . . ?'

The policeman slammed his notebook closed. 'For now. And don't you worry, Miss Fyfe, the truth always comes out in the end.'

CHAPTER FIFTY-SEVEN

The next morning Aunt didn't wake me. I wondered if she had heard me tossing and turning in the night, worrying about Mother. I tried to imagine the turn of events I wanted to happen, as if I could will them into reality.

The police would find all the evidence they needed against Jedders and he would remain in gaol. Mother would emerge from her illness; with no sign of the diamonds the police were looking for, they'd have no evidence against her. Maybe Mother and I could settle in Brighton after all and I could still work at the tea shop with Aunt Bets sometimes, and see Temitayo, Charlie and Mr Lee. And Ghost. Ghost would get better and I'd be drawing him again.

But as soon as I started to doze with these calming thoughts it was as if a green fog descended. Paris Green. Thinking about the girls, eleven-year-old Agnes, thirteen-year-old Martha, the others now without jobs, all of them sick. When I did sleep, I was immersed in nightmares of silver blades, of silver eyes, of the noise Jedders made as the octopus strangled him, of something around my own throat, and I woke, sweating.

The note Aunt Bets had left on the kitchen table read: *Rest, see you later for tea.*

I heated up the porridge on the range, feeling heavy-headed with the sense I had missed something important. I remembered the first day I had woken at Aunt's cottage, how it had been so early I had felt ill. Now it felt strange to be awake so late.

The house was too quiet without Aunt Bets in it, but the rich baking smell was as comforting as always: the yeast of the bread, the hot buttery cakes. I dressed quickly, took a moment to plait my hair and grabbed my cape. It was stained with chalk dust from the smugglers' tunnel, but I fetched a clothes brush and gave it what Aunt would call a 'cat's lick and polish'. Good enough for me.

I arrived at the aquarium, desperate to spend some time

with Ghost. I needed to talk to Mr Lee too, to tell him how Ghost had appeared from the tank—

I stopped halfway down the steps. How could I have forgotten? The weird things I had seen inside the temple just before I had run to catch up with Mother. I needed to tell Mr Lee about them first. I should have woken up early as usual.

Ghost was in his normal place, perched on top of the temple, siphoning water inside. Mr Lee sat at my drawing desk, writing his notes.

'How is Ghost today?' I said.

He spun round. 'Are you well, Vinnie? Oh, my dear girl, it must be quite upsetting to be here again so soon after . . .' He cleared his throat. 'Charlie told me everything. You were incredibly courageous.'

'Charlie and Temitayo were the real brave ones – he used a mop and Temitayo threw a bucket of seal slop over him.'

'Quite amazing. And quite the mess, but none of us were complaining,' he said, with a small worried smile, 'and Ghost seems none the worse for wear after yesterday's ordeal. I am writing a paper on it – how he came out of the tank, it beggars belief – and of course it was only you, Charlie, Temitayo and this villain who saw.'

I didn't take my eyes from Ghost. Had I imagined I had seen those rows of oval shapes inside the den he'd created?

A rush of footsteps across the floor and then arms spinning me round, enveloping me in a tight bony hug.

'Vinnie!' Temitayo almost squeezed the air from my lungs. 'Are you all right? Quite all right?'

I nodded as I disentangled myself.

'Yes, I am, but only thanks to you and Charlie. You were . . .'

'Heroic?' She swung her arm as if she were still holding the bucket. 'Valiant?'

'Yes!' I said, gripping her hand, 'both of those.'

'You'll tell me everything, won't you?' she said more quietly, squeezing my hand. I squeezed it back, nodding as my stomach clenched. I couldn't tell anyone about Mama, even Temitayo after what she had done for me.

'I need to tell Mr Lee something first. I saw something yesterday,' I said, 'as Ghost was settling back into the tank.'

I brought my sketchbook out of my pocket. It was new and unfamiliar. A spare sketchbook to replace the other that had been stolen. I outlined the temple, and then drew those rows of hanging forms.

Mr Lee watched over my shoulder. 'Are you absolutely sure this is what you saw, Vinnie?' he said, his face pale in the flickering aquarium light.

'I think so – it was only for a moment before I escaped down the tunnel, and everything was—'

'Bedlam. Yes, quite. And there is no one's eyes I would

trust more than yours,' said Mr Lee, taking the sketch-book from my hands, peering at it and then back at Ghost.

'Do you know what it is?'

'I do. These are octopus eggs, Vinnie,' said Mr Lee. 'Our Ghost is not a "he" after all. Our Ghost is a "she" – and she's going to be a mother.'

THE DEVIL-FISH CAPTURES A DEVIL

Since the arrival of the giant octopus at Brighton Grand Aquarium, it's been escapade after escapade, from cannibalism to tricks to rival Houdini, not to mention the mystifying friendship between this giant sea beast and a young girl with an uncommon talent for drawing.

But yesterday the octopus apprehended unscrupulous scoundrel businessman Enoch Jedders, who is responsible for the death of two girls in his foul fabric sweatshops in the heart of London's slums. Agnes (11) died over a month ago of arsenic poison, but Mr Jedders was without remorse and immediately set up another workshop, seeming to increase production of the valuable Paris Green fabric with no care for the obvious consequences to his young workers exposed to its poison. In a matter of weeks Martha (13) was the second victim to succumb to arsenic poisoning.

When Mr Jedders arrived at Brighton Aquarium he made an inexplicable attack on the octopus' young friend, but got more than he bargained for when the octopus escaped its tank to apprehend the villain. A beast turned hero.

CHAPTER FIFTY-EIGHT

It was late at night, after the last visitors had just left. Ghost was calm, still, peaceful; she never stopped wafting the water from her siphon into the window of the temple, between her protective tentacles. I tried to capture her calm, to lose myself in her lines, but my pencil wouldn't glide across the page shaping her curves. Instead it juddered, too spiky, too dark.

Mr Lee had already read every book there was about how long it took for octopus eggs to hatch and opinions conflicted with each other, none of them relating to an octopus the size of Ghost. We presumed she had laid her eggs when she took residence on the temple, surrounding her body with the fortress of shells. We had watched and waited and grew more dismayed when Ghost continued to ignore her food. I felt sure that she was just too distracted protecting her eggs and would eat again when they were hatched.

Ghost was a good mother, and she made me think of my mother. She must be safe in a hospital or convalescence home now? Should I be looking for her? I wanted this all to be over, so I could explain to Aunt Bets, Charlie and Temitayo. I felt awkward around Aunt Bets especially – she hadn't questioned whether I had been lying to the police about visiting Mother, or lying to her, and I was so grateful for that. But there was a new thoughtfulness in the way she looked at me and I hated it.

I packed my sketchbook and pencils into my satchel, then when I looked up I gasped. Ghost had changed. She flashed from brick red to white, to deepest purple, and her horns rose above her eyes on her mantle. Then she drifted free of the temple and I finally saw for certain what I knew I hadn't imagined. Rows upon rows of milky capsules.

Ghost swept in a circle, siphoning water urgently across the eggs, giving the impression she was panting. I wanted to fetch Mr Lee in his reading room, but I also didn't want to disturb Ghost, or miss a thing. I watched the rows of pale pods sway, my heart in my throat.

One capsule split.

A tiny spirit of a creature darted out, a baby octopus of lilac glass, tiny dots for eyes, head around the size of my thumbnail. It puffed away from its temple nest and the siphoning gusts of water from its huge mother, up towards the surface of the water. A miniature transparent replica of Ghost. I couldn't stop smiling as I followed its zigzagging journey upwards. It was perfect.

'Well done, Ghost, your babies are here, they are hatching,' I whispered, forehead against the glass as the tiny octopuses now broke free of their eggs in batches, all making their darting journey upwards to float in the top few inches of the tank water.

A gasp behind me. Charlie. 'Talk about good timing,' he said, quietly for once. 'I'll fetch Uncle Henry.'

I was transfixed. Then, aware of Mr Lee's hand giving my arm a squeeze, I turned to flash him a grin and see his smile as wide as mine as the surface of Ghost's tank filled with her tiny babies. The mass of new living things drifted together in the waving weed at the side of the tank, and remained near the surface safe in the swaying fronds.

Then Mr Lee was beside me. We were quickly joined by the other attendants who were on duty and Mr Lee spoke to them in low tones as the last of the babies hatched and drifted up to join the others, only just born but already able to tell where they needed to be.

Then Ghost began to move. She unfurled her arms fully and attached herself to the glass opposite me with two arms, the others drifting behind her in the water. Her colour was still changing but now it was less vibrant: a watery orange chased by pinkish purple. She flashed white for a split second, and glowing blue dots briefly bloomed across her skin before fading back to the washed-out orange.

'You must be very tired.' I mouthed the words without a sound, spreading my hand like a starfish against the glass.

Ghost settled into the corner next to me, wriggling down into the pebbles, arms curled in, eyes closed.

'I need to write to the Royal Society, to Bickerstaff – immediately,' said Mr Lee, eyes flicking from Ghost to her new babies and back again.

'You go, Uncle Henry – we'll wait with her, won't we, Vin,' said Charlie, giving him a gentle shove.

Mr Lee finally tore himself away, muttering. When his reading room door closed Charlie beckoned me close.

'Vinnie. What's that in the temple? Look!'

I followed where Charlie was pointing. Below the ragged bunting of empty egg cases there was something that didn't belong there. Something half buried in the small pebbles. Something very round, gleaming blueish white . . . a thread of silver.

I opened my mouth but had no words.

Mother's pearl. The huge blue quail egg pearl, the heirloom she'd taken to wearing around her neck when we left London.

'How in blazes did *that* get in there?' said Charlie.

The last time I had seen it, Mother had been sitting outside the octopus tank, looking at it.

I wished I didn't know the answer to Charlie's question.

The baby octopuses drifted safely in the weed. Ghost didn't move. Her blue dot pattern. It had appeared after the fight with Jedders, after Mother . . .

The iridescent blue dots were the pearl.

'Stay here and distract Uncle if he comes back. I'm going to hook it out,' said Charlie.

I wanted to argue, I didn't want this to be real, didn't want to understand what this meant . . . but all I said was, 'Be careful. Don't disturb Ghost or her babies.'

Charlie was quick, catching the pearl by its chain so it swung as it left the water. Seconds later I looked at Charlie and he looked at me, then we both gaped at the huge pearl that now sat in my palm as it had once sat in Mother's. Charlie didn't know that. No one but me knew that. And Ghost.

Mother said she had refused any involvement in the workshops. It was all Jedders.

Jedders said she stole his profit, invested it.

Charlie peered at me, no doubt confused by my expression. 'Well, it's certainly a beauty, whoever it belongs to . . .'

I chased the pearl around my palm with my finger. There was no doubt it was Mother's. The chain was joined to it by a filigree top, like a decorative cap upon an egg. It seemed loose. I held the pearl between finger and thumb and tested the top. It unscrewed.

Charlie's eyes widened as I spun the pearl until the fixing came free, leaving a silver-rimmed hole in the top of the pearl.

'It's been hollowed out! Must be one of those clever devices . . . don't ladies keep perfume inside? Or pills, or maybe a lock of hair like in a locket?'

I peered into the top of the hollow pearl. A glint so bright it was as if sunbeams had been captured and sealed inside.

No.

This is what Jedders had told the police.

No.

This didn't make sense with what Mother had explained to me. How could she have this?

No.

I tipped the contents of the hollow pearl egg out into my hand. A small pile of glimmering diamonds tumbled into my palm.

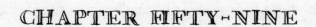

CHAPTER FIFTY-NINE

'Life has definitely got a lot more interesting since you arrived here, Vinnie,' said Charlie, still not looking up from the gleaming diamonds in my palm.

The facts raced around my mind like the horses on a merry-go-round, leaping towards each other but never meeting, never joining because the truth would cause a catastrophic crash. There was only one possible answer. The milliners didn't make enough money to buy diamonds surely – we invested all we earned in better fabrics, Mother said we needed to plough our profits into the business. Quality and perfection was our aim.

Maybe Mother hadn't known there were diamonds

inside her heirloom pearl. I almost laughed at myself, how much I still longed to be fooled. These diamonds must be worth a fortune. I looked around the gallery, still empty, but anyone could walk in or Mr Lee could come back out.

'Here,' I said to Charlie, 'put your hand here to catch any if they fall.'

He held out his hand and I held the pearl – was it even a pearl? – in one hand and carefully trickled the diamonds from my other fist, one by one, back into the hole. I couldn't be fooled any longer. As each diamond tinkled on top of the others realizations glittered sharp in my mind.

Mother had been involved in the poisonous work-shops with Jedders.

Mother stole all their joint takings after Agnes died, and the workshop was closed.

Mother invested the takings in diamonds, hiding them in the pearl.

Mother ran to Brighton with me to escape the man she had stolen from.

When Jedders finally found her at the guest house they must have fought – Mother had his cane, they both had blood on their faces – and he followed her to the aquarium.

While he grappled with me, threatened me, instead of coming to help she hid the pearl in Ghost's den and ran.

Mama. How could you do it?

Then she had sat in the bathing machine hut and told me a string of lies as cold as the glittering stones that had just run through my fingers.

'Why would Jedders bring the jewels here?' said Charlie, voice rising at the end, doubtful. 'Wait – are these your . . . mother's?'

I could tell him everything. I should. I owed Mother no loyalty if she knew about those girls. Did I? But what if she didn't know everything? She had simply stolen from Jedders.

Instead I shook my head.

I was making excuses, trying to make it fit together in the least awful way possible. I knew I had been fooled by her. But she was still my *mother*.

Finally I found my voice. 'I don't know how it got there. I was terrified after the fight, I ran and ran and just kept running until I met the beach and I don't remember much after that.' I looked down. I hated this, hated lying to Charlie almost as much as to Aunt Bets and Temitayo.

'But Mr Jedders must have known about the tunnel somehow, as there is no other way he could have put them there . . .'

I shrugged. Nobody knew Mother had ever been here except me and Mr Jedders, and that was how I needed it to stay.

The door slammed and we spun around, guilty. The last couple of diamonds were stuck to my sticky palm.

If that were the police now . . .

A tinkle against the tiles.

Temitayo. She stopped short and followed our gazes, so the three of us stared at the floor, at the light glancing off the diamond that had fallen. It sent up shards of light, at the final diamond still in my palm, at the hollow pearl in my other hand.

It was Temitayo who finally knelt to pick up the diamond.

First she held it between finger and thumb up to the light, eyebrows continuously rising beneath her boater, then she dropped it carefully back into the pearl, scanning my face.

'They are real, aren't they?' she said.

Both Charlie and I nodded. 'I think so.'

I screwed the little filigree silver lid back on to the pearl, enclosing the diamonds safe inside, then hung the pearl around my neck, tucking it into my blouse out of sight, just like Mother. I thought of her beautiful laughing face, fitting a hat on an elegant lady, the design finished with a cascade of green silk flowers. Then the face beneath the hat was that of Martha, the girl in the workshop with those sores on her lips, her face deathly pale. Of Martha, of the girl with the red hair, of

Ruth . . . all colour drained from them except sickly green.

My hand closed over the pearl, the smooth surface shifting in my fist like bone beneath skin.

Charlie frowned. 'We need to take them to the police, Vinnie. They are Jedders' takings from those awful places . . . now your mother's name will be cleared.'

I crouched to lean my forehead against the tank. The octopus unfurled a tentacle, rippling, but pale. Mother had interfered with Ghost's nest as the mother octopus had nursed her eggs. She must have used the pole with the hook on the end, when I had run to fetch her smelling salts, stupidly believing her ill. She had opened the tank, deposited the pearl in the temple. She would have pushed Ghost aside. She could have hurt the eggs. At least she left the tank open so Ghost could escape and help me, not that she could have known that. And Ghost had tried to show me, mimicking the foreign object in her nest with a new pattern of blue dots. Blue pearls.

Mother had left me to Jedders.

'I'm sorry she disturbed your nest,' I whispered to the octopus. She was such a good mother, protecting her eggs even when it meant never leaving her den, not even eating.

I looked up and caught a glance pass between Charlie and Temitayo, worried about me. I gripped the pearl through my blouse. I knew my friends would help me with what I needed to do, no matter what they thought.

My decision was made.

CHAPTER SIXTY

I sat by the tank two days later, drawing, trying to shake off the fear, the misery, the excitement and, most of all, the betrayal of the last few days.

Where was Mother now? In my darkest moments I wondered if I would ever see her again.

But was her life one I wanted?

The baby octopuses remained near the surface amongst the seaweed and Ghost was pale and unmoving, cushioned into the corner.

Mr Lee watched over my shoulder for a moment as I sketched.

'I don't understand. Now the babies are hatched, why

isn't Ghost eating? She doesn't need to tend them any more,' I said. 'Look.' I pressed my cape right opposite where she was resting. No change in her colour, not even a flicker. Her siphon seemed to pump more slowly, her eyes silver slits.

'Listen, Vinnie, I should have told you this before,' he said. I didn't like his tone.

I stared from Ghost, to the baby octopuses, back to Mr Lee.

'I hoped . . . she's different from other octopuses, not only her immense size; she's shown intelligence and sensitivity that has never been seen before. And the communication between you and her, her colours . . .'

I waited for him to continue despite the ball of dread forming in the pit of my stomach. He sighed and ran his hand through his hair.

'But octopus life cycles are well-documented, and although the time spans vary they all share a vital feature.'

I waited again. Mr Lee's Adam's apple moved up and down as he swallowed.

'Octopus females starve themselves as they tend their eggs, sometimes not eating for months. When the eggs hatch . . . I'm sorry, Vinnie . . . that's the end of an octopus' life. They die.'

'No,' I said, staring into the tank. The octopus' siphon

was billowing in and out so slowly I could barely see it. 'Not Ghost.'

He nodded slowly. Sadly. My heart thumped double-time. I wasn't going to lose Ghost.

'But there must be something we can do, help her eat, revive her?'

Mr Lee laid a kind hand on my shoulder. 'It was inevitable, I'm afraid, Vinnie.'

'She's dying . . . now?' I asked.

'Soon, I think,' said Mr Lee. 'Maybe even today. I'm just going to my office for a little while. You know where I am if you need me.'

He was giving me some time alone with Ghost.

I closed the door marked *Private* quietly behind me. Last time I'd been here, I raced along the tunnel after Mother, never imagining she had just dropped the hollow pearl full of diamonds into the mother octopus' nest to hide them.

That wasn't going to be the last time anyone was close to Ghost.

I found a pair of galoshes hung on a hook and stepped into them. I bunched my skirts inside, adjusted the over-shoulder straps best I could; they were much too big – I would never be able to climb the ladder in them, I would be too clumsy, I could hurt the babies. I stripped the galoshes off, followed by my boots, and rolled down my stockings. I stepped out of my skirts leaving just my cycling bloomers beneath. Finally I left my cape. I padded up the ladder in my bare feet, checking halfway; with my feet level with the bottom of the tank, the water would come up to my chest.

Before I could change my mind, I swung over one leg, then the other, gasping from the cold and reaching out with my toes, this time reaching the floor before I could panic. The water lapped at the top of my chest. Ghost's babies were still so delicate, like crystal flower buds dotted in the seaweed. I didn't want to disturb them. I waded slowly over to Ghost's end of the tank, the water splashing my chin, wetting my plait. I didn't care. Ghost was so much bigger when I was in the tank with her, a mound of jelly twice my weight hiding three hearts, brains in her legs and so much muscle, power and personality. I had flashbacks of when I'd first seen her, sliding out of the gaps in the barrel; she must have already been carrying her eggs inside her. I'd been terrified of her.

I reached down through the water and touched her skin. The first time I'd felt its cool, silky softness she had run her tentacles across my knuckles as Charlie tried to wake her. The second time Charlie and I had grappled with her, so strong, so muscular as she strangled Jedders.

The third time was now, and I stroked my hand across the mantle between her eyes, watching from above through the twelve inches of water, feeling her satin skin, completely alien, from a different world. Was she supposed to be this cold? Had she already gone?

Then a flash beneath my palm, a spreading bruise of red, an island in a sea of pale.

Her metallic eyes opened, my palm between them, and they were still bright, still silvery, but then quickly closed and sunken, gone. A tentacle drifted up from the mass folded under her. It was the smallest one, now almost as long as the others. The one that had grown back. I felt a sudden surge of hope.

'Come on, Ghost, you can mend your own arm, you can escape and trick us all, you can hide from the world and create colours and textures the greatest artist in the world wouldn't dream of. Your whole body is a canvas.'

I took her tentacle in both hands and felt her suckers attach to me, a soft grip despite its size. Colour flickered over the arm, as long and strong as a giant tropical anaconda, yet so very gentle.

'You caught a killer, Ghost. You protected your babies. You saved my life –' my voice caught – 'you're my friend. Please don't die.'

Her colour bloomed into lilac, stripes, checks. The tears ran down my face and dripped into the water with her. Salt to salt. Then with a last pressure from her suckers she released me and her arm drifted, pattern fading, until her last colours had melted away.

CHAPTER SIXTY-ONE

The sobs came in heaving gulps. I waded back to where I had climbed in, blinded by tears, and when I blinked them away I saw I had stumbled too close to the weed, disturbing the octopus babies. Some were dotted around me, translucent lilac. I was relieved to see Mr Lee's concerned face through the glass. He climbed the ladder and leant through the opening.

'It's all right, Vinnie,' he said. 'Just waft the little ones out of the way so none stick to you.'

I did as he said, scooping the tiny octopuses up into pools of water made by my cupped hands and delivering them back to the safety of the weed. I turned slowly. One last one, right by the surface on the far side of the tank, its crystal body catching the light.

I waded over, scooped it up and carried it in the pond of water between my palms. Before I released it I peered close, fascinated by its tiny siphon, black eyes too big for its head, head too big for its legs, but breathing, its eight perfect legs with traces of miniature suckers already forming. I was somewhere else entirely, already framing this scene on paper, an imaginary pencil tracing my hands holding Ghost's beautiful son or daughter. As I reached the weed and opened my hands, the octopus baby clung to my finger. Suckers so tiny I couldn't even feel them, but there it stuck. I waited, hand open, until it released me and propelled slowly to join the others. It already knew where it was going and I couldn't help but smile, before the tears came again.

I reached up to Mr Lee and he helped me climb up and out of the tank, wrapping me in his coat. As we pushed through the door Aunt Bets was right there.

'Oh, there you are, Vin, Mr Lee said he couldn't find you . . . whatever have you . . .'

I threw myself into her chest, into her tight hug, and she held my head until the violent shakes of my shoulders relaxed. I took out my handkerchief and blew my nose.

'Ghost is gone and I'm sorry, I just climbed in the tank . . . look, now I've made you all wet,' I said.

'She needed you to get doing and see her off,' she said. 'I'm proud of you, Vin.'

I thought of my own mother and confusion engulfed me. Ghost died protecting her children. She was an octopus, she didn't even have bones, she had *three* hearts. She was related to a *snail*.

I didn't want to look at Ghost now; I would remember her as colour.

I hadn't noticed Mr Lee had gone but he arrived back with a sturdy blanket and wrapped it around me. Then one of the keepers ran over to us.

'I tried to stall him, to give you a bit of warning, Mr Lee, sir, but you know the captain,' he said.

Captain Bickerstaff entered on cue, stomping across the gallery floor, chest thrust out like a peacock. His eyes flickered over Aunt Bets and me, then found Mr Lee.

'For once I bring good news, Lee – my impressive catch has quite changed the fortunes of this aquarium. The articles in the press have been very useful in spreading—' He paused suddenly, noticing how wet I was and narrowing his eyes as he peered behind me at the tank. At Ghost. 'Lee, I do hope our eight-legged gold mine is in fine fettle.'

Mr Lee shook his head. 'I'm sorry, Captain. The octopus must have been preparing to lay eggs when she was caught. She has done so and they have now hatched.'

Captain Bickerstaff rubbed his hands together. 'Then why the long face, Lee? Get it together, man.' He clapped Mr Lee's shoulder. 'This is excellent news! Almost as if I'd planned it.'

'Ghost has died,' said Mr Lee, and I thought I heard a catch in his voice. Aunt Bets had one hand around me and rested the other on his arm.

'Ah, yes.' Captain Bickerstaff's moustache twitched, revealing a curl of purplish lip. 'I've heard of this, might even have been in your dratted pamphlet. The mother dies after hatching, blasted inconvenient, I say.' He sniffed. 'But let's get a look at these spawn. Only thing Joe Public loves more than a giant beast is its darned children.'

I didn't want to move away from the tank, but couldn't see I had any choice.

Ghost now floated near the surface at the other side of the tank.

'I'm presuming she has recently expired or you would have removed her?'

I blinked back more tears as Mr Lee pointed to the baby octopuses.

Captain Bickerstaff clapped his hands. 'So many! We will keep a small number of the spawn here to grow, and the rest will be sold to private collectors. With the recent press we can expect an excellent price for them.'

I stared at Mr Lee, horrified. Ghost's babies sold off to

strangers? There was no way Mr Lee would allow that.

'A fine plan, Captain. I recommend we nurture them here in the environment they are acclimatized to until they are strong enough to be transported.'

'Exactly, Lee. But only a matter of weeks, for we need to strike while the press is fresh in the public's mind. I might even try to arrange an auction, sell tickets . . .' He drifted into thought, twisting his moustache.

I was shivering. Aunt Bets excused us and left the men talking as we headed back up to the terrace. Once again I was in need of sweet tea. Finally Mr Lee joined us, hair on end and lines of worry etched beneath his eyes.

'Will Ghost's babies be safe? Will they be looked after by people like you?' I said, as he sat down.

Mr Lee gave a sad smile and paused as if weighing up what to tell me.

'*Will* they be safe?' I said, more demanding.

'I'm afraid there just aren't many people like me, Vinnie. It is very difficult to get the water quality right in a private aquarium, and octopuses are sensitive. And who is going to have a tank big enough when they grow to full size? We are quite unique here in that regard.'

Mr Lee and I stared at each other.

'You're saying if we do what Captain Bickerstaff said then they will die?' I said.

Mr Lee stared down at his folded hands, then

straightened his shoulders and blew out a long breath. There was a ghost of a smile on his lips as he checked no one could overhear, then leant in close.

'If we do what he said, then . . . yes.'

If.

CHAPTER SIXTY-TWO

The next day was sunny and I helped Aunt Bets out with the morning rush. Temitayo was at her usual table with Mrs Heap, writing in her diary, and I stopped to sit with them when everyone was served and there was nothing to clear. Charlie arrived at the tea shop looking flustered. He wore a formal-looking suit, too heavy for the bright May morning, had a suitcase at his feet and carried a stuffed carpetbag.

I gave him a questioning look. 'We aren't leaving for another week,' I said.

His eyes were fixed somewhere over my left shoulder. 'I'm not coming with you. I've just told Uncle Henry,

I'm leaving today, going to bunk with my brothers. For a bit.'

But it was all arranged. We were leaving together, the four of us. Aunt Bets, Mr Lee, me and Charlie.

'Why?' I said.

'I had my suspicions,' said Charlie, 'but whoever would have believed it of him?'

I shook my head, utterly confused.

'The octopus articles, Vinnie. The *only* person who could have known all the things we knew was Uncle Henry. I know, I know, I can't believe it either, but he must be the one who wrote those articles.'

As if summoned by his name, Mr Lee rushed across the terrace, face reddened, and hatless. 'Please tell him how ridiculous this is, Vinnie.'

'I had thought you would at least admit it, for it is quite obvious to me. You are already a writer and let's face it, you write much better than I do.'

Now Mr Lee looked angry. 'This is nonsense!'

Charlie turned to me stiffly, a tremble to his lip. 'It has been a pleasure making your acquaintance, Vinnie and Mrs Ruggles.' He gave a slight bow and started across the terrace.

'Charlie! What are you going to do, you can't board with your brothers – you won't be looked after—'

'At least I won't be living with a man who didn't have

the courage to tell me to my face that I would never be a—'

'Oh, for pity's sake, Charlie. Stop this!' Temitayo's voice was so loud all the tables on the terrace stopped talking.

Mrs Heap's mouth dropped open.

We all stared at Temitayo.

'It was me,' she said more quietly. 'The writer. It was me.'

'You?' said Charlie, and plopped down on the nearest chair. Mr Lee joined him, rubbing his whiskers.

'At first I didn't know how much it meant to you; I thought it was fair competition, I heard you even say so yourself. By the time I realized you considered those stories your scoops, I . . . I suppose the excitement of being published when I so wanted to be a writer . . . I admit I got carried away. I vowed not to write again about the aquarium when I knew what it meant to you, but the story about the girls was so important, too important, and although you swore not to tell it . . . I didn't swear that. It felt right that people should know, isn't that the point of journalism, to shed light on shadows? But I'm sorry.'

Charlie's mouth hung open.

'I truly am sorry, Charlie,' said Temitayo. 'I wasn't considering your feelings and understand if you can't forgive me. I was so desperate to see if my writing had worth, even if nobody knew it was an African orphan – a charity case – who was the author.'

It all slipped into place. Temitayo had always been there, throughout everything, quietly writing in her diary. Even I hadn't suspected she could have written those articles. We had all underestimated her.

Charlie stared down at his hands and I worried that he would be so embarrassed that he would leave anyway. Then he looked up. 'Blast it all, you have real talent, Temitayo,' he said, and then held out his hand.

'Are you sure you want to shake my hand? I do feel I've wronged you,' she said, and I saw a tremble on her bottom lip and wanted to reach out to my friend.

'Of course I ruddy do. Maybe I can catch some of your skill, like catching measles,' said Charlie.

Temitayo laughed as she gave his hand a firm shake and I found myself grinning from ear-to-ear. She rested her chin on her hands. 'I don't know how good you are at writing, Charlie, but if you enjoy it you will get better. What I do know is you are exceptionally good at finding things out. You are sneaky and smart, a good combination.'

I looked over at her and she glanced at me out of the corner of her eye.

'You could join the police,' I said.

'I might be a private investigator. They do need more people like me,' said Charlie, rubbing his chin.

'Although you do have a slight tendency to jump to conclusions. You may need to work on that,' said Mr Lee, cheeks still pink from the false accusation.

Charlie stood abruptly and gave a stiff little bow. 'I'm deeply sorry for my mistake, Uncle. I don't know how I could have thought . . . I completely understand if you . . .'

Mr Lee pulled the boy back down to his chair, wrapped an arm around his shoulder and ruffled his hair. 'I think we could all do with a piece of Mrs Ruggles' finest,' he said.

Aunt Bets arrived at the table with a huge tea tray. We pushed Temitayo and her guardian's table up next to ours.

I leant in to whisper to Temitayo. 'Those articles? You – are brilliant,' I said.

'Almost as brilliant as you,' she replied with a grin.

CHAPTER SIXTY-THREE

When Mr Lee and Charlie left, I sat with Temitayo and Mrs Heap.

'Where are your friends today, Mrs Heap?' I asked.

'I wanted to talk to Mary alone, but I don't seem to quite have the courage now it comes to it. Will you stay, Vinnie? You've been such a good friend to Mary.'

This was something new. Mrs Heap looked quite small without her friends surrounding her. Temitayo frowned and we both waited.

'Sir Edgar read your articles and has arranged for you to go to Switzerland, to finishing school, early.'

Temitayo tilted her head to the side with a little shake

as if she had heard wrong.

'I had thought you might be pleased, dear, since you are so very bright and I know I must bore you.'

'How could I be pleased? You know what finishing school is; it isn't a real school at all, it isn't for learning, it's to finish off any interests of your own and polish a girl to a blank slate, ready to please a husband.'

Mrs Heap shook her head. 'But I've not been a fitting guardian for you. I've gossiped with my friends, ignored you. I've really not known what to make of you, Mary, with your clever ways and your languages and music and writing, so I've left you to your own devices, particularly since you've found some friends.'

Temitayo looked at her, wide-eyed. 'Sounds like a perfect guardian to me.'

'I mean it, Mary. You are so much smarter than me, you deserve this fancy school—'

'Piffle!'

'Mary!' said Mrs Heap, glaring through her tiny spectacles.

I giggled.

'See what happens when a young lady is not given proper guidance?' said Mrs Heap, a smile at the corner of her lips. 'I told Sir Edgar the thought of losing you for ever has made me feel surprisingly glum, although goodness knows why.'

'I would hate finishing school and you know it.' Temitayo folded her arms. 'What was the point of writing those articles if not to show there was more to me than performing for other people, that I have ambitions of my own and could do good things with what I have?'

Mrs Heap seemed taken aback but not unhappy.

'Well . . . if not . . . Sir Edgar would require a meeting with us twice yearly to discuss your studies, but no more soirées up at his estate I'm afraid. He mentioned a new tutor – that there have been some exceptionally bright young women who have become quite academic.'

Temitayo clapped her hands, eyes bright. 'Yes! I could study literature. Also history and politics, to enrich my writing. I would love to prepare myself for university one day, then I could travel.'

'Goodness, I can't imagine what you would want with all that,' Mrs Heap sighed fondly. 'But then, you have always been your own person, Mary. Writing for a newspaper in secret, right under my nose. Whatever next? You must write to Sir Edgar yourself.'

Temitayo frowned. 'So where would I stay?'

Mrs Heap pushed her glasses up her nose and cleared her throat. 'You could stay with me. If you'd like. For as long as you like.'

There was a long pause. I found myself holding my

breath and my eyes flicked between them.

'I do like very much,' said Temitayo, covering Mrs Heap's hand with hers. 'But there's one condition.'

'You're not going to start having me on now, madam, I still won't stand for any cheek,' said Mrs Heap.

'I want you to call me by my name,' she said. 'No more Mary. I am Temitayo.'

CHAPTER SIXTY-FOUR

I watched Southampton shrink against the corn-flower blue sky, Aunt Bets and Mr Lee on one side of me at the railings of the steamer, Charlie on the other. I pulled my check cape tight around me, trying to keep out the brisk breeze. This was my first time on a boat. My first time away from England. My first time this far away from Mother. She would come back eventually for the pearl, the diamonds she had left, and she would find them gone, the octopus replaced.

What would she do then?

On the quayside Aunt Bets and Mr Lee told us they would be married in a small service when we arrived in

Madeira. Adults were strange. For years they had been friends, had their little routine, and I never would have thought there was anything else between them, but now their eyes followed each other, and they were barely apart. It made me feel warm inside, but I caught a fair amount of eye rolling from Charlie.

'Let's go and find a table in the salon before they are all taken,' said Aunt Bets.

'I'll join you shortly,' said Mr Lee, although it couldn't be more than an hour since he'd checked on the baby octopuses back in the cabin. They were in large glass jars, inside a specially built wooden chest that kept them upright. Mr Lee had told Bickerstaff that there had been an accident with their aquarium tank, the filter had broken and the water turned foul, and all the young octopuses were lost. The story was that Mr Lee was so devastated by the loss of his beloved octopus and the babies that he left for Madeira. Still, I knew he was jumpy about the deception – I'd had enough unwanted experience of lying myself – and would spend as much time as possible during the five-day journey in his cabin, with the chest.

'I'm going to stay here a bit longer, then I'll come and find you,' I said.

I wasn't ready to go inside with the others. I wanted to catch the very last glimpse of England, to watch until the horizon was the same on all sides, until we were completely free of the land, yet as surely trapped as animals in a giant circular tank of sea and sky. I leant on the rails, gazing down at the frothing wake blending into dark teal blue. It was a long drop and the back of my knees felt watery, as if I might jump over controlled by an invisible madness, like a puppet or automaton.

I smiled at my fanciful self, then took the deepest breath I could of the fresh air. I found my new pocket sketchbook in my skirts and outlined the back of the ship, its foam wake drawing a line back to the disappearing coast of England. I remembered how once all I would draw was hats. Now my sketchbook and pencils were like extensions to my hands.

Someone beside me, very close. Too close, elbow touching mine. I started away from her: a tall woman in a veiled dark-blue hat, dressed in a smartly cut but plain grey skirt suit.

'Lavinia, dear heart.'

I gasped. 'Mother?' I stepped forward as if to hug her, the habit almost too strong. But something stopped me.

'Of course. I wouldn't leave you all alone, on the first day of our big adventure.'

I didn't know what to say, what to think. A tiny corner of my treacherous broken heart was still pleased to see her.

'I'm not alone, Mother. Aunt Bets, Mr Lee and Charlie are just in the—'

'But they aren't your real family, darling. I'm here now. I've found you like I said I would.'

We stared at each other, her face a shadowed outline behind the thin veil.

'I am sorry to have underestimated you, Lavinia. If I had known how grown-up you were, I would have included you from the beginning.'

'Don't tell me you knew about those girls, that you knew where the money was coming from,' I said on impulse. 'I don't want to hear you say it.' My heart throbbed. I had the same feeling I'd had looking over the railings, dizzy.

I wanted to nurture the tiniest seed of doubt that she hadn't done those things, that the truth was a lie, that a lie was the truth. I wished I could live in a trick of the light, a clever illusion. *Pepper's Ghost*. If she confessed everything, things could never go back to how they were. If I never found out the truth from her mouth, then I could, at least, sometimes . . . pretend to believe the illusion.

'Mama.'

I stepped forward into her arms and she held me tight and I was a small child again, tears soothed after a nightmare. A tiny girl, Mother winding my hair in rags at bedtime in a matching nightgown. A larger girl, fussed over at the millinery, admired for how well I could bring Mother's visions to life. Her pride and joy.

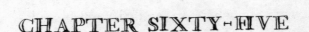

CHAPTER SIXTY-FIVE

Mother held me back from her and my hands dropped from her waist to my sides.

'Now, no more secrets, dear heart. I know the details of how we earned our profits were distasteful, I fully agree, and of course that has upset you deeply. But there is a bigger picture. Jedders is rightfully rotting in gaol, so we are free. I am proud of you, Lavinia –' her finger touched the slight lump in the centre of my chest beneath my blouse – 'for you found my heirloom and I see you are keeping it safe for me. For us.'

I stepped backwards. She wanted the profits, the diamonds. That was what she had come here for, not me.

'Please don't gape, dear heart.' Mother reached out to touch my chin but I shied away from her. Her face changed beneath the veil, eyes wide, a tremor at her lips.

'Oh, Lavinia, I love you so much – you are my daughter, my only child. We are connected, and deep down you are like I am, talented and driven, you just don't see it yet, you don't yet know what it takes to make a way in the world.'

She stepped towards me and I stepped back.

'You knew what was happening to those girls. It was your workshop where Agnes died,' I murmured.

'That was Jedders' fault. That girl was too young – and it was up to him to take care of production. And the second workshop was nothing to do with me. A shrewd businessman knows when to move on, and I am shrewder than any man.'

I gazed out to sea for a moment before I could bear to meet her stare. I'd always thought the blueness of Mother's eyes was like the sky. But it was more like the sea. Unknowable. Hidden depths.

'Jedders would have tricked me as I tricked him. You saw for yourself that man is more than suited to gaol.'

Yes, I had seen what he was truly like, at the workshop but also outside the octopus tank with a knife to my eye.

'You left me with him, Mother! You had already

fought with him at the house, hadn't you? You knew he was coming for you, but you *left* me.'

'Dear heart . . . of course I waited, but then thank goodness that plucky girl with the bucket arrived, and the boy too.'

So she had waited? She had seen what was happening through the glass, and *watched*. I wasn't sure if that was worse or better than leaving me.

'You aren't even sorry that the girls were sick and dying from your Paris Green. You . . . you . . . *killed* them for money.'

'Of course I am sorry. But those girls are like a million others, urchins who would have died of childbirth in a few short years, if they managed not to succumb to typhoid or cholera before. They aren't like *you*, Lavinia.'

With her words I stumbled across the invisible line I was walking. I felt sick. I wanted Aunt Bets.

'Agnes and Martha were just girls who didn't know who to trust. Exactly like me,' I said.

Mother lifted her chin, adjusted her veil, and smoothed her skirts. 'You've had a very unpleasant time, my dear heart, and I am truly sorry for that.'

I believed her but it didn't change anything.

'As you grow older you will grow tired of serving tea, Lavinia. I am happy for you to reside with Elizabeth until that day.'

I frowned, confused.

'My blue pearl, Lavinia,' she said, holding out her hand. 'Now, please.'

CHAPTER SIXTY-SIX

I reached into the neck of my blouse and hooked my finger around the chain. I drew out the iridescent pearl, glossy blue against the darker water.

Mother's eyes widened and she reached for it, but I found my palm closing around its smooth surface, still warm from where it had been hidden against my heart. To remind me.

'You left it in the tank with the octopus.'

Her eyes narrowed. 'Don't be ridiculous, dear heart. What are you and cousin Elizabeth going to do with something so valuable?'

My mother wasn't who I thought she was. I'd obeyed

her without question every single day of my life. Trusted her. No more. I didn't want the hollow pearl, with its nasty secret. But I didn't see why she should have it either.

I yanked the chain over my head, the pearl still inside my fist, then shot out my hand towards the edge of the railing. Mother was quicker. She yelped and darted at me, snatching my other arm so hard it wrenched my shoulder.

'Mama, you are hurting me!' My wail was caught by the wind.

'This is for your own good, Lavinia, you don't know—'

She twisted my arm behind my back. I screamed in shock, and released the pearl. It landed right at the edge of the deck, rolling, precarious in the sway of the ship. The silver chain hung over the edge and before she could get to it, it slithered off, dragging the pearl with it.

Mother shrieked.

We both stared down over the railings. The chain was caught on a knot in a rope that held rubber buffers against the hull of the ship. The pearl swung out in the breeze. It wouldn't hold for long. As I stared, Mother flung off her hat and swung herself up and over the railings, so her heeled boots were on the rim of the deck, now the wrong side of safety. With one hand she held the bar, knuckles white, and with the other she reached down, snatching at the air, inches from the swinging pearl.

'Mother! Stop it!' My yells were snatched by the wind, which was billowing Mother's skirt like a sail. I pressed both my hands over her cold gripping fingers. 'Stop it, Mother, please, the pearl is empty!'

She couldn't hear me, she couldn't hear anything. Her eyes were glued to the pearl. She stretched out further than before, now only clawing at the rail with her fingers. I reached through and grabbed her wrist as she snatched the pearl with a grunt of triumphant effort. The pearl was in one of her hands but the other had slipped. No. Not this.

'The pearl is *empty* – we gave the diamonds to the girls and their families. They are gone!'

For less than a second I held her wrist in mine, then her hand, then her fingers.

Then I was holding only air, screaming, and Mother was falling, gripping the pearl, triumph turning to disbelief as her back hit the sea. Her skirts folded over her, followed by the waves, and she vanished into the churning wake.

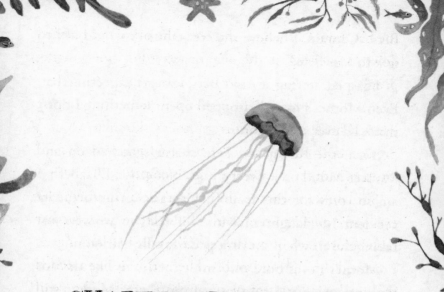

CHAPTER SIXTY-SEVEN

Mother sat in the captain's office, soaked through, shivering and hatless but with her chin held high. I couldn't take my eyes from her and wanted to embrace her as much as I was revolted by her. Instead I held tight to Aunt Bets' arm.

'Now would someone like to explain why one of my crew just risked his life?'

A group of people had seen my struggle with Mother and alerted the boat's staff, which was why a strong young sailor had already been on hand with a life ring, and had bravely leapt into the foam after my mother.

'I'm sorry, Rosamund, but this is enough,' said Aunt

Bets. 'Captain, I believe the constabulary would like to talk to Mrs Fyfe.'

I gasped, staring at Aunt Bets. I wasn't expecting that. Even Mother's mouth dropped open, something I don't think I'd ever seen before.

Then the Rosamund Fyfe charm switched on and Mother pasted on a sweet smile. 'Nonsense, Elizabeth. I am so sorry for this trouble, Captain, an unfortunate accident. My daughter Lavinia will tell you, we were just taking the air when she dropped a family heirloom.'

Mother's eyes bore into mine, her gaze like threads binding me. But I tore away from them. Mother still believed that I would never turn against her. I was so glad, to the depths of my heart, that she wasn't drowned. But Aunt Bets was right: it was enough now, all of it.

The captain raised his eyebrows. 'On my ship, I am the law,' he said. 'Madam, I would like to see this trinket. I do not wish to ask one of my cabin maids to search you for it, but I will do so if necessary.'

I couldn't meet Mother's eyes, but I saw her unfold her palm.

The captain held up the necklace. The pearl seemed to have lost some of its lustre.

He frowned. 'An uncommonly large specimen. Extremely rare if it is genuine, which I doubt. Does anyone have a pin?' he said.

'I beg your pardon? That is an heirloom, Captain,' said Mother, eyes darting. 'How dare you suggest it is not genuine.'

I realized Mother hadn't heard me tell her the pearl was empty. Hadn't heard me tell her what we had done with the diamonds.

There was no getting them back. It would be easier to find them if they were at the bottom of the sea.

This time all three of us had gone to London, Temitayo refusing to be left behind after I told them everything. Charlie had helped me, keen to work on his skills of investigation. Disguised as a chimney sweep he'd found Ruth easily, down the other end of Litcham Street. I'd poured the diamonds into her fist myself, trusting her to share whatever she could get for them with the other girls from both of the factories.

In a way, by giving the diamonds to the girls, I had helped Mother. There was no real evidence against her except the pearl itself.

'Mother will have a pin,' I blurted. 'She always carries hatpins.'

Mother shook her head at me, whipped out her pin purse and slapped it into his hand.

'You'll find it quite real, gentlemen. Do you think I would have risked my life otherwise? I am but a widow, a hard-working milliner, and this small but important piece represents all myself and my daughter have in the world . . . please do not damage it.'

I stared at her in amazement and she lowered her voice.

'Dear heart, Lavinia, it was all for you.'

Mother thought I didn't know what had been inside the pearl, but this time it was she who was in the dark.

The sailor lit a match from his pocket and held the sharp end of the pin to it until it glowed red. Then with a little scream from Mother he put the pearl on the desk and pressed the needle to it. A smell of burning filled the room and the pin passed deep into the pearl. A crack formed across its surface, then spread.

The pearl split clean in half, as if made of plaster. Like something was hatching.

Mother darted forward. She expected a spill of glittering diamonds.

'Hollow as an egg,' said the sailor. 'Just as you expected, Captain, it is nothing but paste.'

CHAPTER SIXTY-EIGHT

Five days later

I stared out of the hotel window at the deep blue of the Madeira sky, my head thumping. Our first night on land I'd hoped I would sleep better. The hotel was just along from the port of Funchal where we had docked, and was an old stone building, cool inside, simple but comfortable. Despite the breeze from the window, it had been another sleepless night, waking in sweats after my mind replayed Mother's fall over and over. My arm and shoulder still ached from her grasp; now and again I found myself shivering, the shock of it lingering.

Mother had been detained in the cells on the ship and would be returning to England and the police. Aunt Bets had betrayed her but I didn't know if I had too. There were no diamonds as proof against her . . .

I couldn't feel glad or sad. I was simply numb.

I dressed quickly, my lightest striped-blue cotton dress. We'd get more clothes made for us out here to suit the hotter climate. A knock sounded on the door between rooms and I called Aunt Bets inside, dressed in her pantaloons and a linen jacket.

'Good morning,' she said. I gave her a quick tight hug. When her strong arms held me, I felt like I could see ahead, to a time when the foaming wake closing over Mother wouldn't linger behind my eyelids. When I wouldn't keep seeing Martha's lost face.

I wished I had three hearts like an octopus, like Ghost. Then maybe it wouldn't hurt so much if one got broken.

Aunt Bets and I smiled at each other. The daytime was easier: more distractions. We would set up our new life in Madeira, the first stage of which was finding an appropriate place for Aunt Bets' tea rooms. I was looking forward to exploring the old town streets with her, searching for a shop with an apartment above, that she could afford with the sale of her house in Brighton. But there was something even more distracting today.

Charlie gripped the side of the rowing boat, as it rocked. I seemed to be less nervous than he was. If anyone had told me that, when I sat on the steps of the bathing machine with Aunt Bets, I wouldn't have believed them. I don't think it helped Charlie that the boy rowing us was barely older than him.

'So your family brought in the giant octopuses? That is so fascinating. And your name is . . . ?'

'Alfonso Pinto,' said the boy, with a grin. 'Me, my brother, my father. *Polvo*.'

He understood English but didn't seem to speak it much, but was entranced when I'd shown him my drawing of Ghost and her babies.

The boy rocked the boat, pulling a scared face. 'Big, very big.'

'And Captain Bickerstaff?' I said. He took his hands off the oars to grab a scrap of netting from the base of the boat. He thrust it beneath his nose, holding it in place with his top lip as he thrust out his chest and sniffed.

I laughed; that was him all right.

I grabbed Charlie's arm as he stumbled from the rowing boat after me with a sigh of relief, then gave me a withering look that turned into a smile. He had been confined to his cabin, seasick, on the ship and wouldn't be keen to get back on the little fishing vessel that had taken us from Funchal round the rocky headland, to this cove. Now we needed to find the sheltered tide pool that the Portuguese naturalists had described to Mr Lee as the perfect place for the release.

Aunt Bets followed Charlie, landing neatly on the rocks, her hair blowing from its usual bun. Lastly, Mr Lee – I was now trying to think of him as Uncle Henry – who reached back, anxiously directing Alfonso to be careful with the heavy trunks containing the jars and the baby octopuses.

Aunt Bets took one trunk, despite a minor fuss from the still wobbly Charlie, Mr Lee the other.

The large tide pool was easy to find, an irregular-shaped turquoise jewel in amongst the jagged volcanic rocks. We circled it, finding an area of green weed, similar to the weed that Mr Lee had transplanted into the jars.

Mr Lee and Aunt Bets put down the trunks, panting. We all stared at the landscape. The sea further out was wavy, tipped with white foam, the breeze gusty but warm. The sun seared bright, sparking diamonds off the pool. I found a rock to sit on and drew my sketchbook from the satchel as the others removed the jars. Temitayo had made me promise to draw the tiny octopuses one last time and send it to her to join her last octopus article in the newspaper. I crouched close, outlined one of the tiny creatures inside. Its arms were growing to match the size of its head and eyes, its transparent body now scattered with deep-red dots, the colour its mother had been when calm yet playful. Ghost's babies were getting their colours. Not a single one had died on the way over. Mr Lee had protected them as well as the mother octopus had tended her eggs. They were much stronger then they looked, these miniature devil-fish.

Aunt Bets tapped me on the shoulder. I turned. She held up an item of clothing. A short sky-blue dress, a sailor collar and stripes around the base of the skirt, with matching bloomers. Behind it hung a matching outfit in navy. The swimming costumes we'd used in Brighton when she taught me to swim.

'I thought we could give these little ones a proper send-off,' said Aunt Bets. 'Boys' changing hut behind that rock, girls' behind this one.'

'I'm going to be the sensible land beast,' said Charlie. 'After all, who gets into a pool with hundreds of devil-fish?'

CHAPTER SIXTY-NINE

We all laughed as we rushed to change into our swimming costumes. I looked around nervously, but the rocky shore was deserted. Still, Aunt Bets and I helped each other to pull on the costumes beneath our chemises. I couldn't even imagine what Mother would think. She'd always said swimming was undignified at best, scandalous at worst. Tears darted into my eyes and I looked over at the trunks, the baby octopuses, and when I thought of their miraculous little glassy bodies, I found the water in my eyes subsiding like the tide.

We emerged, sun on our bare arms, calves and feet, the rest of us covered only by thin cotton. I felt free. Mr

Lee – Uncle Henry – joined us in his own one-piece swimsuit, baggy grey cotton to the elbows and knees. I stifled my laugh, and he gave me a wry grin.

We found a place to lower ourselves into the cool water, and I felt for the rocky bottom of the pool with my bare feet without thinking. The water came to the base of my chest and I remembered the last time I had stood in the water, in Ghost's tank.

We've looked after them for you, my friend.

Charlie passed Uncle Henry the first jar and I watched him hold it against his chest as Aunt Bets twisted the cork free. He lowered it into the water, and we watched the tiny octopuses puff out into the pool.

My turn. Aunt Bets and I held the jar between us, then she stepped back as I dipped it beneath the water and watched more of Ghost's babies float out with darting movements into their new home. The water was clear and they stayed near the surface, already gathering in groups. I thought of Ghost, the best of mothers, and blocked thoughts of my own mother, at least for now. I lifted the jar from the water and emptied it, looking down into the long glass cylinder. Right at the bottom, one of the babies clung to the glass, tiny arms splayed and clinging in an eight-pointed star.

'I know it's scary, but you have a whole new life ahead of you,' I whispered.

I reached into the jar, which came right up to my shoulder, and gently eased the baby from the glass with my finger. It clung to my fingertip, and in the week and a half since they had hatched, their suckers had grown strong enough that I could now just about feel it clinging on. I raised it to my face. Two tiny horns rose behind its eyes and the dots on its body flashed dark then white.

Ghost. Here in every baby. Yet each would be their own creature, quite different from their mother.

I lowered the miniature octopus into the turquoise pool and ducked my shoulders under the water. I felt my own strength as I stretched out my arms, lifted my feet, and floated. Not held by the ground, but by the water. I laughed in delight.

After a few seconds the octopus detached from my finger and swam away with juddery wafts of movement as new waters propelled it, powering its three tiny, but growing hearts.

OF FICTION AND OF FACT

Mr Henry Lee

Henry Lee really was the aquarist at the Brighton Aquarium, and he really did love octopuses. He wasn't a famous man, but he did write articles that were bundled together into a booklet: *The Octopus: or, The 'Devil-fish' of Fiction and of Fact*. Although Henry Lee is a real person, I have fictionalized him. He actually lived from 1826 to 1888, but I wanted to set this book slightly later in 1893, when the aquarium wasn't as popular and people had grown more used to seeing ordinary octopuses. But they still would have been amazed by an octopus the size of Ghost!

Brighton Aquarium

The Brighton Aquarium opened in 1872, making it now the oldest continually operating aquarium in the world. When it first opened all aquariums were extremely popular and octopuses were the stars of the show – the newspapers called the craze for them 'cephalomania', as octopuses are cephalopods, a class of marine animals that also contains squid and cuttlefish. By the end of the Victorian era aquariums had started to go out of fashion; some were closing down, and others were used as music halls or theatres and for travelling circus acts.

You can still visit the Brighton Aquarium; it became Sea Life Brighton in 1991 and now has the UK's largest collection of sharks and rays under one roof. It is also home to Noodles the octopus, who I was lucky enough to meet in person in 2021 as I was writing this book. Noodles is a common octopus, the type that can be found around the shores of the UK. This little octopus was only young at the time, but very friendly and curious. It enjoyed exploring my hand with its surprisingly strong suckers and squirting me in the face three times!

Victorian Factory Workers

The Victorian era is known for being a time of great industry, when new factories were thriving. Unfortunately, the difference between the quality of life of rich people and poor people was also greater, and many employees worked in dangerous, unhealthy conditions for less pay than they could survive on.

The girls working with the toxic green dye were inspired by the true story of Matilda Scheurer, a nineteen-year-old who worked applying arsenic green dye to fake flowers. She was gradually poisoned, so that even the whites of her eyes turned green. Before she died in 1861, she claimed that 'everything she looked at was green'.

The strange thing is doctors *knew* this was happening.

Drawings in newspapers depicted skeletons dancing in green dresses. *The Times* newspaper commented, when a case of mild arsenic poisoning was traced back to some green socks: 'What manufactured article ... can possibly be trusted if socks may be dangerous?'

You would think these stories would have caused people to immediately stop wearing the colour, but, of course, they didn't. The risk was much less to the wearer than to the workers, and the Paris Green colour became incredibly fashionable.

The Octopus

Ghost the octopus is fictional. I've based her on the giant Pacific octopus but have taken all the amazing things I've read and seen about octopuses and other cephalopods to inspire her abilities and character.

I have always loved sea creatures, particularly mysterious ones. In April 2016, an octopus at the National Aquarium of New Zealand squeezed out of its tank and made an eight-armed dash for a drainpipe that – luckily for him – led directly to the sea. That was when I first thought I'd like to write about an octopus. Later at a school visit in 2019 I told some young people some of the ideas I'd like to write about in the future, including something about an octopus. One boy put up his hand and said: 'Your octopus could be very kind.'

I was intrigued and asked why that would be, and he replied, 'Because an octopus has three hearts.'

That moment stuck to me with all of its suckers.

FACTS ABOUT THE OCTOPUS

Octopuses . . .

. . . have three hearts.

. . . have nine brains – because, in addition to the central brain, each of their eight arms has a mini-brain that allows it to act independently.

. . . have blue blood.

. . . can grow to nine metres wide from the tip of one arm to the tip of another, and can weigh up to twenty kilograms.

. . . can change colour in one-tenth of a second.

. . . have short lifespans of only two to three years on average.

. . . have 2,140 to 2,240 suction cups on their arms, giving them a powerful grip and sense of taste and smell.

The plural of octopus is octopuses. The word 'octopus' comes from the Greek, *oktōpous*, meaning 'eight foot'; it is pluralized as a Greek word, too, so an 'es' is the suffix. (Sorry – no octopi, octopodes or octopussies!)

RECIPE

A Victorian Recipe to Try at Home:
Petits Fours à Thé (1867)

This recipe for petits fours comes from Jules Gouffé's *Royal Cookery Book*, first published in French in 1867. It was translated into English by Jules' brother Alphonse, head of the pastry division in the royal kitchens under Queen Victoria. This cookery book along with others would have been commonly used by bakers such as Aunt Bets.

INGREDIENTS

125g flour
70g caster sugar
35g unsalted butter, cubed, at room temperature
1 pinch of salt
25ml cream or whole milk
The zest of 1 lemon
1 egg, separated
Decoration, for example raisins, candied peel, candied
angelica, blanched almonds or pistachio nuts

METHOD

1. Sieve the flour. Make a well in the centre and add in the sugar, butter, salt, cream, and just over half of the egg

yolk. Mix well, but fast and lightly. Do not overwork, but form it into a dough which should be slightly sticky and firm. Wrap in plastic wrap or put it into a bowl with a plate on top and leave to rest in the fridge for an hour.

2. Remove from the fridge and roll out on a well-floured worktop. Aim for a thickness of around 6mm. Using what the Victorians would have called fancy cutters, cut out shapes and lay them on a baking sheet lined with greased baking parchment, or a silicone baking mat.

3. Beat the egg white and leftover yolk together with a small pinch of salt and brush this over the surface of your biscuits. Decorate each one with a raisin or piece of candied fruit or nut.

4. Bake at 180°C (170°C fan oven) for fifteen minutes until just golden brown. Cool on a wire rack before serving.

These biscuits will keep for at least a week in an airtight container (though they might have been eaten long before then!).

Credit: www.english-heritage.org.uk/visit/inspire-me/the-history-of-the-biscuit/

ACKNOWLEDGEMENTS

It takes more than three hearts and nine brains to write a book! With heartfelt thanks to:

My agent, Clare Wallace. You sold 'octopus idea' on proposal within weeks of me signing with you, and I am not only incredibly impressed but forever grateful for your enthusiastic support, guidance and knowledge. Our shared vision and your meticulous care has given my writing new direction and boosted my confidence. I am empowered to write so many more books with you in my corner! Thanks also to the excellent team at Darley Anderson.

My friend the editor, Rachel Leyshon. Our creative collaboration has shaped me as a writer, and changed my life. This book baby had an easier birth than the previous two, and I credit that to our partnership and your input from the very outset. From blue pearls to green poison to stabby canes, you pick up on which of my crazy ideas might work, then challenge me to make it so, and I love you for it!

My publishing team at Chicken House – Barry, Elinor, Jazz, Esther, Olivia, Kesia and all the Chicken House coop – for your continued trust, imagination and support.

The cover crew, Rachel Hickman, Steve Wells and sublime artist Gordy Wright. For the first time I've been rendered speechless by my cover and the whole design package. I will love this one for all eternity; it is beyond perfect in every detail.

My sensitivity reader, Adamma Okwonko. Your insightful observations and suggestions enabled me to build authenticity and nuance into my characterization, and I'm so grateful for your input. Any errors are wholly my own.

My Friend the Octopus is the first book I have finished as a full-time author. I thought that leaving teaching after twenty years would be a difficult transition, but I love my new life and feel hugely privileged to have been able to start anew, halfway (hopefully!) through my actual life. But it could only happen with the support of the following:

The reassuring and inclusive #writementor community and particularly Stuart White; your trust and encouragement mean so much, and my work as tutor and mentor has supported me financially, enabling me to follow the full-time writing dream.

All my friends – the uni group; my ex-colleague teaching friends particular Kate, Anna and Helen; the home gang, the Seaford massive. It's been A Year, and in the face of a global pandemic it's seemed ridiculous to ask people to get excited about just another book . . . but my cheerleaders never fail.

All my supporters online, particularly #edutwitter and the indie booksellers, bloggers and bookaholics who spread the word about *Darwin's Dragons* – delayed for a year and then with a lockdown release – with such verve that it became that most precious of things, a 'word-of-mouth bestseller'. Your support made this happen. I'll never forget that.

To all the teachers, librarians and young people who have invited me to their classrooms either in person or digitally. I have loved sharing time and ideas, and appreciate every single one of you.

To my writing friends online, Jenni, Emily, Rachel, Emma, Sinead, Louie, Lucy, Zillah, Olivia, Antonia, Giles, Perdita, Ravena, Piu, Claudia, Eve, Lex, Anna, Andy, Jenny and many more. You are my treasured colleagues and fellow travellers.

Sarah Harris. Always there; I wouldn't want to be on this wild ride without you.

Jo Hogan. You, reader, will never know the two painfully honest but essential notes Jo gave me that were relatively small tweaks, but which transformed this book. I hope you will always be my first reader, you utterly brilliant human.

My bestest, Sally, and the Gasson 'framily', for everything always, my anchors.

The Moakes side of the family, and in-laws, for always

being there. The extended Galvin clan who all read and celebrate.

My Seaford family, Mum, Dad, Kathryn, you are the scaffolding holding up this slightly crumbling fortress. I wouldn't be me without you.

Rob, Jo, Arlo and Jem who have created the most cherished of boltholes.

Beloved furry wallies, Flinny and Saffy.

Extraordinary sons Edward and Oscar – my favourite thing is being your mum.

My love, Bill, who nourishes me – both literally and in my heart and soul. This year you've put so much faith in me; thank you.

DARWIN'S DRAGONS by LINDSAY GALVIN

-1835-

Cabin boy Syms Covington is on the voyage of a lifetime to the Galapagos Islands with the world-famous scientist Charles Darwin. But when Syms falls overboard during a huge storm, he washes up on an unexplored island. Stranded there, he makes a discovery that could change the world . . .

Now it's not just his own survival at stake – the future of an undiscovered species is in his hands.

'A striking and original adventure . . . just the sort of story I love.'
EMMA CARROLL

Paperback, ISBN 978-1-912626-46-5, £6.99 • ebook, ISBN 978-1-913322-15-1, £6.99